As I climbed the porch stairs, I spotted my five-foot-nothing Aunt Sherry standing behind two six-foot folding tables that blocked the front door. A coatrack held small baskets of woven hemp and willow, and larger baskets made of those and other materials were scattered on the porch floor. A long swath of blue gingham fabric lay in and around the fallen baskets, the edges fluttering as if agitated by the swirling emotions instead of the mild breeze.

Opposite my aunt stood the snarling star of the showdown in progress. She leaned over the folding table, her bloodred fingernails scary long and lethal-looking as she pointed at Sherry.

"You'll come to an agreement with me, Mrs. Cutler, and you'll do it soon or you'll be very sorry."

"But, Ms. Elsman," my aunt began.

"No 'buts,'" the Elsman woman interrupted. "I want that option on your land, and I will by God have it."

She tucked her asymmetrically cut black hair behind an ear, lifted a stiletto-shod foot, and deliberately speared one of the medium-sized hemp baskets lying on the porch.

Blame it on being tired and stressed, but the woman stomped on my last nerve, and my temper flared in a sonic boom of fury.

"Back up and back off, lady," I snarled.

I heard heavy footfalls behind me—Detective Shoar's, I guessed—but was too incensed to let him take the lead.

The woman casually turned and arched a brow. "My name is Elsman, Ms. Jill Elsman, and I suggest you stay out of this. It does not concern you."

"Actually, it does." The black-haired, black-eyed demon woman towered over me, but I stood straight and let her have it. "It so happens that Mrs. Cutler, the woman you just threatened, is my dearest aunt."

Basket
Case

NANCY HADDOCK

BERKLEY PRIME CRIME, NEW YORK

An imprint of Penguin Random House LLC
375 Hudson Street, New York, New York 10014

BASKET CASE

A Berkley Prime Crime Book / published by arrangement with the author

ISBN: 978-0-425-27572-6

PUBLISHING HISTORY
Berkley Prime Crime mass-market edition / September 2015

PRINTED IN THE UNITED STATES OF AMERICA

10 9 8 7 6 5 4 3 2 1

Cover illustration by Ann Wertheim.
Cover design by Diana Kolsky.
Interior text design by Kristin del Rosario.

Penguin
Random
House

Acknowledgments

I love acknowledgments because I get to publically thank everyone who helped make this book a reality.

I fear acknowledgments because I know I'll forget to thank someone. It's happened before. Sooo, if you aren't listed, it's only my, ahem, mature memory at fault. That, or I'm protecting your identity as requested (wink, wink).

Giant hugs go to Leis Pederson, extraordinary editor and fabulous friend, for being her amazing self. I can hardly wait to see you again, Leis!

More giant hugs go to Roberta Brown, amazing agent and soul sister. Words fail, but you know how I feel, Roberta!

Huge thanks to the people of Magnolia, Arkansas, for welcoming me, answering my questions, and clarifying so very many points. Among my research angels are Dana Thornton, Columbia County Library; Megan, CID secretary, and Heather, sheriff's secretary, both of the Columbia County Sheriff's Office; Brenda, Columbia County Prosecutor's Office; and Randy Reed, Columbia County coroner. Angela Flurry Lester, former owner of Loft on the Square, and Deb Baker of Magnolia Cove also provided inspiration and information in and on Magnolia, and Frank Harrington of Field's

Cadillac in St. Augustine, Florida, answered car questions. Any goofs I may have made are my fault, not theirs!

Although I've dedicated this book to the Allens, I have to thank them, too. Magnolia native Yvonne Allen and her dear hubby, Tom, of Sapulpa, Oklahoma, met me in Magnolia to drive me around their old stomping grounds and share stories of the past. I've known Yvonne and Tom since I was a tyke, and it was a gift to spend such a quantity and quality of time with them as an adult. Thanks, Yvonne and Tom!

Big ole tubs of thanks to my critical reader Katelin Maloney, and to writing buds Julie Benson, Sandy Blair, Lynne Smith, and Lorraine Heath. And for my Writer Retreat cohorts, Neringa Bryant and L. A. Sartor, well, words aren't enough. We worked and played together. You gave me the space and encouragement to finish the book. Ma'am, yes, ma'am, you did, and then you joined my celebration afterward. I love you both, and I can't wait to do another retreat . . . whenever and wherever it might be!

As always, deep and abiding appreciation for the caffeine and support from my friends at Starbucks #8484, Barnes & Noble #2796, and Second Read Books!

Last but never least, thanks and love to my hubby for his support and brainstorming and charting help, and to my children for their love and unwavering encouragement.

Chapter One

I, LESLEE STANTON NIX, NIXY TO MY FRIENDS, HAD never been called on the carpet for anything. Up until four days ago, that is.

Now I had third-degree rug burns and the risk of being jobless.

Why? Because my boss at Houston's Gates Fine Arts Gallery, Barbra (like Streisand) Vole, had blown her nonexistent fuse when the Lilyvale, Arkansas, police detective Eric Shoar had called me at work. His fifth call in the last month, the second in the past ten days. Shoar's deep, dreamy Southern drawl had stirred my feminine interest, but deep and dreamy hadn't softened his complaints.

"We had another incident at Miz Sherry Mae's yesterday," he'd begun. "Neighbors across the road reported booming sounds and smoke coming from the kitchen."

"Is anyone injured?" I'd asked on a gulp, my cell phone slick in my suddenly moist hand.

"Thankfully, no."

"Did the fire department respond?"

"They don't respond anymore unless I call them, but do you want whatever the problem is to go that far?"

"No, how can you think that?"

"Then prove you care. You have one week to get up here and see to your aunt and her housemates."

"A week?" I'd echoed stupidly.

"This needs to be an in-person visit, ma'am. Not a phone call."

"I hear you, but why the rush?"

"First, because the situation—whatever it is—seems to be escalating. Second, because my chief of police is asking questions about all the complaints coming in and why I'm taking the calls instead of the patrol units. I can't deflect him much longer."

"You're investigating, so you're doing your job. What's there to question?"

He coughed. "My reports might be on the sketchy side."

And the light dawned. "You're protecting Sherry."

"Miz Sherry's ancestors founded this town, and she's served on the city council. Even been the mayor."

"That's enough to cut her some slack?"

"That and having had her for a teacher, but understand me, Ms. Nix. This is serious. I don't want a tragedy on my hands, and I don't want Miz Sherry and her friends to be declared wards of the court."

"What?" I'd gasped.

"If the chief believes that Miz Sherry and her friends are a danger to themselves or others, he'll have to act."

"You'd tell him they're dangerous? You'd take away their independence? Their freedom?"

"Not if I can help it." He'd paused, then continued, "I understand that you don't think you know Miz Sherry well enough to stick your nose in her business, but none of her housemates have people left. We need this resolved, and you're the only relative in sight."

"I'll get up there as soon as I can," I'd said as I sagged against a wall.

"Good. Come by the station when you're in town. I'll be happy to help you if I can."

With the threat of legal action against my aunt, I might've panicked and dashed off to Arkansas then and there. My mother, Sue Anne, had been a late-in-life child, ten years younger than Sherry Mae. I was a surprise late-in-life baby, too, and we'd lived in Tyler back then. Though Sherry and her husband, Bill Cutler, made trips to visit us in Texas, I didn't remember visiting them in Arkansas. The families exchanged cards and letters and phone calls, but I didn't know my aunt well. Not until my mother had suffered a stroke a year and a half ago and Sherry Mae had come to say good-bye to her sister.

Sherry's husband had died just over three years earlier, but she had housemates—a temporary arrangement that had become permanent. Because she didn't have a deadline to be home, she'd been able to stay and support me through my mom's death and through the myriad of funeral arrangements. Always calm and steady. Always ready to advise me without being the least bit pushy. Always ready to share stories of herself and Mom as girls and young women. I'd grown close to Sherry Mae during those weeks, and I was grateful for the chance to relate to her as an adult. It had been fun to stay in touch since then with regular e-mails and holiday cards, phone calls and photos. So many photos that I should recognize each blade of grass and every plank of the original hardwood floor when I saw it.

Surprisingly, Barbra had given me time to be with my mom those precious days before she died, and time to take care of the services. After that, I'd used my weekends to wrap up her estate. Now, however, livid as Barbra was about my "sordid involvement" with the police, she wouldn't give me emergency leave. She had demanded that I finish out the week to complete our latest art installation—work overtime, in fact. Four days of Shoar's deadline shot, and Barbra had given me just until the middle of next week to return.

Which is why I'd packed a small suitcase on Thursday night, finished every task Barbra dreamed up until we closed on Friday, and then finally hopped into the no-frills white Camry I'd inherited from my mom. Purse. Check. Directions to Sherry's. Check. Sunglasses. On. I was ready to fight the weekend traffic leaving downtown Houston.

At least the April weather was on my side. Not too hot, not too cold, not storming. I had daylight saving time in my favor, too, though I saw more buildings than roadside bluebonnets on the way out of town.

Daylight melted into dusk, then dark, and my thoughts turned back to what waited in Lilyvale, southwest Arkansas.

Lilyvale. The town my mother's family had founded, but I'd never visited.

Lilyvale. The town my stupid portable GPS unit probably couldn't find.

Lilyvale. The place I didn't want to be, or at least not now. Not when I was so close to earning a promotion at the gallery.

Okay, so I was only next-in-line to the assistant director's assistant. Still, I'd made the gallery my life since owner Felina Gates had hired me. I'd busted my butt to earn double majors in fine art and art history, a minor in marketing, and a masters in art history. I excelled at my job, and I'd paid my dues. And now that Barbra was supposed to retire, I deserved the promotion.

I deserved a massage, too. The Shreveport motel bed I'd fallen into after midnight left me with more aches than I'd had after my first and final kickboxing class. Up again at the crack of dawn, I showered, went through my pre-drive checklist, and hit the highway for the last leg of the trip.

Though Sherry had mentioned that winter had lingered in Lilyvale, the day was sunny and clusters of early blooming wildflowers lined the two-lane country roads. The sight

brightened my mood as I mentally made my schedule for
the day. First, drop in on Detective Eric Shoar at the police
station to prove I was in town as ordered, and then visit Aunt
Sherry Mae.

Just after nine, I cruised north on what appeared to be the
Lilyvale main drag. The British male voice on my portable
GPS kept telling me to make a U-turn as soon as it was safe.
I ignored it.

Not a minute later, I found the picturesque town square my
mother had spoken of, and felt the oddest tug of comfort. A
sign proclaimed that Hendrix County Courthouse stood before
me, a two-and-a-half-story limestone structure on slightly
elevated ground surrounded by magnolia trees and a riot of
lilies. Lilies graced the base of a small white gazebo on the
courthouse grounds, too. Businesses lined each side of the
square, and yet more lilies, tulips, and even daisies bloomed
in large cement planters outside the shops.

Spring had not merely sprung here. Spring had reared up
and slapped the soil into giving up riots of color.

As I looked for the police station, I circled the entire square
and noticed how it was laid out. An inner circle ran closer to
the courthouse and served through traffic. Two outer sections
opposite each other held two rows of diagonal parking spaces
for shopper convenience, and parallel parking slots lined the
other two streets that bordered the square. After circling the
inner street twice, I hadn't seen the police station, but did spot
a shopkeeper opening her clothing store.

In a sleepy Southern town, I didn't give a second thought
to asking for directions, so I parked in a diagonal slot next
to a behemoth Buick land-boat with an elderly woman hunkered behind the wheel. The pristine powder-blue paint
gleamed as much as the woman's coifed gray hair, and I
gave her a friendly nod as I beeped my locks and took the
two steps up to the broad sidewalk.

"Honey. Oh, honey," I heard behind me.

I turned to see the blue-Buick lady beckoning.

"Yes, ma'am?" I put my sunglasses on top of my head as I neared her.

"Honey, would you do me a little favor? Would you go in there"—she paused and pointed—"and tell Miss Anna that Miss Ida Bollings is waitin' for her medicine."

I glanced up at the picture window reading simply PHARMACY in old-fashioned lettering. Mental shrug. I didn't have an actual appointment with Shoar and had decided not to forewarn Aunt Sherry I was coming. Why not do a good deed? I'd deliver Miss Ida's message and ask directions to the station.

"That's Miss Anna for Miss Ida's medicine?"

"That's right, honey. They'll put it on my account."

Right, and let a perfect stranger walk off with a prescription. Possibly a controlled substance.

The inside of the store was as quaint as its sign. An antique oak glass-front cabinet dark with age sat along the left side of the space. Wood shelves filled with typical drugstore products ran down the middle and along the right wall of the store.

"Help you?" The question came from one of the two middle-aged clerks seated behind the oak cabinet.

"Um, yes. I'm a visitor in town, but Ida Bollings is outside and wants me to tell Miss Anna that she's waiting for her medicine."

"Sure. That's Miss Anna in the back."

I'd expected a clerk to take over, but what the heck. I approached Miss Anna, another woman of middle years who stood behind a raised counter, also made of oak, and also glowing with a dark patina.

"May I help you?" she asked brightly.

"I'm a visitor in town, but Miss Ida is in her car outside waiting for her medicine."

"Good. I have it right here." Anna produced a brown glass bottle that looked like it had been made in the 1930s. "Now tell Miss Ida to take just one tablespoon full at a time. A tablespoon from her silverware drawer will do, and no more or it'll make her drunk."

"One tablespoon," I echoed, feeling like I'd landed in a time warp.

"The directions are right here," Anna said, tapping the white label, "but we like to remind Miss Ida."

"Do you ever remind her in person?"

Anna titled her head. "Come again?"

"I'm just wondering why Miss Ida didn't come in herself."

Anna chuckled. "She doesn't like to fool with dragging her walker out of the car unless she's shopping for a spell.

"So she sends strangers in for her prescriptions all the time?"

"Oh no. She's discerning about people, our Miss Ida is. You have a good visit in Lilyvale."

She handed me the bottle and reached for the ringing phone. At the front desk, I mentioned again that I was only a visitor just to see if the ladies would take over. They didn't. They waved me off with a cheery "Tell Miss Ida hi, now!"

Still stunned that I was walking out of a pharmacy with a concoction that could make its recipient drunk, I delivered the bottle and one-tablespoon message to Miss Ida. Her eyes twinkled when I mentioned the drunk part.

"I'll be careful, never you fret."

I nodded. "Miss Ida, do you know where the police station is?"

"A'course, honey. You go to the end of the block, turn right, and go two blocks. The station is on the corner and the fire station is across the street."

I'd no more than thanked her and returned to the sidewalk when the Buick's engine revved and Miss Ida peeled out like an Indy champion. Must be eager for a hit of her medicine.

The Ida-and-her-walker episode had me wondering, though. Were my aunt and her housemates as physically well and mobile as Sherry had told me they were? Did they still drive? I didn't talk with Sherry daily, not even weekly, but we'd chatted at least twice a month. When she'd mentioned the cold weather, she hadn't mentioned she or her friends had caught the flu. Not even a mild cold. She had never indicated that any of the Silver Six, as they called themselves, were ill or infirm in any way.

Of course, she'd never mentioned explosions and cooking accidents either.

Gripped by a sudden urgency to meet Detective Shoar, I drove to the cop shop, a building that turned out to be modern and bland compared to the pharmacy and the other downtown buildings. Tiled lobby floor with white walls, a reception window, and a green door to the inner sanctum of the station.

A young black man with a T. Benton name bar on his crisply pressed tan uniform took my name and request, and made a call. A moment later, Detective Shoar blew through the green door and introduced himself in a rush.

"You're Leslee Nix?"

"Nixy," I said automatically, stunned at his brusque manner. Not to mention he had a chiseled handsome face, and in short sleeves, well-worn jeans, and boots, he had a body artists would kill to paint. He smelled fine, too. Spicy with a mysterious undertone.

Detective Shoar narrowed his brown eyes. "You look about eighteen."

Not the first time I'd heard that, especially when I wore cargo shorts, a T-shirt, not-so-white tennis shoes, and my blah-brown hair in a ponytail. Never mind that I'm only five foot three.

I gave him my stock reply. "I'm twenty-nine. Our family has youthful genes."

"Hunh." He blinked then frowned. "You know where Sherry Mae lives?"

"Uh, sort of." I had Internet directions.

"'Sort of' won't cut it. You can follow me out there," he said as he closed a big hand around my elbow and guided me to the glass front door.

"Why the hurry?"

"Because I just got a call that there's trouble at the house."

Chapter Two

I SCRAMBLED TO MY CAMRY AND TOOK OFF BEHIND Detective Shoar. He didn't use his lights or siren, so it wasn't a challenge to keep up with the patrol car he drove. Not on the relatively level and straight streets with nearly zip traffic. It wasn't as easy to keep calm. Though he'd said "trouble" at the house, not "emergency," my breath clutched in my chest as I imagined a fire or worse raging at Aunt Sherry's. True, no screaming fire trucks followed us, but I'd forever blame myself if I'd come to Lilyvale a day too late.

I'd about worked myself into a baby ulcer when Detective Shoar's brake lights flashed and snapped me out of my head. I refocused my attention on the line of vehicles parked in the newly green grass just off the two-lane blacktop road. More cars, bearing license plates from as far away as Kansas and New Mexico, nosed along the split rail fence a few feet higher than the road. Beyond the cars, portable white tents rose in neat rows, and behind those, at the apex of a gentle upslope, sat a sprawling two-story farmhouse.

Sherry's home. I knew it immediately from my mother's

and Sherry's photos, and I breathed easier just seeing it
perfectly intact with no smoke boiling from the windows.
But was Sherry hosting a giant garage sale?

Then I spotted a banner lashed to the rustic fence rippling
in the breeze: FOLK ART FESTIVAL.

I mentally smacked myself for not remembering. Aunt
Sherry's last letter had brimmed with news about the event, but
I hadn't paid attention to the dates. Not important now. The
crux was that the house looked fine. No one ran screaming
from the grounds. So what kind of trouble call had Shoar taken?

His patrol car hung a right at the mailbox enclosed in a
skinny-mini version of Sherry's farmhouse, and I followed
him up the gravel driveway. To my left, on a chain-link
fence, hung hand-lettered signs that read HANDICAPPED,
POLICE, and FIRE. Talk about being prepared.

Shoar wheeled into the police-marked space, and as soon
as I parked by a blooming dogwood, I shot out of my car and
dogged his steps past clusters of people. Unnaturally quiet
and watchful people.

Except for one man who stepped in Shoar's path.

"What's going on?" I heard Shoar ask the man, but I
hustled past them.

As I climbed the porch stairs, I spotted my five-foot-
nothing Aunt Sherry standing behind two six-foot folding
tables that blocked the front door. A coatrack held small
baskets of woven hemp and willow, and larger baskets made
of those and other materials were scattered on the porch
floor. A long swath of blue gingham fabric lay in and around
the fallen baskets, the edges fluttering as if agitated by the
swirling emotions instead of the mild breeze.

Sherry held one hand to her chest, the other hovering
over a barrette in her hair. Her eyes held annoyance and a
hint of fear. Three women and two men flanked her, looking
on with concern but saying nothing. These were her housemates, I realized. The rest of the Silver Six. I remembered
their faces from the Christmas card Sherry had sent.

A blonde, rawboned, big-chested woman wearing jeans and a summer sweater stood off to the side, her eyes wide with horrified fascination.

Opposite my aunt stood the snarling star of the showdown in progress. She leaned over the folding table, her bloodred fingernails scary-long and lethal-looking as she pointed at Sherry.

"You'll come to an agreement with me, Mrs. Cutler, and you'll do it soon or you'll be very sorry."

"But, Ms. Elsman," my aunt began.

"No 'buts,'" the Elsman woman interrupted. "I want that option on your land, and I will by God have it."

She tucked her asymmetrically cut black hair behind an ear, lifted a stiletto-shod foot, and deliberately speared one of the medium-sized hemp baskets lying on the porch.

Blame it on being tired and stressed, but the woman stomped on my last nerve, and my temper flared in a sonic boom of fury.

"Back up and back off, lady," I snarled, whipping off my sunglasses.

I heard heavy boot steps behind me—Detective Shoar's, I guessed—but was too incensed to let him take the lead. I stormed to Sherry's tables.

The woman casually turned and arched a brow. "My name is Elsman, Ms. Jill Elsman, and I suggest you stay out of this. It does not concern you."

"Actually, it does." The black-haired, black-eyed demon woman towered over me, but I stood straight and let her have it. "It so happens that Mrs. Cutler, the woman you just threatened, is my dearest aunt."

"Nixy?" a voice said faintly.

I barreled on. "In addition, you happen to have flattened a fine piece of folk art."

"That little basket?" Hellspawn snorted and gave the basket a shove with her shoe. "What do you know about real art?"

"According to my art degrees and my position at the

prestigious Gates Gallery in Houston, I know quite a lot. I know something of the law, too, and I believe we'll be filing charges of harassment, criminal mischief, and property damage. Or is it called malicious mischief in Arkansas, Detective Shoar?"

I looked over my shoulder and caught his expression of surprise.

"Criminal mischief covers it," he drawled, but then his eyes turned all cop. "I suggest you leave now, Miss Elsman."

"Suggest all you like, Detective," she sneered, "but this event is open to the public."

"However, since you're creating a disturbance, ma'am, I think it best if you go now."

She huffed, glared at me, and then snapped her fingers. "Trudy."

I whirled to see sweater girl jump to attention. Aha. Hellspawn's minion, it seemed. She scuttled after the wicked witch like a faithful, fearful dog at heel.

And Shoar? You could've knocked me over with one of Sherry's minibaskets when he winked at me before he leisurely followed the routed twosome. I hoped he'd be certain they left because I needed to find out what the heck was happening here.

"Pixy Nixy?"

I had no more than turned when I was enfolded in Sherry's gentle hug. Although I winced at the grade school nickname Sherry had resurrected, the strong wave of warmth from my aunt comforted me in a way I hadn't known I missed. My mother had hugged me like this, and emotion swelled as I returned the embrace.

"Dear child," she said as she released me, "I hardly recognized you with your hair up like that. Did I miss an e-mail telling me you were coming?"

"Um, no, Sherry." She'd taken the barrette from her hair, and bangs fell over her left eye. She no longer looked frightened, but the sweep of bangs made her seem more vulnerable for some weird reason. I reached for a fast white lie. "I just thought I'd surprise you and experience the folk art festival. You've told me so much about it."

"I see." She gave me an *I know you're fibbing* teacher look, and since she'd taught junior high and high school, the expression fit. Then she smiled. "Well, I'm glad to see you, but I'm afraid I'll be rather busy today."

"That's okay. I'll pitch in and help."

"Not until the rest of us properly meet you."

A tall, dapper man with a full head of white hair pulled up one side of his baggy khaki pants, then the other side, but they settled back on his bony hips as he moved to stand beside Sherry. He took my hand and bowed slightly. "Dwight Aloysius Baxter, at your service."

"Dab, don't hog the girl," said a woman with short steel-gray hair. She wore a shirtwaist dress and an apron so blinding white, it could've been seen from space. Her facial structure held traces of American Indian ancestry a couple of generations removed and care lines etched her skin. "I'm Maise Holcomb, and this is my sister, Aster Parsons."

Maise's erect bearing gave me a flash of memory. Sherry had spoken of Maise and Aster, her first roommates, in the days after my mother's death. Maise had been a U.S. Navy nurse during Vietnam, and Aster had been something of a flower child. Not antiwar, but pro-peace. The differing ideologies hadn't split up the sisters, Sherry had said. They'd remained close.

Aster was more tanned than Maise, wearing her faded brown hair in a long braid, and decked out in more tie-dye than I'd seen since the gallery hosted a retro exhibition. She hugged me and I caught the essence of herbs. Rosemary? Lavender? Something both fresh and soothing, though I couldn't place it before Aster released me and my beaming Aunt Sherry took over the introductions.

"Last but never least, Nixy, this is Eleanor Wainwright and Fred Fishner."

I had to stop myself from gaping at the lovely and nearly wrinkle-free black woman with short salt-and-pepper hair decked out in an amber designer suit. I offered my hand to both Eleanor and her polar opposite, Fred. He was almost completely bald with a slight paunch covered by a white T-shirt and crisp light blue overalls. Screwdrivers and pliers and a dozen more tool-type gadgets poked out of every pocket. Even the two cargo pockets on both legs bulged. Then there was his walker, an overflowing tool belt strung across the front of it.

Fred banged his walker. His tools clanked, and arm muscles bunched. "Enough chitty-chat. I'm behind at my fix-it booth. See you later, missy."

"I do believe Fred is correct," Eleanor said in a cultured drawl as Fred clumped around the porch swing toward the driveway where I had parked.

"Right. We have tables to man, sales to make," Maise said. "Quick time, now. Let's get these baskets reorganized."

I moved to help as Sherry untangled the blue gingham checked cloth from a willow basket. She draped the fabric on the table and arranged her display with Aster and Eleanor helping, Maise supervising.

I handed Sherry the last item—the basket Big Bitch Foot had stomped. "Aunt Sherry, I really need to know what's going on here."

"With the sale or that basket?" she asked innocently. "I can repair the basket, you know."

"With that Hellspawn woman, Sherry. Please don't dodge the question."

"Elsman, dear, and, truly, it can wait."

"No, it can't," I said more quietly because boot steps approached behind me. "I want to be prepared if she comes back."

"She won't," Sherry said, smiling at someone over my shoulder.

"I agree," Detective Shoar drawled. "I'm pretty sure the lady and her assistant will stay away for the duration of the festival."

"Pretty sure?" I challenged.

"You lit into her hard. I don't think she'll want to go another round with you today."

"And after that? Do you know why she was badgering Aunt Sherry?"

"I've seen her around town. Miz Sherry, mind if I borrow your niece for a few minutes?"

"Borrow away," she said with a shooing wave. "Better yet, go shop."

Shoar gestured for me to precede him, so I stomped down the porch steps, then ended up following him to his patrol car. He leaned his fine butt on the trunk and crossed his booted ankles.

"What?" I asked after seconds of silence. Yes, I knew about the cop silent-treatment trick. I watched my share of crime shows. Didn't mean I couldn't hurry Shoar along.

"It took you so long to get here, I sure didn't expect you to jump to Miz Sherry's defense."

"I couldn't leave my job until last night," I said, sounding more indignant than I'd meant to.

"I'm not talking about just this time. I've been trying to get you to visit your aunt for a month."

"Well, I'm here now, and I don't do bullies. Which begs the question, why didn't you call Hellspawn on her threat?"

"I didn't hear her make it. I came up just as you went ballistic." He paused and gave me a stern look. "You sure had a mouthful of legal terms handy. Why is that?"

"I've dated three lawyers. Now about Hellspawn. Do you know her?"

His lips twitched. "Three lawyers?"

"Different specialties. Hellspawn?"

"I don't know her personally."

"You want to expand on that?"

He shrugged. "She's a land developer, from what I hear. I've seen her at the courthouse, and I've seen her having lunch with a couple of city councilmen, but I didn't think much of it."

"Why not? If she's after Sherry's land, I'll bet she's greasing palms."

"That's worth considering, but the lunches all took place at the Lilies Café."

"Why do you make that sound unimportant?"

"Clark and Lorna Tyler own the Lilies Café and the Inn on the Square. The building was Lilyvale's original saloon and hotel, and that's where Elsman and her assistant are staying. That's also where Jill Elsman had lunch with Clark Tyler and the other councilmen and women. Nothing smacked of clandestine meetings."

"For a cop, you're not very suspicious."

He gave me a slow smile. "You seem suspicious enough for both of us, but I will tell you this. Sherry's not the only landowner Elsman has approached, and a few have called in complaints about her."

"No one will press charges?"

His expression darkened. "To my knowledge, she hasn't done anything illegal yet, Ms. Nix."

"Nixy."

"Nixy, then. I suggest you talk to Miz Sherry and her friends about Elsman," he said as he took a business card from his shirt pocket, "and keep me updated. Call anytime."

I accepted the card. "Updated about Hellspawn or the kitchen incidents?"

"Both. Elsman may be all snap and no dragon, but better to keep her claws at a distance. If Miz Sherry wants, I can have a friendly chat with Elsman about her people skills."

"What people skills?"

"Exactly."

He gave me a quick smile, pushed off the trunk, and started for the driver's door when I remembered something bugging me.

"Hey, Detective."

"Eric."

"The call you got at the station. That wasn't through the nine-one-one line, was it?"

"Nope. Eleanor phoned me directly." He beeped open his door. "I left another card with her when I was out here Monday evening. I think she has me on speed dial."

We shared a smile that hung in time and space. I finally looked away, then back.

"Thank you," I said, and he raised a brow. "I mean for taking a personal interest in my aunt and her housemates. That's above and beyond."

"Lilyvale isn't that big. We look after our own." He opened his car door, then glanced back at me. "But never doubt I have a job to do, Nixy. Protecting the public includes protecting people from themselves. Remember that."

Chapter Three

ERIC SHOAR HAD PROVED FRIENDLIER THAN I'D imagined he'd be, was for sure handsome, and oh my, his deep, dreamy drawl was more potent in person. However, his cop stare left no doubt where he'd draw the line. A line I wasn't eager to cross.

As he drove away, I checked my mental to-do list: Get my aunt and her friends to spill about the explosions and kitchen fires. Observe the mental and physical condition of the Silver Six, especially Aunt Sherry. Discover who Hellspawn was and what she wanted. Hopefully I'd have answers by tonight. Scratch that. I *would* have answers by tonight. I didn't have time for Sherry to stonewall me.

Besides, I mused after I snagged my wallet and cell phone from the car and headed back to the porch, Sherry should be tired enough tonight to give me straight answers. Every problem had a solution; every challenge could be overcome. The sooner I had the scoop, the sooner I'd sort things out and be home in Houston. We'd all go back to our normal lives, except that I'd keep closer tabs on Aunt Sherry in the future. Just in case she needed me.

I reached the porch to find she'd clipped her bangs back
with the barrette again and was merrily chatting with several
customers. It took a moment for her to see me, and when she
did, emotion flashed in her eyes. Distress? Panic? Okay, I
should've called to tell her I was coming. My mother had
taught me better manners. But catching Sherry off guard was
the point if I wanted to get to the truth and keep her and her
housemates from winding up in court.

"I'm fine right now, but I'll take a break later," she said
after I bagged a bread basket of woven white oak for a customer. "Go enjoy the festival for a bit. Stretch your legs before
I put you to work."

She waved me away as more customers approached, but I
didn't leave. No, she seemed too eager to run me off, so I stood
at the porch railing, pulled out my phone, and began to take
pictures while surreptitiously eavesdropping. I didn't overhear anything important, and soon was looking more than
listening.

The first detail I noticed suggested that Sherry and her
friends kept the property in excellent repair. The porch looked
more or less recently painted, and so did the house itself. A
lone crepe myrtle sapling about six feet tall stood near the first
of the booths, mulch surrounding its base. Mulch-covered
flower beds lining the porch teemed with iris blooms, the old-
fashioned purple bearded iris my mother had grown. I recognized what my mom had called pinks, too, but couldn't name
the white-flowered ground cover. Sherry's four forsythia
bushes with their bright yellow flowers anchored each end of
the beds. My mom had loved forsythia, too.

I gazed beyond the cars and booths to the far side of the
yard and the thicket of pines and pin oaks interspersed with
redbuds and dogwoods that defined the southern property
line. Sherry's farmhouse sat on a half square block of land,
and the miniforest ran along the back of the house and on
part of the north side, too. I remembered that from the many
photos Sherry had sent, all labeled to give me the feeling of

being here. And while I did recognize the general layout of
the yard and garden, moving in a space was always a different experience from seeing it in pictures.

"Nixy? Nixy, are you all right?"

I blinked at Sherry's upturned face. "I'm fine."

"You were a million miles away, child."

"I was thinking about how Mom used to talk about this
place. You want a break now?"

"Not yet. Go shop. Buy that nice boss of yours a little gift."

Nice boss? Barbra? I managed not to grimace, but with
nothing else to do, I took Sherry's suggestion to browse.

All art holds value to me, be it fine, folk, or way out there. One
of my majors was in fine art, but I only squeaked through. Why?
Because I can barely draw a recognizable stick figure. An eye
for arrangement, for design, is more my thing, and I used that
talent at the gallery to showcase the works of those who have
true artistic gifts.

According to one of my professors, folk art was originally created from whatever natural materials were at hand,
and esthetics took a distant second to function. Baskets were
made for gathering food, gourds for carrying water, and the
prettiest of aprons doubled for dust rags in a pinch. But folk
artisans had long blended beauty with practicality, and as I
strolled through the festival, that truth slammed home. In
fact, the high quality of craftsmanship blurred the lines
between fine and folk art at every turn.

The horde of shoppers must've felt the same way.

I drifted from display to display, snapping photos with
my cell phone, astounded by the variety of items. Made of
every kind of material from fabric to wood, clay to metal,
artists offered quilts, furniture pieces, birdhouses, wall
hangings, multimedia paintings, jewelry, and more. Very
few vendors repeated goods, and when they did, the prices
were comparable. No undercutting one another here.

In chatting up the several dozen artists manning their

stations, I noticed distinct trends. That is, aside from the Southern drawls and Southern hospitality I found at each stop.

The first trend was that the artists were in their fifties and older. Second, they all lived in the area. Third, they'd all been doing this festival since Sherry started it three years earlier. Last, and most telling, they all sold their art for one driving reason: to supplement their limited incomes. Unlike other art and crafts festivals I shopped, not one vendor handed out business cards or directed shoppers to their websites for Internet sales. No one took special orders. The artists clearly loved creating their works of folk art, but none of them wanted to invest the time or money to run a web sales operation. Whatever customers wanted had to be bought today, or they were out of luck until the fall festival.

Were Sherry and her housemates supplementing their incomes out of necessity, too? Were any or all of them in financial trouble?

I searched my memory for the facts Sherry had dropped about her housemates in her letters. I knew each of the Six was retired, although I didn't know what fields they had worked in. Well, except that Sherry had taught school, and Maise had been a nurse. I knew they were all over sixty-five, too, so it was a safe bet they were each getting social security benefits. Sherry may have a retirement fund or pension through the school system, and some of the others might have pensions, too. Of course, that was no guarantee any of them pulled in much monthly income.

As for coming to live with Sherry, Maise and Aster's home had burned, I recalled. They'd stayed with Sherry as a stopgap, then the three decided to share the farmhouse. The arrangement gave Sherry companionship and security so she wasn't ambling around the large farmhouse alone. Eleanor came to live with Sherry next. I dredged up something said about an evil landlord. On the circumstance of Fred and Dab joining the ladies, I drew a blank, but Sherry had happily quoted the *more the merrier* adage. Simple logic dictated that the house-mates pooled their financial resources, too.

If the Six did need extra money, even mad money, I needed to do my part.

With that in mind, I sought out Aster's booth on the south side of the farmhouse. Aptly named Aster's Aromatics, her setup stood in front of a large garden of plants I couldn't begin to name, and her tables overflowed with herbal everything—soaps, bath salts, lotions, eye packs, teas. No wonder Aster smelled of herbs. Maise manned the booth with her sister, and they put on a show of being delighted to educate me about the properties of herbs and aromatherapy in general. Still, I felt an odd undercurrent as I selected soaps and lotions for my boss and friends at the gallery. Hard to pin down, but a distinctly different energy from their cheerful welcome when we met on the porch.

Across the way from Aster and Maise, I located Eleanor and Dab presiding over tables featuring carved wood art. Human, animal, plant; and free-form figures; wall art; boxes; boats; and more drew buyers. Some figures were executed with amazing detail; others were more representative. None were painted, and the gorgeous natural wood grains took my breath.

I fell for exquisite napkin rings with a lily motif and bought a set of eight for my roommate Vicki's wedding gift. Which reminded me. With Vicki leaving, I needed to get serious about apartment hunting. Soon. I couldn't swing our two-bedroom place solo, not without touching the nest egg my mother had left me. I wasn't about to deplete those savings unless I invested in buying a place of my own.

Eleanor treated me cordially if a bit coolly, even after I bought the napkin rings. Then again, I sensed a natural reserve from her. Dab acted jovial, but I felt the key there was acted. That, or I was being paranoid and the housemates were simply interested in selling instead of gabbing. Made sense if they had money worries.

Or did they resent me for waiting so long to come visit?

Or resent me for visiting now?

I sighed and reached the backyard as a group of musicians launched into a lively bluegrass tune. No stage for these performers. They stood in the mown grass, the miniforest of trees the backdrop. With fiddles, guitars, banjos, basses, and mandolins they played and smiled at the crowd. Young children pushed closer to dance to the music.

After toe-tapping to two numbers, I went to investigate Fred's display. He didn't have a mere table or three. He had a whole shed that stood opposite the farmhouse back porch and deck. The shed's double doors were thrown open and a banner overhead read FIX-IT FRED: BEST MECHANIC ANYWHERE, I FIX ANYTHING. The shelves inside held small appliances like electric griddles, blenders, and a waffle iron I'd swear had been new in 1960. He also had a few old suitcase-style record players and vintage radios.

Fred himself sat on a tractor-seat stool at a wooden workbench marred with pits and scars. Glasses perched halfway down his nose, he tinkered with a toaster as I approached. Even now, using fine motor skills, the muscles of his upper and lower arms subtly flexed. No wonder, considering the loaded walker he lunged around.

"Mind if I take a peek inside?" I asked when he noticed me.

"Look all you like, but ain't nothin' for sale in there. Owners haven't picked them up yet."

"Not even that stand mixer?" I eyed the white KitchenAid that had to date from the 1970s.

"It's a beaut, ain't it? Lady who owns that still has all the attachments. She's visitin' her daughter for a spell." He gave me narrow glance. "You cook? Bake?"

"Not much, but that mixer is a classic. It's great that you can fix it."

"Lotta classics around here, but it don't mean they're disposable."

I met his serious, faintly warning gaze, and knew he spoke of more than household appliances.

"Fred," a voice called, and I lost my chance to say more.

As I poked around in the shed, I overheard Fred consult with customer after customer about their lawn mowers, tractors, cars, and appliances needing repair. I'd about tuned out the conversations when one caught my ear.

"You better fix that stove in y'all's own house, Fred. Maybe you wouldn't have smoke pouring out the windows ever' other durned day."

I edged closer to eavesdrop, but stayed out of sight.

Fred humphed. "Stove's not the problem, Bob. It's Maise. She's a helluva cook, but she don't know 'come here' from 'sic 'em' about making fancy desserts."

"What kinda desserts?" Bob asked, emphasizing the "de" in desserts.

"The woman's obsessed with lightin' fruit on fire. Pours good liquor over it, flicks that long barbeque lighter, and whoosh."

"What fool kind of thing is she trying to make?"

"She calls it flambé but it always goes flambooey. She's too stubborn to quit, though. Says she won't give up until she gets the dish right."

I heard the man chuckle. "Well, we're just across the road, you know. Can see your place easy from the kitchen window. You have our number, right?"

"We do," Fred confirmed.

"Then holler if you ever need us."

Fred greeted someone new, and I slipped away from his shed, considering what I'd heard. Igniting booze certainly explained the kitchen fires, but not so much the explosions. Not unless Maise was the mad scientist of cooks.

Hmm. Bob had to live in the subdivision across the way, one that looked to date from the 1970s. A drainage ditch, then a brick wall separated the neighborhood from the road. I recalled seeing it as I followed Detective Shoar. I'd lay odds Bob was one of the complaining neighbors, but he wasn't testy with Fred. That was good.

I blinked, realizing I'd been staring into space again, and looked around. Three vehicles were parked off to my left near the fence—a rather beat-up red pickup, a blue Corolla, and a dark gray Cadillac. The Corolla was Sherry's. I remembered her driving it when my mom died. Also on the left, some ten yards from Fred's shed, were two country-red outbuildings a little wider and deeper than single-car garages, and beyond those a barn the same color. Not a ginormous barn, but with typical high double doors. I startled when a standard-sized side door swung open. A harried woman about my age hustled out, shooing two children in front of her. I was a second from confronting her for being in a nonpublic area when I noticed the RESTROOM sign beside the door.

It seemed beyond progressive to have a bathroom in the barn, but it made sense for the festival. On-site facilities kept customers on the grounds ready to spend more money, yet renting porta potties would cut into the profit margin. Toilet paper, paper towels, and soap were cheap by comparison.

The woman and her children hustled away, but I spotted someone else skulking by the back of the barn. I blinked, squinted, whipped out my cell to take a picture. She'd covered her blonde hair with a blue ball cap but hadn't changed from the jeans and summer sweater she'd worn earlier. The one that enhanced her Dolly Parton chest.

Shoot fire. If Hellspawn's minion was here, was Hellspawn herself far behind?

Detective Shoar had been wrong about the troublemakers staying away, but I'd routed them once, and I'd do it again.

The minion peered out from behind the corner of the barn, spied me, and gave me a *come here* wave, but I was already on the move.

Chapter Four

I STOMPED THROUGH THE MOWED FIELD GRASS TO where the woman stood at the corner of the barn.

"What are you doing back here?" I demanded.

"Finding you." Coming from a tall, big-boned gal who looked like she could snap me in half, her breathy voice startled me. Deep but breathy. Like Marlene Dietrich doing Marilyn Monroe, and yes, I'd dated an old-movie buff.

The minion craned her neck, her gaze darting from me to the main yard and back. "I'm Trudy Henry."

"What do you want, Trudy?"

She hesitated, bit her lip, and again scanned the area as if looking for spies. "I want to buy one of your aunt's white oak baskets. One with the rope handle braided in with blue gingham fabric. I have money."

She wedged a fat roll of twenties from her jeans pocket, and I couldn't help but stare.

"Your boss pays you big bucks, huh?"

Trudy made a sour face. "This is from my savings. May I buy a basket?"

Sincere as she sounded, I shook my head. "I don't think it's a good idea to come back to the festival today."

Her shoulders slumped. "Can I buy one later if your aunt has any left over?"

"I'll ask her for you," I said more kindly. The girl was about my age but reminded me of an awkward puppy. "Is that all you wanted?"

"Actually, no. I need to warn you about Ms. Elsman. I'm not supposed to talk about her business, but you need to know she's, uh, pretty determined to get, ah, what she wants."

I stiffened. "Which is what?"

"You need to ask your aunt about that. Like I said, I shouldn't be talking to you at all, but I'm worried about how far Ms. Elsman will go." Trudy looked close to tears. "I just don't want anyone to get hurt. Please, talk with your aunt."

With a wave, Trudy galumphed off toward the back of Sherry's property and disappeared into the woods that extended to the next street over. In spite of not having visited Sherry before now, I *had* listened when my mother talked about playing hide-and-seek out behind the house. She'd mentioned her old home often in the weeks before her stroke, had longed to visit again. Then it had been too late to bring her.

It wasn't too late to help Sherry. Trudy's warning worried me even more than the kitchen fires, and my resolve to get these mysteries sorted out doubled.

I spent the rest of the morning selling handwoven baskets to a steady flow of festival customers. Sometimes Sherry stayed with me for a spell. More often I manned the wares without her, although she flitted back to check on sales or to introduce me to groups of people. I met two women who had taught with Sherry at the junior high school and three others about my age who had been Sherry's students. A former-student fireman and four city and county bigwigs stopped by, too.

The young women didn't shop Sherry's baskets. They flirted with Ben Berryhill, a tall, muscles-on-muscles fireman, and with the equally tall Bryan Hardy, introduced to

me as the county's deputy prosecuting attorney. Though I
kept expecting Ben to mention Sherry's kitchen fires, he
never did. Bryan Hardy's baby face belied the age he had to
be to have finished law school, practiced law, I presumed,
and now hold an important office. His black-framed glasses
made his face look even broader and younger, but he also
seemed quiet, almost shy for a guy in his position. The
Houston attorneys I'd dated had been more flash and brash,
and I found myself liking Bryan's hazel eyes and soft-spoken
voice. What little I heard of his voice.

Shopping took a backseat with the teachers, too. They
schmoozed with Mayor Patrick Paulson and councilper-
sons Kate Byrd and B. G. Huff. Were they two of the council-
persons Detective Shoar had seen lunching with Hellspawn?
How many others were there? I put Huff and Byrd in my
mental Rolodex.

Not one person mentioned Sherry's explosions or fires,
and I wondered if she had asked them to keep mum. Not
one of them bought baskets either, except for the mayor. He
scored points with me when he purchased an egg basket
before he wandered away with the others.

Sherry's behavior puzzled me yet again. She talked easily
with everyone else, but with me she acted jittery, her eyes
never quite meeting mine. Even in the one moment we had
without shoppers surrounding us, when I apologized again
for arriving without notice, her gaze only skimmed my face.

"At least let me order pizza or go pick up dinner," I said.

"No need, child," she said, waving away the offer. "We
have supper all set. Ham salad, chicken salad, cottage cheese
with olives and tomatoes, and Maise's famous fried okra.
You'll stay with us, no arguments. I'll share Eleanor's room
and you'll have mine."

"I don't want to put Eleanor out, Sherry. I can bunk with you."

She gave me another of her near-panicked glances.

"Or I'll take the sofa," I amended. "Or find a hotel room.
I'll only be here a few days."

"No, no, it's all settled. Now, will you watch the baskets again for a while?"

"Sure, I will. And thank you."

She cocked her head, peering at me like an inquisitive bird, then patted my arm and took off.

What had happened to the serene, never-ruffled Sherry Mae of eighteen months ago? The question nagged at me, but I shoved it to the back burner of my brain and sold more baskets.

WHILE PEOPLE CAME AND WENT THROUGHOUT THE day, the crowd never really thinned. In the late afternoon, when artists began packing up what little seemed to be left of their wares, shoppers hustled to score last-minute buys.

Sherry had fewer than a dozen baskets remaining in her stock, two made of rough jute that I learned were crocheted, not woven. As I packed the wares in a large cardboard box, I remembered Trudy's request to buy one of Sherry's white oak baskets. Sherry made distinctive long hemp rope handles wrapped in fabric with the ends artfully frayed. Two were left. Should I hold one out for Trudy now? No. If she followed up on her request to buy a basket, I could find one for her quickly enough. I finished packing and broke down the rest of the boxes for easy storage.

At five fifteen, the last of the vendors wheeled her SUV out of the gravel drive and the yard looked pristine. The crepe myrtle sapling didn't have so much as a bent leaf, and there wasn't a scrap of trash anywhere. Impressive, especially considering the number of people who'd been on the grounds today.

I folded Sherry's tables and leaned them long way against the porch rail, then strode to the south part of the wrap-around porch to help Aster, Maise, Dab, and Eleanor with their tables. I knew they were capable of folding the tables on their own. They'd managed the setup, after all. But, hey, they were all in their early seventies and had been on their feet all day.

Besides, I needed all the brownie points I could get with his group.

I found the Silver Six in a hushed-tone huddle. Folded tables rested on two hand trucks along with a couple of intact boxes—packed with their own festival leftovers, I guessed—and more neatly folded boxes. I couldn't overhear them, so I took a moment to observe them more closely.

No outward signs of illness, and they all seemed mentally sharp enough. Heck, I was beginning to droop from the long drive and the long day, while the seniors seemed to have reserves of energy. Sherry stood tall as a five-foot woman can, and had kept a trim figure. Eleanor had, too, while Maise and Aster had figures like my mother. Matronly, Mom had called it. Dab was thin but not emaciated, Fred rounded but not morbidly obese. Except for Fred using a walker, he didn't look the least bit infirm, and neither did the other compatriots. Or would that be conspirators?

Eleanor looked up and spotted me, all conversation halted, and every face turned my way. Yep, they were plotting. At least they all looked healthy doing it.

I waved and bounced down the stairs, weaving my way through the herb garden. "That was a wonderful festival," I said as I approached. "Shall I move these tables for y'all?"

Sherry smiled. "Certainly, Nixy. They go in the barn. Dab and Fred will show you where, right, gentlemen?"

"Whatever you wish," Dab said gallantly.

"And your unsold baskets? There weren't many, and they all fit in one box I left on the porch."

"Those go in the basement, but I'll take care of them."

"You sure? It's a big box."

"But not heavy. Now, when you finish moving the tables, Nixy, bring your things and come on in for supper."

"I'll even break out my dandelion wine to celebrate," Aster said.

I expected immediate action, yet, except to shift from foot to foot, no one moved. Maise glanced at her watch, gave a small nod, and they all turned toward the road.

I turned with them, having to shade my eyes against the intense western sun, even though I wore my sunglasses. Birds chirped, but nothing moved. No cars passed. The rustic rail fence didn't appear to be damaged, and the cute farmhouse mailbox enclosure was intact and upright as far as I could see. Nothing seemed out of place because, again, there was not so much as a gum wrapper in the yard.

Impatience got the best of me.

"I'll bite. What are we looking at?"

"Not looking at," Maise said. "Waiting for."

Sherry linked her arm in mine, and I had another flash of memory about my mother. "Jill Elsman has been driving by each afternoon about this time," she said. "We wave at her."

"Just being friendly?" I asked doubtfully.

"Psychological warfare," Maise snapped. "She thinks she's intimidating us. We retaliate with a peaceful show of force to keep her off balance."

"She's already unbalanced," I muttered, but waited shoulder to shoulder with the Six until another few minutes passed.

"Don't look like she's comin' today," Fred barked. "I'm hungry."

"All right, then, let's move out. Ladies, with me. Men, show Nixy where to stow the gear."

I spent the next thirty minutes bemused and bumping table-laden hand carts through the yard and into a storage room in a front corner of the barn. Fred and Dab escorted me on the first load run, but Fred stayed in the barn to tinker with the riding lawn mower parked there. I also caught sight of plastic bins on a workbench holding blocks of wood, wood slats for baskets, and coils of white and tan rope. Even without an artistic gene in my DNA, my fingers itched to touch and test the textures of the art supplies.

With my suitcase and my brown suede hobo bag, I entered

the house through the back to get a look at the country
kitchen, which took up nearly a quarter of the downstairs. I
glimpsed Maise at the oven, Aster at the counter, and Eleanor
standing at a round pedestal table but saw no telltale scorch
marks before Sherry intercepted me. She'd removed the barrette in her hair again and bangs flopped over one eye.

It struck me as odd that she was finally looking at me
directly when she hadn't done so most of the day. I didn't
have time to puzzle on it, though. With a firm grip on my
arm, Sherry steered me away from the heavenly smells of
dinner to the back hall and staircase.

"Did Sue Anne tell you much about the Stanton homestead?"

"She did, and you sent photos to me, Sherry, but the
house is even nicer than I imagined." I eyed the original
hardwood floors and the plain but gorgeous banister and
spindles. A large window splashed late-afternoon sun on
the landing, and we turned to the second set of steps.

My mom had talked about the Stantons being a larger
clan at one time, so I knew the house had four bedrooms
upstairs and boasted three full bathrooms. Bathrooms were
as rare as closet space in a house this old, but my ancestors
had been forward thinking enough to build both as they
added to the house. Or desperate for bathrooms.

"We womenfolk are up here with Dab," Sherry said.
"Fred's downstairs. My Bill couldn't handle the stairs at the
last, and since we had two parlors, we converted the back
one into a bedroom and cut another door to the downstairs
bath. Dab and Fred share that one."

Bill, I recalled, had suffered a stroke several years before
my mother did. Unlike my mom, Bill had lived another year
before a second, fatal stroke.

Sherry stopped at the end of the hall, opened the door on
the right, and I sucked in a breath. The room was painted a
soft spring green with white sheers on the four windows. A
burl wood dresser, dark wood night table, and overstuffed

chair with a needlepoint footstool had perfect places in the room, but the centerpiece was the homemade quilt with a spring flowers motif covering the four-poster bed.

"Your great-grandmother made the quilt," Sherry said softly. "It's a bit faded, and it's been mended over the years."

"It's beautiful, Aunt Sherry," I breathed. "The whole room is you."

"Thank you. I like it, though the morning sun will wake you, so sleeping late is nearly impossible. The master bath is through there," she said on a smile and pointed to the right. "Do you want to freshen up before we eat?"

"I'll just wash my hands and be right down."

"Don't dawdle."

I didn't. I didn't even take time to snoop. Hunger pangs hit like a hammer, and, besides, the doors were closed in both the upstairs and downstairs halls. I followed the sound of voices to the front of the house where a double wide doorway opened onto the dining room. A long, dark wood sideboard held candle sticks and decorative bowls, and an old farm table, equally darkened with age, was set for seven and laden with food. Three glass beverage pitchers, and a bottle surrounded by cordial glasses. Everyone but Dab was seated, and he came through a swinging door with another chair he plopped down next to Sherry at the far end of the table.

"Nixy, sit there at the foot so we can all see you," Sherry said as she pointed to the chair closest to the foyer.

With Fred on my left, Eleanor on my right, I took my seat, and after Aster gave thanks for the bounty, we dug in. Saucers piled with homemade bread, big bowls with the cold meat salads and crisp, evenly browned fried okra, and small bowls with condiments made the lap around the table. I opted for sweet tea and accepted a splash of dandelion wine.

I expected dinner chatter about the festival, but the Silver Six ate in silence so profound, they'd give vow-silent monks competition. And, okay, I shoveled down fried okra so divine, my taste buds had a religious experience.

But I needed answers, and at this moment, I had a captive audience.

"Aunt Sherry, I mentioned that I have to leave Tuesday, right?"

"It's not the least bit inconvenient to have you longer."

"Thank you, but the point is I have only a few days to help out. And first, I need to know what's going on with the explosions and kitchen fires."

"Detective Shoar's been tattling on us?" Her tone went for playful. I didn't buy it.

"He's concerned about your safety and the safety of your neighbors."

Fred harrumphed, and Maise cleared her throat.

"It's my fault," she said. "I have a lovely recipe for bananas flambé, but it always goes flambooey. Same when I try it with peaches and berries. I don't know what I'm doing wrong."

"No offense, Maise, but coming from someone who can fry okra this perfect, that story sounds like a lot of baloney." I set my fork on the plate, sat ramrod straight, and gave each of the Six a hard stare. "Time to come clean, ladies and gentlemen. What's really going on?"

Chapter Five

SILENCE HUNG OVER THE TABLE AS THE SIX EX-
changed glances. Then Aster shot out of her chair and grabbed
a blue bowl from the sideboard.

"Let's enjoy a little calming lavender," she said as she
sprinkled tiny purple buds down the center of the table,
deftly avoiding the food.

Fred growled and slapped his thick ham salad sandwich
on his plate.

"I do believe Fred is immune, Aster," Eleanor said.

"Bet my last nuts and bolts, I'm immune. I'm mad and
I'm stayin' that way. Who's she to be askin' questions when
she don't know nothin' about—"

"Fred!" cried the women.

He crossed his arms. "I'm just saying she's awful nosy
for a niece who hardly pays attention to her aunt."

"Fred, please don't," Sherry cautioned.

"Well, she is, dadgumit." Fred shifted his gaze from
Sherry to me. "We're the ones who've been with Sherry
through thick 'n thin these past years, and she with us. Me

after my accident, Dab after his Melba died, Aster and Maise when their house burned, and Eleanor when—"

"That's quite enough, Fred." Aster spoke with steel in her tone and smacked the bowl of lavender on the table.

"Point is," Fred went on, "we've been knowin' each other long before we started sharin' this house. You don't know diddly squat about us, and you shouldn't be stickin' your nose in our business."

I took a measured breath.

"You're right, Fred. I don't know nearly enough about any of you, and I haven't been the best of nieces to Sherry Mae. But I want to be a better niece, and I want y'all to be safe. To do that I need information. So educate me. Please. Let's start by talking about the explosions."

"That's my fault," Dab said, "but it's a boom, not an explosion. I distill Aster's herbs in the basement, you see, and every time the old furnace down there rumbles, the vibration messes with the pressure valves on my stills."

"When we have, uh, a boom," Aster added, "we have a system. Maise sets off a smoke bomb in the kitchen window, and I crank up the garden fans to blow away the smoke."

Eleanor sniffed. "And blow off whatever that noxious smell coming from the basement is."

I narrowed my eyes at Dab. "Why don't you tell Detective Shoar the truth?"

"'Cause Dab thinks Shoar will arrest him for moonshinin'," Fred grumped. "Old Dab's family was bootleggers back in the day, and he stores some of the old hooch down there."

"It's just some jugs of vintage home brew his family made," Sherry added. "It's not much different from having a wine cellar."

"I see. Are you making anything illegal, Dab?"

He puffed up. "Now listen here, I am a chemical engineer with years of experience. I would move out before I'd put any of us at risk."

"Okay, then let's talk about Hellspawn. From what I heard, she wants an option on your land, Sherry. Is that like an oil lease?" Yes, my Texas roots showed, plus I'd dated a geologist who worked for an oil and gas company.

Sherry folded her hands on the table, and I saw they trembled slightly. "No, child, she wants an option to purchase the entire property. We looked up the term on the Internet. Eleanor, you explain it."

Eleanor folded her hands in her lap. "A developer draws up a contract to buy your house or land. You agree on a set purchase price, and the developer then pays the landowner a fee for signing the contract."

"How much of a fee?"

"According to the article we read, it's five to ten percent of the purchase price. There's a time limit in the contract, but the selling price remains the same, even if property values go up."

"Ms. Elsman told us most of our neighbors have signed her contract," Sherry added.

"Bullies lie, Aunt Sherry. Have you talked to the neighbors to check out her story?"

Sherry looked shocked. "Heavens, no. One doesn't talk about religion, politics, or money with people one doesn't know extremely well, Nixy."

"Perhaps not even then," Maise said, "We're not nosy parkers."

"I know your mother taught you the same rules," Sherry added.

"She did, but, Sherry, you're being threatened. If asking questions gives you facts, it's time to be a little nosy." I paused and glanced around the table. "Does anyone know what she's planning to build?"

"No," Dab chimed in, "but Eleanor tried looking her up on the Net. Nothing came up except an Elsman obituary. Oliver James Elsman owned OJE Development Company out of Little Rock."

"Is that a land development company?" I asked, and Eleanor nodded. "Then unless there are a lot of Elsmans in Arkansas, I'll bet the company and Hellspawn are connected. Did she leave you a business card?"

"Yes, but it only lists her name and phone number," Eleanor said.

"Then maybe she's not legit. Have you called the OJE office to ask if they've heard of her?"

Sherry looked sheepish. "We haven't had time, what with getting ready for the festival."

I nodded and put calling OJE on my to-do list.

"I heard Hellspawn say you'd be sorry for not selling to her, but has she made specific threats?"

"She has. She's visited for thirteen days now, and every time she made threats. At first they were verbal, like telling the city powers that be that I'm unlawfully running a boardinghouse."

"At first?" I echoed, feeling the okra suddenly churn in my gut.

Another of those looks passed around the table, then Sherry sighed.

"We can't be sure Elsman is behind these incidents, but just Tuesday morning we found a dead bird on the porch steps. Its little neck was broken. Wednesday morning, we discovered a break-in at the barn."

"What was taken?" I asked, willing myself to remain calm even while remembering the tidy barn and art supplies.

"The barn was a mess with things tossed all over, so it took a while to pin down that anything at all was missing. Eventually, I discovered some of my basket weaving supplies were gone. Some blue gingham fabric strips, some hemp rope, and my old white cotton gloves. Well, they weren't white anymore. I use them when I crochet with jute twine, sometimes with hemp twine, too, so I don't tear up my hands."

"And we wear cotton gloves after we treat our hands with lanolin," Eleanor added. "Although I do believe I've come

to like my gardening gloves more for whittling. The rubber-
ized ones give me a better grip."

"We also discovered," Dab said, "that a crow bar and an
old hand drill were gone. A few other things, too. Nothing
worth much, but the drill was my dad's."

"That weren't the worst mischief, though," Fred growled.
"Tell her, Sherry."

"Someone put a cherry bomb or some such thing in the
mailbox. I found the damage Thursday morning."

"A bomb?" I said, managing not to screech.

"Back panel landed in the front yard," Fred said, "and
the mailbox door blowed clean across the road. Dab and me
put a new mailbox in right quick and fixed the enclosure.
And we're keepin' the doors on the barn and t'other outbuildings padlocked."

"Oh. My. God."

My hands clenched the chair arms while every muscle
vibrated with anger. This went beyond bullying into terror-
ism. A deep breath then another four calmed me enough to
speak again.

"Does Shoar know about all these incidents? Surely he's
investigating the mailbox bomb."

"Naturally," Sherry said. "Why, even Mayor Paulson and
Chief Randall came by with our county deputy prosecuting
attorney, Bryan Hardy. You met the mayor and Bryan today.
They assured us they'd find the culprits."

"Does the detective have suspects?" I asked tightly.

"He thinks it's kids pulling pranks," Dab said.

Sherry nodded. "I've known Eric Shoar since he was a
boy, and he's been very attentive and helpful. He's doing his
best, what with our other detective out for surgery. I'm only
surprised he didn't tell you all this when he took you aside
this morning."

"So am I," I muttered with visions of retribution next
time I had Shoar in my sights.

"I ain't surprised a'tall," Fred grumped. "To tell it true, we think Shoar believes we're losin' it, and that's why you showed up. Shoar wants you to take us in hand, get us to go to an old folks' home."

I collapsed against the chair back on a whoosh of breath. No wonder they'd all been so leery of me at the festival. Why they were huddled together afterward. Why they kept exchanging speculative glances.

Why Fred blew up at me.

"You're wrong," I said firmly. "In the first place, I wouldn't dream of making you move, even if I had that authority. Second, within the limits of his job, Detective Shoar has been protecting y'all. It's true he gave me an ultimatum to come check on Aunt Sherry Mae, but he doesn't want you in a seniors' home."

"He told you that?" Sherry asked.

"He told me Lilyvale takes care of their own, but the explosions—"

"Booms," Dab corrected.

"—have to stop. No more smoke bombs either."

Dab heaved a defeated sigh. "I'll dismantle the stills tomorrow. Now that the festival is over, Aster won't need me to distill herbs for a month or so."

"Hotcakes on the griddle!" Fred crowed. "That'll give Eleanor a chance to redesign the stills and me to build 'em."

"Eleanor designs stills?" I asked.

"Not in the general way of things, but she is a mechanical engineer."

I said, "Oh," but thought *wow*.

"Now, wait a minute," Dab sputtered. "I want to reassemble at least one of those stills in the barn."

"Why, Dab?" Eleanor asked.

"Because I'm working on my own project and never you mind what it is. I just need one still to be operational."

I held up a hand. "Dab, as long as it's legal, and there are no booms, and no fire dangers, have at it. That will take care of one issue, but, Sherry, you have to talk to your neighbors.

You need to find out if Hellspawn is lying about those option contracts. Tomorrow's Sunday, so most of them should be home by the afternoon, right?"

Sherry's worried expression transformed into a beaming smile. "Even better, Nixy. Most of them will be at services tomorrow morning."

"Not only that," Aster broke in with a grin, "it's also Break Bread Breakfast Sunday at nearly every church in town."

"It's what?"

"The church ladies of various denominations serve a buffet before the first service," Eleanor said.

"It's designed to build community," Aster added with a twinkle in her eyes, "but it's also the best time to pick up gossip."

"Not that we gossip," Eleanor said primly.

Dab and Fred snorted a laugh.

"Then are you in for some snooping?" I asked. "All of you?"

Heads nodded, and Maise rapped the table with the heel of her knife. "It's unanimous. At oh-eight-hundred tomorrow, we commence Operation Sink Hellspawn."

LATER I PITCHED IN TO CLEAN THE DINNER DISHES— policing the kitchen, Maise called it— and listened to Sherry and crew strategize which of them would visit which churches the following morning. From their discussion, I learned none of them were strangers to any church in Lilyvale. That, Sherry said, should make asking questions less offensive. Maise declared they'd operate at maximum efficiency if she went to the Baptist breakfast, Eleanor and Aster hit the Methodist church, and Sherry, Dab, and I attended St. Mark's Episcopal.

Fred decided he'd stay home and on guard in case Elsman and her assistant tried to pull any shenanigans. When Maise pushed him, he promised he'd guard without shoving his prized Colt .45 in an overall pocket.

I kept my mouth firmly shut during that exchange but shuddered at the image of Fred with a gun in hand. Or tucked into his walker tool belt.

When Maise pronounced the kitchen shipshape, the Six gathered in the dining room again, this time to add up their festival receipts. Pointed looks from Eleanor and Aster made it clear they wanted privacy. Part of the *don't discuss finances* rule, I supposed, so I said good night to a chorus of "Sleep tight," and headed to Sherry's bedroom to unpack my meager wardrobe and figure out what to wear to church.

I hadn't seen the need to bring a dress. Definitely *not* one of my gussy-up-for-the-gallery suits, and my work clothes from Friday wouldn't do either. I had, however, packed a decent pair of navy slacks and black loafers. With a white, modestly scoop-necked T-shirt and my throw-it-over-anything navy jacket, I should pass even Maise's inspection. I should be perfectly comfortable, too, because my weather app showed average highs in the midseventies all week, lows in the fifties. No rain predicted until Saturday, by which time I'd be home.

Sherry's claw-foot tub beckoned, so I hung my church outfit on the shower rod to steam out the minor wrinkles and ran a hot bath with a sprinkle of lavender bath salts carrying the Aster's Aromatics label. Sinking into the fragrant heat relaxed my stiff muscles and general tension, but it didn't ease all my concerns.

I didn't know quite what I'd expected to feel being with Sherry Mae again, but something was off. Though she'd been grieving for my mom, too, the Sherry of eighteen months ago had been rock solid. She'd kept me organized and on task whether the job at hand was making lists for the mountain of thank-you notes to be written, or sorting items to keep or donate.

In contrast, today's Sherry acted unsure, tentative. More passive than assertive. The woman who'd helped me account for every dime of the funeral expenses had accepted Hellspawn's claims without blinking.

Then again, I didn't want to question the obnoxious Hell-spawn about the time of day either. I wanted her far away. Mars could be far enough.

I just *had* to help Sherry get rid of her by Tuesday.

As for determining if Sherry and her friends had money troubles, that was information I doubted I'd get at all.

However, knowing the explosions and kitchen fires were only booms and smoke bombs was a huge relief. Once Dab dismantled the gitlly, no more booms, no more bombs, and the neighbors would have nothing to complain about. Detective Shoar would have nothing to investigate. Nothing to plague me about.

I bit my lip as I drained the tub, toweled dry, and considered not Eric Shoar's many manly attributes, but his manner.

It bothered me that the Six assumed Shoar wanted them out of their home. They lived in this town and had done so most of their lives from what I gathered. They knew how things worked in Lilyvale. So what if I was wrong about the detective? What if Hellspawn was indeed greasing city official palms and he was a pawn to do their bidding? I didn't for a second consider he'd be complicit with an underhanded scheme. Instinct told me he was too honest, too honorable. Besides, if he wanted the Six out of the farmhouse, he'd want me staying put in Houston, not visiting Lilyvale. Right?

I plugged in my tablet and phone to charge them and thought about Fred's outraged defense of Sherry. Of them all, I'd surmised from Sherry's letters and cards and e-mails that she shared a close bond with her housemates, but I'd had no idea how strong their ties were. I couldn't claim to be that close to my roommate, Vicki, although I counted her as a friend.

Sadly, I had to admit she was one of my few friends. I had drinks with acquaintances now and then, and I used to date often, but I hadn't met a man who really tripped my romantic trigger. Without fail, sometime between dates one and three, either I got fed up with a guy, or I became his pal instead of a potential partner. I learned a lot of interesting tidbits about a lot of subjects, from law to car maintenance to longhorn cattle ranching, but each relationship that lasted past three dates quickly became platonic. All fizzle, no sizzle.

I snuggled down in Sherry's bed with a promise to myself that I'd get a life when I got home.

Sunday morning, I dressed for another beautiful Arkansas day. Makeup and hair done, I met the Six in the kitchen. Except for Fred, the seniors wore church clothes. Eleanor again looked elegant enough to belong in a fashion magazine.

Maise handed me a list of people we should be able to corner at the breakfast. Each name was followed with a brief physical description and a notation about where they lived and how long they'd been in their homes. Also where some of them worked. I didn't know the area, so the addresses didn't mean a thing to me, but I did note some of these people had been Sherry's neighbors for thirty years or more.

"We thought this would help you keep everyone straight," Sherry said.

"Seein' as how you haven't been here before," Fred added, his tone just shy of snide.

Winning Fred over was going to be a challenge. Maybe when I came back for another visit, he'd forgive me for being a bad niece. Make that twenty or thirty visits.

Riding in Dab's prime-condition Cadillac soothed my nerves somewhat, although they jumped again when we entered the already crowded fellowship hall just after eight. Dab steered us to the buffet tables even as he pointed out some of the neighbors on the list. Sherry hovered over the dishes but didn't help herself to much of anything. Dab insisted on scooping a serving of egg-and-bacon casserole onto her plate, then served himself.

I had a half serving of the casserole, too, and then all but fell on the platter of biscuits. "Dough Belly," my dad used to call me, and he was right. Sandwich bread didn't tempt me, but corn bread, rolls, and biscuits were siren songs to my stomach. With butter and honey? Bliss on a paper plate. Good thing I burned off carbs with ease, though that supposedly changed after age thirty. Fair enough. I refused to worry about it until then.

My guide-to-the-neighbors cheat sheet in my jacket pocket, I followed Dab and Sherry to the last three seats at the end of a table near a concrete block wall. Sherry introduced me to John and Jane Lambert, the couple who owned the house at the end of Sherry's block. Both wore green—a green shirt and gray tie for him, a long-sleeved shirtwaist dress that looked vintage for her.

Sherry didn't have to question them, though. A couple of how-do-you-dos, and John lit into her.

"Sherry Mae Cutler, you have some nerve showing up here. Your family must be rolling in that graveyard out back."

Chapter Six

SHERRY GAPED, AND I WAS RIGHT THERE WITH HER.

"What on earth are you talking about, John?" Dab snapped.

"That developer woman told me you up and sold her the property option on your place. That place has been in your family since they founded Lilyvale. And after all the work you and Bill put into it over the years, too. It's not right. Just not right."

Sherry sputtered before finding her voice. "I haven't sold Jill Elsman a thing, John."

He lowered a forkful of hash browns. "You haven't?"

"No. She told me *you* had. That all my neighbors had sold to her."

"Why, that lying—"

"Now, John," Jane said, a hand on his coat sleeve. "We're in church."

"We're in the fellowship hall."

"God can still hear you."

I choked on a bite of biscuit, but Sherry kept her eyes on John.

"Have you signed her contract yet?" Sherry asked John.

"No, I have not. I told her I wouldn't unless she showed me *your* contract, signed and sealed."

"I declare, John. Why would you tell her that?"

"Because of your standing in this town. You were the mayor. I figured if you signed, the deal was legit."

"What are you talking about?" a big man in blue bellowed from the next table. "Is it that pesky Elsman woman?"

"Sure is, Big George," John called back.

That name I remembered from the list. Big George Heath looked like a bear in a brown suit. He owned the hardware store.

Heads lifted, chairs scraped on the dull linoleum, and suddenly people swarmed to the table, drawling their words double time. The Southern accents weren't that different from the Texas drawl I'd grown up hearing—heck, the one I had myself—but the noise grew in volume and bounced around the room.

A rare attack of crowd-induced claustrophobia gripped me, so when Sherry stood, I did, too. Shoulder to shoulder with her, I grabbed my cheat sheet from my pocket. Dab stood behind and between us.

"She's the rudest person!"

"Marie Dunn," Dab whispered as the neighbors voiced their agreement with Marie, a petite woman wearing a black pantsuit.

"She acted like she was doing us such a big favor. Just because our home is small and more than seventy years old doesn't make it worthless."

"Pauletta Williamson," Dab provided even as I glanced at my list. Gray permed hair, denim dress, squash blossom necklace.

"That fool woman sets a toe on my property again, and I'll use Barker to comb her hair with buckshot."

"Now, Duke, don't be saying things like that," Sherry chided. Duke Richards, I remembered after a peek at my crib sheet. The suit-wearing man with collar-length hair. He owned the Dairy Queen.

"You've been the mayor, Sherry. You should do something about that land shark."

"Bog Turner." Dab identified the bald man who jerked at the knot of his black striped tie. Ironically, he owned the barber shop.

Silence reigned for seconds. Then Sherry straightened her spine.

"I can't do anything about her by myself, Bog, but together we can. I'll organize a meeting, so everyone write down your name and contact information, just in case I can't find my church roster at home."

Scribbling quickly ensued, and Sherry turned to me. "You take notes on that list Dab gave you."

"Yes, ma'am," I said as she clapped for attention.

"Friends, I need a show of hands. How many of you have signed contracts with Jill Elsman?"

No hands went up. I dutifully recorded it.

"How many of you were told that I had signed the contract?"

Thirteen hands waved, and I marked the number, though I didn't have time to mentally connect hands with people's names.

"Did Jill Elsman tell any of you what she planned to build?"

No one answered, and I jumped in with a question.

"Did she threaten any of you?"

"Who's asking?" Pauletta demanded.

"I'm Nixy. Leslee Stanton Nix. Sherry Mae's niece."

"Sue Anne's girl? Oh, honey, we prayed for your mama."

The comment blindsided me. My throat clogged and tears threatened, but I swallowed hard and took a breath. "Thank you, Mrs. Williamson. Now, about the threats. Anyone?"

"She didn't threaten me, but I heard about the trouble at your aunt's place," Bog said. "You think this woman's behind it all?"

I shrugged. "Detective Shoar thinks kids are pulling the pranks. Back to what this project could be, what about contacts at city hall? Does anyone have an in with a secretary? A clerk?"

"I play checkers with Scooter Morgan at the shop," Bog admitted. "But he's the janitor. I doubt he knows much."

"The thing is," John said, "if there were plans afoot to build anything new in Lilyvale, it'd be all over town."

While voices raised in general agreement, a bell sounded in the hall, the signal that services would begin in ten minutes. The exodus began.

"We did good, didn't we, Nixy?" Sherry said quietly.

"You did great, Aunt Sherry, and you didn't have to be nosy."

She beamed. "You're right. I hope the others had as much success."

"Whether they did or not," Dab said, "we have a good start on the resistance movement. I think Elsman's days here are numbered."

I HOPED WE'D BE ABLE TO LEAVE RIGHT AFTER THE service. That plan pretty well tanked with the last "Amen" when one person after another stopped to say hello. Sherry introduced me, and while I understood the small-town social convention, what touched me was hearing the pride in Sherry's tone. Pride in me. Shoot. I *had* been a bad niece. I'd make it a priority to come back soon to spend a weekend.

I spotted several people who looked familiar from the folk art festival and one man I absolutely recognized from yesterday. Bryan Hardy, the county's baby-faced deputy prosecuting attorney, escorted a middle-aged lady across the church lawn—a lady who seemed to be talking Bryan's ear off. The sum total of his responses? Nodding like a bobblehead doll. Was the woman his mother?

"That's his aunt."

I startled at Dab's voice beside me.

"Was I staring?" I asked.

He grinned. "I don't think anyone else noticed. Most people avoid Corina Hardy because she talks nonstop."

"Mostly about herself and her exalted pedigree," Sherry added.

"She's hot stuff around here?"

Dab snorted. "More a legend in her own mind."

"Sherry Mae," a new voice called. "I need a word with you!"

Dab, Sherry, and I turned in sync. A lady in her early fifties wearing a pretty sky-blue shirtwaist dress hustled to my aunt's side.

"Nixy, this is Lorna Tyler. She and her husband, Clark, own the Lilies Café and Inn on the Square."

I'd met a lot of people in the last day, had a lot of names tossed at me, but Detective Shoar had mentioned the café and inn.

"Where that horrible Elsman woman is staying, God help me," Lorna said, not bothering to lower her voice. "Nice to meet you, Nixy. Hello, Dab. Clark's playing golf later, so I made him take the early shift at the café, but I heard about the to-do y'all had here during the church breakfast."

"To-do?" Dab echoed when Lorna ran out of breath.

"You know. The discussion about the trouble all y'all are having with Jill Elsman," Lorna clarified. "She can't get our property even if she wanted it, but I'm right sorry about the problems she's causing. I'd kick her out if it weren't that she and her assistant are our only paying guests since your festival is over."

Sherry patted Lorna's arm. "It's not your fault, dear."

"No, but I can't wait to see the back of her," Lorna fumed. "She's buttering up Clark like he's hot toast about getting approval for this project of hers when the time comes. I swear, we're going to come to blows if she doesn't leave Clark alone."

"Has she told your husband about her project?" I asked.

"Not that I know of, but, Sherry Mae, you know him. He's tight-lipped about city business when he needs to be."

"Which is an admirable trait," Sherry said. "We don't need unfounded rumors flying around town."

"So true, especially when any news at all flies through town like lightning." She paused and smiled. "Well, at least you know you have my support. Now, you bring Nixy by for lunch when you have time."

Lorna departed, and Dab offered Sherry his arm. We started toward the all-but-empty parking lot when my steps faltered.

"Dab, isn't that Detective Shoar hunkered under the back end of your Caddy?"

"Looks like him, but why's he holding a paper bag?"

"Let's find out."

I led the charge, ready to nail him about those vandalism incidents he'd failed to mention.

I made no attempt to be stealthy, but stopped short when Shoar suddenly stood. "Did you pull litter patrol this morning, Detective?"

"In a manner of speaking," he replied, all cop-faced.

"Then nothing has happened at the house?" Sherry asked as she and Dab came up behind me. "Fred is okay?"

"Everyone is fine so far as I know, Miz Sherry Mae. I'm here for another reason." He opened the bag and tilted it toward us—well, mostly toward Dab, but I got a quick look at the partly black, partly rust-colored metal rod inside.

"Mr. Baxter, is this your tire iron?"

"Nope, and I don't remember the last time I even saw a tire iron like that, though Fred had one for prying off bicycle wheels," Dab answered. "There's a four-way wrench in the trunk with my spare. You want to see it?"

"I'd appreciate your permission to look in the trunk," Eric said.

I bristled. "What's going on, Detective?"

"About an hour ago, Jill Elsman reported vandalism to her Hummer," he said, his tone flat. "From the dents in the car, looks like a tire iron could've done the damage. The one I bagged has flecks of blue paint on it. I found it under Mr. Baxter's back bumper."

"Let me get this straight," I said, hands on my hips, temper suddenly on high simmer. "Hellspawn is accusing us of wailing on her Hummer, and then leaving the evidence in plain sight? Seriously?"

He didn't answer me. He simply stepped around me to look into Dab's trunk. "Thank you, Mr. Baxter. How long have you been at church?"

"We arrived for breakfast," Sherry answered. "We've been here since about eight this morning."

"And we got an earful from Sherry's neighbors," I said as I stepped into his space. "Hellspawn has lied left, right, and sideways about who's sold property options to her. I wouldn't put it past her to lie about this and have done the damage herself."

"That's a theory, and I'll investigate every angle."

"Like you're investigating the dead bird, barn break-in, and mailbox bomb at Aunt Sherry's? You could've told me about those incidents yesterday. Or, gee, you could've called anytime last week to give me a heads-up before I got here. So what's that about, buster?"

"I told you that you needed to talk with Miz Sherry to get answers."

"Which I obviously did, but you still could've prepared me, and I resent that you'd think even for a minute that Sherry would vandalize someone's property."

"Now, Nixy," Sherry said, patting my arm when I ran out of breath. "We've wondered if Ms. Elsman is behind the vandalism at my house. It's not a stretch for her to believe the same of us."

"I disagree," I shot back. "It's a stretch from here to

Houston that you'd bash on her car, but it's a devious way to divert suspicion if she's the one who . . ." A thought hit me. "Uh-oh."

I rushed to the front passenger side of Dab's Caddy, ran my hand over the smooth fender while peering at the hubcap.

"What are you doing?" Shoar testily asked.

"Looking for damage."

"I did that," he said with exaggerated patience. "There's not a ding or scratch on the Caddy."

"This wheel cover is scratched."

"Where?"

I hunkered down by the tire as he moved nearer. Reached to touch the lug nuts. The loose lug nuts.

"Where is the damage?" he asked.

I pointed. "There. And look at the nuts. Somebody's messed with them."

Sherry made a sound of distress, but I stayed focused on Eric as he looked, really looked at where I'd pointed. In a few heartbeats, he let out a low whistle as he pulled out his phone and snapped several pictures. "Dab, you ever have trouble with these lugs coming loose?"

"Never, and the car drove fine this morning. Just like always."

Shoar stood and faced Dab. "If you'll get your four-way wrench out of the trunk, I'll get these tightened so you can be on your way."

Dab hurried to the trunk while I glared at the not-so-eagle-eyed detective. He merely took more photos until Dab handed him the X-shaped tool. Then he knelt by the tire and I stood right over him.

"You know that tire iron wasn't used on those lugs," I said conversationally. "You'd use it to pop off a hubcap but not to loosen the nuts. You tested the wrench end against Dab's lugs, didn't you?"

"I did against one of them," he said without looking up.

"And they didn't fit."

"Nope." Still no eye contact.

"That type of lug wrench is old and probably came with a particular make and model of car. They aren't all interchangeable."

He finally looked up at me. "How do you know?"

"A guy I dated. Matt the mechanic."

"He taught you about lug nuts, huh?"

"How to change a tire, check my fluids. All kinds of car things." Not that I put most of Matt's lessons into practice, but Shoar didn't need to know that.

"Good for you," he grunted as he finished with the front passenger tire. When he rose to inspect the other three tires, I followed. He only tightened four more lugs, and that seemed more for my benefit, not because they were dangerously loose.

"So," I began when he returned the wrench and closed the trunk, "do we need to file an official criminal mischief report, Detective?"

"I'll start the paperwork myself and bring it out for you to sign, Dab."

"Are you sure filing a report is necessary?" Aunt Sherry asked, her eyes huge and concerned.

"Absolutely," I said just as Shoar answered with an emphatic, "Yes."

"Well," Dab said as he opened the passenger door for Sherry, "I hate to take you out of your way. Let me know if you want me to come to the station."

"Will do."

Dab headed for the driver's side. I gave Shoar a last glance and half turned away when I felt his hand brush my shoulder. "That was an excellent catch, Ms. Nix. If that tire had come off, it could've caused a bad accident."

"I know."

He arched a brow. "More lessons from your boyfriend Mitch the mechanic?"

I gazed into those chocolate-brown eyes of his, saw the

corner of his mouth tilt, and had to smother an answering smile. "It was Matt. And he was just a friend."

"Well, I promise you, I will investigate this, just as thoroughly as I'm investigating the vandalism and theft at Miz Sherry's. This is another piece of a pattern, Ms. Nix, and I don't like it."

"It's Nixy, and thank you, Detective."

"Eric," he said with a slow, full smile.

Chapter Seven

SOON AS WE ARRIVED HOME, I DOVE IN TO HELP GET Maise's big Sunday dinner on the table.

No surprise that the car incident trumped the church reconnaissance report. Sherry's friends were aghast over the news and discussed it all the way through the meal of pot roast, veggies, rolls, and apple pie. I could see that Dab and Sherry were still a little shaken, and each of their friends was rightfully incensed at Dab's car being targeted.

"It just doesn't make sense," Aster said. She'd sprinkled lavender down the center of the table before we sat to eat. Now she forked up a last bite of pie. "If Elsman is responsible for any of the vandalism here, why would she risk tampering with the car in broad daylight and in a public place in view of anyone passing by?"

"I do believe she's becoming desperate," Eleanor offered as she stood and began clearing dishes.

"Dab, are you sure you didn't feel a difference in the way the Caddy drove this morning?" Maise asked. "The lugs might've been loosened last night and become looser on the way to church."

"Nope," Fred said. "If them nuts were loose, Dab woulda noticed. 'Sides, I checked out the Caddy bumper to bumper on Wednesday. Wasn't a thing wrong with it, 'cept needin' more wiper fluid. Tell you this, though: we all need to be extra alert."

"High alert and combat ready," Maise added. "First order is KP duty, then we can get comfortable and reconvene for the church report. We need to stop this harassment before someone is injured."

I shuddered remembering that Hellspawn's minion Trudy had made a similar statement. And wondered how far her employer would go to get what she wanted.

"I'll tell you this," Aster said as she dried a dinner plate, "that woman's a karmic nightmare. Her bad juju will come back a hundredfold."

"I thought the saying was tenfold," Maise ventured.

"I thought it was threefold," Sherry said.

Aster waved a hand. "Three, ten, a hundred. When you're that nasty, you're sure to get walloped. Mark my words."

Judging by the silent nods, we all dutifully marked.

Dishes done and kitchen cleaned, we scattered to change out of our church clothes. Well, everyone but Eleanor came back to the kitchen dressed casually. In black slacks and a silky geometric-print shirt, she still looked like a fashion plate. Maybe this was as casual as she got.

Armed with my computer tablet, I joined the Six, who crowded around the kitchen table. Dab had a copy of the list he'd given me this morning, and to that he added the names of the neighbors Eleanor, Aster, and Maise had questioned. Sherry had yet another list but in a dark, large-sized font, and kept track of how many total neighbors were accounted for with big, bold tick marks. Did she have eye trouble? I hadn't seen her wearing glasses, had I?

I checked off my own list, but when my head swam with all the names being called out, I interrupted.

"Wait, y'all, I'm confused. Can you sketch the neighborhood and fill in who lives where?"

"Why do their locations matter?" Eleanor asked.

"Because I'm betting we'll see a pattern in where these people live. If we do, it'll tell us more."

"A battlefield overview," Maise said with a nod. "I like it."

Eleanor began sketching the areas where the target neighbors lived and filled in property owner names. With Aster and Maise kibitzing over Eleanor's shoulder, I opted to pull up Google Earth on my tablet.

Fred eyed the drawing. "I'll be dadgummed. There is a pattern."

"I see the residential blocks and the three farm parcels at the far end," Sherry said, "but I don't know what it means. Nixy, does it tell you anything?"

"I'm not sure." I eyed Eleanor's sketch on the lined pad, then the aerial image, then pointed at the drawing. "Are those rectangles the farms?"

Sherry nodded. "They're right outside Lilyvale proper. Once you cross the road at the end of our block, you're on county land."

"How many acres are the farms?"

"Twenty each, I should think, except a bit of Stanton Lake cuts through the end of each parcel, so not a full twenty acres."

"Stanton Lake?"

"Named after our ancestors. Samuel Allan Stanton owned all the land here on Eleanor's sketch and much more. Granddaddy W. R. Junior sold off parcels in the 1920s and late 1930s when oil was found hereabouts. Those were Lilyvale's boom eras back when the oil workers moved in for a spell."

"Are there houses on Lake Stanton?"

"There could be a cabin here or there. It's not a recreational lake with boating and fishing for the public. Lake Stanton is more of an extra-large pond."

Nixy looked at Eleanor. "Did these farmers sell property options?"

"Elsman talked to them all, but just one sold. He didn't figure the county zoning folks would approve whatever she planned, so he saw it as free money."

"Same with two ladies a block over," Maise supplied. "But three couples in the same block turned Elsman down flat."

"Some property owners are absentee," Aster chimed in, pointing at the map. "In this block far catty-corner from Sherry are duplexes and an apartment building. Eleanor and I talked to a renter, but he pays a management firm. Oh, but Elsman approached Ida Bollings. She rents out a house up the street."

"Miss Ida?" I asked. "Does she drive a big blue Buick?"
Sherry smiled. "How do you know Ida, child?"

"She sent me into the pharmacy for her medicine yesterday morning."

"She does that from time to time," Sherry said. "I'll bet she gave Elsman the sharp edge of her tongue, too."

Aster smiled. "She sure did. Elsman threatened to steal Ida's rental house out from under her by paying the back taxes. Of course, Ida is sure she paid the property taxes, so she'll be raising a ruckus at city hall tomorrow."

"Good for her." I typed on my tablet. "All right, a city block is a little over six acres, so that's thirty-six acres plus close to sixty acres in the farms. Nearly one hundred acres in all, and around forty landowners. That's a lot of cash layout, but the big question is, why would she want so much land?"

"What about a big-box store?" Dab asked. "We hear rumors about that from time to time."

"We hear about Magnolia getting one," Maise drawled. "Not us."

"It's worth a look," I said, already typing a search on the tablet. I felt all eyes watching as I went through several possibilities, then looked up. "Most stores like Walmart only need thirty acres for a typical store site."

"Maybe Elsman is planning to build a factory," Eleanor mused.

"To make what?" Dab said. "We have some light industry here, but most of the forestry and manufacturing concerns are over at Magnolia."

"One of them could be expandin'," Fred offered.

"From what I see," I said, "between the options, actually buying the properties, and then permits and building costs, a developer would have to be pretty darn sure the project would return a small fortune."

Sherry snorted. "Lilyvale is a nice little town, with light industry adding to our tax base, but it's no place to make a fortune."

The kitchen again fell silent for a moment.

"Do we need a plan of action?" Dab asked. "Sherry, you mentioned having a meeting of the neighbors."

"We could do that, just so everyone knows where everyone else stands."

"How about holding the meeting Tuesday afternoon?" Aster said. "We need to clean the parlor tomorrow anyway."

"I'll make snacks," Maise declared.

"Sherry and I can make the calls," Eleanor added.

"But Nixy has to leave on Tuesday," Sherry put in.

"So what?" Fred barked. "She won't be here to see this through anyhow."

"Now, Fred, you know Nixy has a job she needs to get home for."

"She has vacation time, doesn't she?" he groused.

"Not enough, and not right now, but I can leave after the meeting, Aunt Sherry. And"—I paused to give Fred the stink eye—"I'll call every day next week to check on you."

"That's somethin' more than you have done," Fred said with an *I won* look while Sherry patted my hand.

"Well, then," Maise said as she rose, "there's nothing more to do other than be sure we're locked up tight at night and leave the yard lights on. Now, if you'll excuse me, I'm off to read my Navy Seal book."

"Which one are you reading?" I asked, as any book lover would.

"One with a very handsome model on the cover, Miss Nosy."

The men harrumphed, I snorted a laugh, and Maise sailed off.

Sherry grinned at me. "Your laugh reminds me of Sue Anne's, Nixy. It's good to hear it."

Emotion blindsided me again. While I blinked away the second teary lump in my throat of the day, the rest of Sherry's friends began drifting away.

Aster strode off to her garden, and a minute later a Jimi Hendrix song blasted from the south side of the house.

"What on earth?"

Sherry giggled. "That's Aster. I'll bet you thought she'd play classical music to her plants."

"I didn't think about her playing any music to them, but acid rock is, uh, a bold choice."

"She says it gives her herbs extra oomph."

"Uh-huh." If I hadn't seen her garden, I'd wonder what kinds of herbs Aster grew.

Dab came through the kitchen with a handful of tools, declaring himself ready to break down the stills as promised. Eleanor offered to help, and with only a slight hesitation, Dab accepted.

Fred clomped his walker to the back door. "I'm gonna mow old lady Gilroy's yard."

"Old lady Gilroy?" I echoed as Fred and his walker clanked out the back door and onto the deck.

"I guess we shouldn't call her that, but she's ninety if she's a day." Sherry carried her tea glass to the sink. "She lives in the small house next door. Irascible woman. We take meals to her every few days. Not that we see her in person, but the food disappears off her porch right enough."

"I'm guessing that's one neighbor Hellspawn never talked to."

"It's Elsman, dear."

"Not in my book. How does Fred get the riding mower over there?"

"There's a gate in the chain-link fence. You can't hardly see it if you aren't standing there, but the barn is set a good ten feet from the fence. The gate is there, so Fred has plenty of room to maneuver the tractor."

"I noticed her yard goes back to the next street like yours, except she doesn't have all the trees. I suppose that was part of your homestead once."

She gave me a sideways glance. "Um-hmm."

I felt like I was missing something, but plunged ahead. "So, what do you usually do on Sunday afternoons?"

"This and that," Sherry said. "Today I want to spend time with you. What would you like to do?"

I smiled as an idea occurred. "Will you show me the family cemetery? I'd forgotten about it until Mr. Lambert mentioned it this morning."

Sherry's breath caught and she blinked rapidly. "You're a Stanton, child. Naturally you should meet your ancestors."

WHEN I'D CAUGHT TRUDY BEHIND THE BARN YES-terday, I'd only glimpsed a sea of pink azaleas. Now I saw the azalea bushes surrounded a three-sided whitewashed picket fence, which in turn enclosed the cemetery. The south edge of the cemetery reached almost to the edge of the barn, and the chain-link fence, bare of bushes, sealed the north boundary of the graveyard.

Chain-link fences, in fact, outlined the back and side yards of each home all the way down the block. I counted six houses, three facing west as Sherry's did, and three facing east. One fat cat lounged on a round wicker table in the nearest yard, but I didn't see or hear a single dog. Perhaps they were all too old to be bothered to bark at us.

"Sherry, which house is the Lamberts'?"

"The last one on the right. It's blue with white shutters on all the windows. Jane's a bit of a nut about shutters, and John indulged her."

I had to smile because I imagined Sherry's husband, Bill, had indulged her, too.

We continued strolling past the south side of the cemetery to the gate on the east side, not far from the woods between Sherry's land and the street behind her house. The azalea bushes at the gate were trimmed back to allow access, and the cemetery was so well maintained, the hinges didn't even squeak as we entered. An oak tree outside the fence spread its limbs over the upright, mostly modestly sized markers. Tombstones were engraved with names and dates and short epitaphs that Sherry didn't need to read.

"I've known each grave by heart since I was a tyke," she told me. "In fact, I taught your momma about the Stanton ancestors."

With that, Sherry reeled off names and family history. Samuel, his family torn apart by the Civil War, had survived the battles to move his wife, Yvonne, and their children to southwest Arkansas. Samuel had bought a huge tract of land from a widow named Hendrix, then he and Yvonne founded Lilyvale, named after Yvonne's favorite flower. Sherry made the past come alive as she shared more stories of Stanton descendants, both those who had lived long lives on the land and those who had died young. Two American flags represented Stanton boys who'd died in World War I but had been buried overseas.

I absorbed her enthusiasm as much as the stories. It didn't even bother me when she expressed her hope that I'd want to keep the property. Much. And, okay, I diverted her attention with questions.

"Why are there only twenty graves? It seems like there should be more."

"Samuel laid out the cemetery for thirty plots, but some of the Stanton clan moved away, as people do. Then, too, burials had to stop along about 1925 after Lilyvale annexed part of Stanton land."

"The same time your granddad sold off land?" I asked.

"Yes," she said on a sigh. "After that, family started being buried in the city cemetery. Sissy was the only original Stanton child who lived here most of her eighty-nine years but had to be buried in the city cemetery because of the annexing. She ordered markers for herself and her husband, Josiah, to be put in here so she'd be with family."

"Is that why the stones read 'in memory of'?"

"It is. Sissy had memory markers made and installed for my great-grandparents, too. She even left a trust for things like upkeep of the markers. I paid to add the stones for my mother and dad, your grandparents. I think it's nice to see their names with the rest of the family."

"It's lovely, Sherry, but did you say Sissy lived to almost ninety? When was she born?"

"Long about 1860, if I remember right. Sissy was some kind of character. A feisty go-getter, rather like you."

I sidestepped that comment and pointed at the three-foot-high angel on a short pedestal spreading its wings over the small markers in the children's section. Four graves were grouped slightly apart from the rest.

"What about these graves in the children's area, Sherry? You didn't mention any McAdoos on the family tree."

"The family legend is that the McAdoos were passing through when their children died from influenza. Samuel and Yvonne had just lost their little Vera, so they offered plots and gravestones to the McAdoo parents. The parents accepted, and they stayed for a few months to work for Samuel, but they moved on to Texas. I guess they couldn't bear being reminded of their loss."

When Sherry's family stories wound down, I wanted to stroll in the wooded area behind the house. The tree house my mother had fondly recalled was long gone, but I enjoyed the soft wind singing through the trees.

We didn't go far, though. The path was somewhat over-grown with low bushes and young trees. I stopped and looked harder at the path. Hadn't Trudy galloped through here just yesterday? How had she known there was a path at all, much less known where it was located? Because she'd helped Hellspawn burglarize the barn?

I mentally shrugged. I supposed it didn't matter now. I let those thoughts go. As I did, neighborhood sounds receded, too, and I felt the peace I saw reflected in Sherry's expression.

"Sherry," I began as we turned back to the house. "Did the married Stanton children live with their parents? I know the house is large, but it seems that would get awfully crowded."

"No, child. Back when we owned more property, they were offered tracts of land as wedding gifts to build their own houses. Some did that, and some moved to town. Why do you ask?"

"Just curious. Have you ever considered applying for a historical landmark designation for your house?"

Sherry linked her arm in mine. "The county historical society suggested we do that back in the eighties. I found trunks filled with family papers and mementos that Sissy had gathered. I even had most of the research together, but I always got sidetracked. Besides, I don't know that the house is any finer example of architecture than a dozen others in the county. Other than being used as a courthouse for a spell, nothing particularly historical happened here. It's simply where the Stantons raised their families."

"It can't hurt to apply. If the application goes through, I think it will protect your house from being torn down. At least make it harder to do. Do you still have your research?"

"I imagine I packed it all and left the trunks in the parlor."

"The one that needs cleaning?"

She waved a hand. "It's not really dirty. We do some of our crafting in there and in the dining room, and just haven't tidied it yet."

"Then are you up for a little digging with me?"

"I would love that!"

Sherry gave me a smile of near rapture and a hard hug before she bustled inside. I admit I walked on air a bit as I trailed her, happy that I'd suggested a project that excited her. If we didn't finish it on this trip, I'd make another one to work on it later. Or I'd ask Sherry to let me take the information home.

Or so I thought until I saw the sheer volume of treasures packed in a trunk and two cedar hope chests.

I dragged the trunk and chests out of a storage cupboard in the lower part of the floor-to-ceiling bookcases built into either side of the fireplace. Magnificently crafted bookcases that made the parlor look more like a library. Then, at Sherry's direction, I arranged them in a semicircle around two wing-back chairs. She moved basket-making supplies and labels for Aster's herb concoctions out of the way, retrieved a large magnifying glass from the desk near the front porch windows, and we were soon elbow deep in Stanton family detritus.

I latched on to copies of deeds, Samuel Stanton's Civil War records, a delicate journal that had belonged to Samuel's wife, Yvonne, and other papers. Age had faded the ink, so the magnifying glass came in handy. Sherry held up daguerreotypes, ambrotypes, and tintypes from the 1800s, and photographs going back to the early 1900s. I *ooh*ed and *aah*ed over each one, partly because that's what Sherry expected, but mostly because I got caught up in a feeling of family history I'd never experienced before. We reverently examined each memento, from leather shoes and kidskin gloves to watches and rings, brooches and bracelets. Nothing escaped our attention as I peppered Sherry with questions. I even went to the kitchen to grab my tablet so I could take photos and type notes.

The exercise reminded me a little of going through my mother's things with Sherry, but without the aching sadness. I was so deep into the discoveries, I startled when Maise poked her head in through the pocket doors we'd left partially open.

"Time for the drive-by."

Sherry folded a lacy christening cap her grandmother had tatted. "Do you think she's coming? She skipped yesterday."

"She set Shoar on you this morning. She'll show."

"Maise's right." I put aside an open photo album. "Let's go."

Sherry offered me a place on the porch swing with her and Eleanor, but I opted to sit on the porch step for a front-row seat.

"Attention, troops. Here she comes. Prepare to wave and smile. No, wait. Belay that. The woman isn't slowing down. What in the world?"

I shot to my feet as the dark blue Hummer wheeled into the driveway, spewing gravel. The vehicle veered across the yard, plowed over the crepe myrtle sapling, and rocked to a stop spitting distance from me.

Chapter Eight

THE SIX WERE ON THEIR FEET, TOO. I COULD TELL by their voices closing in behind me.

"My poor tree!" Sherry.

"That woman's a menace." Dab.

"Her bumper's a goner." Fred.

"She's gettin' a thousandfold backlash now. I need my lavender." Aster.

"I'll give her a backlash. Where's your Colt, Fred?" Maise.

"I do believe I'll call Detective Shoar." Eleanor.

Good thing someone thought of placing a call, because I seemed to be frozen. I gaped at the women through the Hummer windshield. Trudy, hands still braced on the dashboard, sat in the passenger seat visibly shuddering. And Hellspawn?

The witch climbed out of her car and stomped toward the porch. In spiked heels and on grass, the stomping lost a lot in translation, but her face, contorted in rage, made up for the lack.

Trudy, I noticed, more or less tumbled out of the passenger seat, grabbing the open door with both hands. I guessed to keep from falling on her face. She let out a moaning "Now, Jill, don't say something you'll—"

"Shut up, you cow," Hellspawn barked.

For a second, Trudy's eyes blazed with hatred. Then, lips tight, her expression became resigned. I'd have punched Hellspawn's lights out. Heck, I was tempted to do just that on Trudy's behalf. Never mind Sherry's.

Instead, when Hellspawn turned back to me and took a step closer, I descended a stair tread to confront her. She had to stop or plow into me. She stopped, and in spite of our height difference, I held the high ground.

"What the devil are you trying to pull?" she demanded, hands planted on her hips. "You vandalize my Hummer, then sweet-talk that detective into believing I did something to your car? That's bull!"

"First, I didn't sweet-talk Detective Shoar. Second, none of us touched your car. Until now, I didn't even know what it looked like."

"Liar," she spat. "You saw me leave yesterday."

"No, I didn't. I was busy putting my aunt's baskets back on display. The display you ruined."

Hellspawn didn't have the grace to look even a smidgen ashamed. She went right back on the attack. "You can't deny that you're conspiring with other landowners to shut me out. Three of them slammed doors in my face in the last hour, and one held a shotgun on me."

"With your winning personality? Imagine that."

Hellspawn reddened and oozed closer. "I'm offering a good deal to these people. More than they'd ever see in a conventional sale."

"Why?"

She opened her mouth again, closed it, and blinked. "Why what?"

"Why do you want the land? What are you building? A big-box store? A mall? A factory?"

Her nose went higher in the air. "What do you care?"

"I don't, but you'd get more cooperation from people if you let them in on your plans."

"They don't need to know my plans. I promise you, they'll take the money and thank me, and there's nothing you can do to stop me."

"I have no interest in stopping you. My aunt and her neighbors make their own decisions, and they've decided you're a manipulative liar."

Hellspawn's sudden smile would make a rattlesnake wary. "I will have this land, and I'll do whatever it takes to get it."

I narrowed my eyes at her. "Is that a threat?"

"Let me put it this way. Mowing down that little tree is nothing compared to what I'll do to get my way." She gave me a long, cold glare, then snapped her fingers. "Come, Trudy."

Hellspawn slammed the car door, ran back over the sapling, and swung out of Sherry's drive in another spray of gravel right into the path of an oncoming car. Brakes screamed, wheels screeched, and time suspended as the brown sedan rocked to a stop in the middle of the road.

I turned to the Six, who stood huddled around Sherry, staring in silence.

"Are y'all okay?" I got murmurs and nods, so figured heart attacks weren't imminent. Aster looked ready to bolt inside for her lavender, but she stood fast.

"I'll go check on the people in the car," I said.

I started down the steps, but the driver backed up the sedan, angled into Sherry's driveway, and parked. Before I reached the yard, two men got out. I recognized the driver. Bryan Hardy.

"Was that the crazy Elsman woman?" the older man with the full beard asked as he crossed the lawn, his gaze more on the Six than on me. I pegged him being in his early fifties. Tall and physically fit, he wore brown pants and a yellow cotton shirt with a scorecard and several golf tees sticking out the top of his breast pocket. He also sported one of the bushiest full beards I'd ever seen.

"It was," Sherry said shakily as she descended two steps. "Clark Tyler, this is my niece. Nixy, this is Lorna's husband. We spoke with her at church today."

"I remember. Nice to meet you, Mr. Tyler. How was your golf game?"

When he looked blank, I added, "Lorna mentioned you were playing golf today."

"We were," he said, and turned back to Sherry. I was dismissed. "Did Elsman hurt anyone?" he demanded.

"Just my crepe myrtle."

"But she made more threats," Maise said as she joined Sherry. "It's an outright declaration of war."

"Now, Ms. Holcomb, let's be calm." That was Bryan. He'd joined the group so unobtrusively, I hadn't noticed him. He wore navy pants, a white polo shirt, sneakers, and those nerdy black-framed glasses. "You don't want to do anything to escalate the problem."

Maise shook a finger at him. "Then the law in this city and county better do something about that harridan."

"We will." He spoke firmly enough, but for a prosecutor, he still struck me as atypical. "You file a complaint and I'll personally call the city PA."

Clark gave Bryan a sideways glance I couldn't interpret, then focused on Sherry. "We'll get rid of the harpy, don't you worry. She has to leave sooner or later."

"I'm counting on sooner," Maise said. "We're organizing a meeting of all the neighbors she's harassing. If we stand firm, she'll run out of steam."

"That's a good plan, Ms. Holcomb," Bryan said with a nod. "We'll let you get to it. Clark?"

Clark opened his mouth as if to say something else, but just waved and walked back to the car. As he stepped around the sapling, I noticed that the treetop canted off to one side like a broken neck. Which reminded me of the dead bird left on Sherry's steps, its neck broken.

I shuddered and pivoted back to the porch.

Maise clapped her hands for attention. "All right, troops, let's move. Fred, Dab, see if you can save the crepe myrtle. Ladies, we'll make those calls to set up the Stop Hellspawn meeting. Nixy, you wait for Shoar to show up." She cocked a brow at Eleanor. "Or is he coming?"

"Should be here any minute," Eleanor said. "But I do believe he'll want to talk with all of us, won't he?"

Maise waved a hand. "Nixy can take point filling him in."

And I did, more or less. Shoar wheeled into Sherry's drive eight minutes later. I timed him. He drove a late-model extended-cab truck, dark gray and dusty, but with nary a scratch or dent that I could spot. He looked a little dusty, too, in wash-worn jeans, a faded short-sleeved shirt, and boots. I wondered what he'd been doing in what was apparently his off time.

We met at the sapling where Fred solemnly gazed at the cracked top of the tree. Dab joined us with a shovel.

"I take it this is the hit-and-run victim," Shoar said.

"Not funny, Detective," I snipped.

He held up his hands. "You're right. Eleanor was whispering when she called, so I'm not sure I heard everything right. Did Elsman really run over the tree with the Hummer?"

"Twice," Fred told him. "Mowed it down roarin' in here, snapped the top when she roared off."

"She also," Dab added, "nearly T-boned Bryan Hardy's car as she left."

"What was he doing here?"

I waved a hand. "He and Clark Tyler were driving home after a golf game. They only stopped after Hellspawn nearly creamed them. The point is, if Hellspawn spins you a story about us damaging her bumper—"

"She's lying," he interrupted. "Got it. Here, Dab, let me do the digging while you and Nixy push the tree upright."

"We didn't call you out here to garden," Dab protested. "You take Nixy's statement so we can get on with filing the complaint."

Shoar hesitated and I could see his wheels spinning. Insist on helping the seniors, one of them using a walker, or give them their dignity? The latter won.

He turned to me and motioned toward the porch. "Mind if we sit?"

I shrugged and led the way. I plopped down in a bent willow rocker, and he, small spiral notebook in hand, took the wicker chair next to me.

"Tell me what happened."

I turned to watch his expressions as I recounted Hellspawn's hissy fit in detail, including the semiveiled threat.

"And why were you all sitting on the porch when she drove up?"

"Hellspawn apparently drives by every evening, Maise thinks to intimidate them. So Sherry and her friends smile and wave at her."

"Why?"

"Maise calls it psychological warfare."

"Maise would." The corners of his mouth quirked as he scribbled in his spiral again. "Did Elsman drive by last night?"

"No, and that seemed to be the first evening she's missed." I exhaled hard enough to flutter the pages of Eric's notebook. "This woman is a danger, and I'm worried about leaving Sherry to deal with her."

He frowned. "You're going home already?"

"Tuesday morning. I have to get back to my job. Can't you do something about Hellspawn before then?"

"City's fresh out of tar and feathers, I'm afraid," he deadpanned.

"Again, not funny. You want to talk to everyone else?"

"Will they have anything different to report?"

"Overall, I doubt it, but Sherry will be the one filing the complaint. I'll go get her."

I sat in on Sherry's interview, and I managed to keep quiet. In fact, I tuned them in and out, but kept my eyes on Sherry. Her hands trembled a little. Probably still stunned as well as upset about her tree. She'd let her hair fall over an eye again. I thought the style made her look younger, but she kept brushing it back. Did she need a trim? Is that why she wore barrettes off and on? I'd see about taking her to a beauty shop tomorrow.

It wasn't long before Shoar closed his spiral and stood.

"Thank you, Miz Sherry Mae. I'll write this up and the car-tampering report, too. Will you be home tomorrow? I'll need you to sign the complaint."

Sherry put her hand on his sleeve. "I'll come to the station. I want to show Nixy around downtown, and I have some business there anyway."

"Wait," I said. "Is that all? Aren't you going to go talk to Hellspawn? Follow up right now? I mean, that's how one investigates, isn't it?"

"You learn your police procedure from TV?"

"No, another guy I dated."

"Let me guess. Carl the Cop."

I flushed. "Pete the PI's assistant."

He shook his head but I caught the small smile. "Miz Sherry Mae, if I'm not in when you come by tomorrow, I'll leave the paperwork at the front desk. Tell Dab I'll have his car vandalism complaint ready to sign, too."

"That's fine, Eric. Thank you."

"You're welcome and get some rest."

He stopped to speak to Fred and Dab, who had the mulch scraped away from the hole and the sapling more or less upright. Again I saw him hesitate, but Dab waved him off. I understood the seniors wanting to keep their dignity.

However, while the detective resisted his urge to help out, I didn't resist mine. I pitched in to assist, and after another half an hour, the crepe myrtle was properly replanted. The men hadn't objected to my aid, but then dignity didn't do much to ease sore muscles. At any rate, I felt that I made a few points with Fred.

The Sunday evening meal consisted of leftovers from both Saturday's and Sunday's lunch. Maise encouraged me to hog the fried okra, saying, "We can have my okra anytime, but you're leaving. Eat up."

The dinner table mood was more subdued than I expected, and I didn't think it was due to the lavender oil Aster had sprayed in every corner of the dining room. The Six didn't chatter about Hellspawn's visit, though Aster and Eleanor did confirm that the neighborhood confab was scheduled on Tuesday at five in the afternoon. That way, they said, those who still worked would be able to attend.

I had hoped for an earlier meeting time so I could be there. How late could I leave Lilyvale and still be awake enough to work on Wednesday? By seven or eight at the latest. Make a motel stop, sleep a few hours, then go straight to the gallery. Not ideal but doable.

Except I didn't feel good about leaving as long as Hellspawn was at large.

"That gives us two days to clean the parlor," Eleanor said.

"And for me to prepare refreshments," Maise added.

"I'll cut fresh flowers and put out my lavender and other calming oils," Aster offered.

"What a wonderful idea, Aster." Sherry smiled. "Angry as I am with Ms. Elsman, we'll need cool heads to plan."

"I'll type up a short agenda and print copies at the vo-tech tomorrow."

I turned to Eleanor. "Are you teaching classes?"

"I volunteer teach," she said. "Three days a week at the technical college."

"We all volunteer at the vo-tech." Fred waved his fork to encompass the Six. "Even me."

"It's a mentor program," Dab explained. "Students get lectures and demonstrations from professionals. In our case, former professionals."

"And from those with particular expertise," Aster said.

"Aster is a master gardener and certified herbalist," Maise declared with obvious pride. "I work with the culinary arts students."

"That's awesome. Those students are lucky to have you. Sherry, are you a reading skills coach at the junior high or high school?"

Her fork clattered on the plate. Eyes widened. Her friends shifted in their chairs. What had I said wrong?

"Reading and history, and I help out wherever I'm needed. But I'm skipping tomorrow so we can go to the square. Well, you heard me tell my favorite detective we'd be in town tomorrow morning. I want to spend time with you, and I need to go sign that complaint, too. Don't let me forget, Nixy.'"

Forget? Was Sherry worried about her memory? She had recited chapter and verse about the family history all afternoon, but that was long-term memory, right? Did Sherry fear she had a short-term memory problem?

And what was with the babbling? Sherry wasn't the least bit taciturn, but she didn't babble. Or she hadn't when we'd spent time together after my mom's death.

I was a rank amateur on senior issues, but it didn't take a specialist to see that something about Sherry was off. Way off. Should I chalk it up to Hellspawn stress syndrome, or should I dig deeper?

Sherry didn't seem open to confiding in me, and her friends were obviously protective of her. They wouldn't readily share her secrets either.

I heaved a silent sigh and stiffened my resolve. I'd get to the bottom of as many issues as I could in the time I had left. And hope that none of them other than dealing with Hellspawn were critical.

Chapter Nine

SHERRY WAS RIGHT ABOUT THE SUN STREAMING into her room. I was awake by seven, did my morning routine, and Googled both Jill Elsman and OJE Development in Little Rock. I found it beyond weird that Hellspawn didn't have a single entry in the search results, not even a Facebook page. OJE seemed equally cloaked in mystery. No website, only a physical address and phone number.

I called the company at eight on the dot, but was stonewalled as soon as I asked if Jill Elsman worked there. The gatekeeper said she was unable to answer my questions, but I could call after Wednesday to talk with Jeanette Anders.

After their breakfast, the seniors set off in two cars. Dab took Fred—whose overall pockets still brimmed with tools. Eleanor took Sherry's Corolla to drive Aster and Maise. Dab's Caddy seated five, and I idly wondered who had to squish in the back or drive another car when they all went the same place at the same time. Or maybe that never happened.

"I told Eleanor you'd drive to town today," Sherry told me, though why she felt she needed to explain, I didn't know.

"You don't mind, do you? I thought we'd stop at the police station so I can sign the complaint, and then have breakfast at the Lilies Café. It's one of Lilyvale's historic spots."

"I don't mind, but isn't the café attached to the inn where Hellspawn is staying? You want to risk running into her?"

Sherry's eyes twinkled. "It's Elsman, child, and I'm hoping to be there when my favorite detective comes in to arrest her."

"She'll froth at the mouth."

"We'll simply cover our food with Lorna's lovely, large napkins."

"You have an evil streak, Sherry."

"Well, I did teach junior high and high school. I learned from the best."

I snorted and led the way to my Camry. Sherry and I almost matched today, she wearing black jeans and a white cotton blouse, me in black capris and the white T-shirt from my thrown-together church outfit. We both wore white tennis shoes, too, though Sherry's looked much cleaner than mine. She wore her bangs loose today. I still wondered if I should offer to take her to the hair salon, if I could suggest it without offending her.

The sun shone brightly and the temperature was mild again. Purse. Check. Sunglasses. On. Directions. Sherry, my navigator. We were off.

I powered down the windows as Sherry pointed me back to the square, which was almost deserted at this hour of the morning. She explained that most businesses didn't open until between nine and ten, though city and county offices opened at eight. Lilies Café opened at seven to catch the early bird workforce and vo-tech college students.

Once in town, we stopped by the police station, but Shoar was out. He had, as promised, left the paperwork for Sherry to sign.

I could tell she was disappointed that he wouldn't be tearing over to arrest Hellspawn, but we stuck to our plan. I slid into a parking space smack in front of the Lilies Café, which sat next to the pharmacy. I hadn't noticed the café on Saturday morning, but then I'd had other things on my mind.

"Come make yourselves comfortable," Lorna Tyler greeted as soon as we entered the café.

She ushered us through the empty dining room to a round table for two at the front window. She was dressed in a blue flowered apron over black slacks and a black polo shirt, and her black waitress shoes hardly made a sound on the wide plank pine floors.

"Morning rush is over, so you get the best seats in the house."

We thanked her and settled in. The white tablecloth was pristine, and the mismatched bentwood chairs added charm. Not original Michael Thonet bentwood pieces, but the style fit the café perfectly.

Lorna handed us each a single-sheet menu listing the breakfast selections, and Sherry told me what she liked while Lorna went off to get our coffee and water. I'm more of a breakfast-protein-bar person, so I opted for an English muffin and mixed fruit. Sherry asked for a half order of eggs Benedict.

Lorna disappeared into the kitchen behind an oak bar right out of the set of a Western movie. I gawked at the former saloon with its historic pictures of old Lilyvale lining the walls, a staircase at the back of the room. I didn't know how much of an old West sort of flavor Lilyvale had back in the day, but I could almost see cowboys clomping their way up that staircase to the rooms they let for the night. Accompanied by a saloon girl perhaps.

"You can almost smell the boot leather, trail dust, and whiskey, can't you?" Sherry said with a faraway smile. "Lorna's great-great-grandfather was an original owner of the saloon and took over when his partner died."

"A gun fight?"

"A mule kick. The Stanton family's general store was across the square where the antiques store is now. We'll go over there later."

"Great. So, Sherry, who turned the saloon into a diner?"

"Lorna's grandparents did that, and modified the rooms upstairs. Lorna helped her parents modernize more, and got interested in hotel management, or whatever the term is now. She studied at Oklahoma State, got a job in Shreveport, and came back here when her parents died."

We held a respectful silence for a moment, then Sherry said, "The guest rooms are very nice. Two are suites with their own bathrooms, and two share a bath. Some of our folk art festival patrons stay here."

"How many rooms did the saloon originally have?"

"At least seven, as I recall. They were much smaller rooms, but then the baths and the outhouses were out back. Some say outlaws came through here, though there were never any reliable records about that."

I grinned. "So Lilyvale wasn't always a sleepy little town?"

"My, no, child; we had our rough and tumble times. The upstanding and the scoundrels, and both groups created a few scandals in their time."

"Too bad Lorna has to put up with a scoundrel now."

"At least there's no sign of her this morning. I'd hate to be put off of Lorna's excellent food."

There isn't much you can do to ruin English muffins and sliced fruit. Still, Sherry's eggs Benedict looked tantalizing, and the homemade cherry marmalade Lorna served with my muffin had me vowing to come back next time I visited.

That train of thought reminded me again that the clock was ticking to help solve the Hellspawn problem.

Lorna refilled our coffee cups once and left us to eat. I wondered if her bushy-bearded husband was in the kitchen but didn't ask. The second time she brought refills, she plopped in the third chair to visit.

"What are you girls up to today?" she asked with a smile.

"I'm showing Nixy Lilyvale," Sherry said, and I couldn't miss that note of pride in her voice.

"You've never been here? I didn't realize." Lorna waved

a hand. "But then I stay so busy running the inn and café, I'm not always paying attention."

Sherry shook her head. "Lorna, you know about everything and everybody in town. You just don't gossip."

Lorna grinned. "But I occasionally pass along news."

"Is there news this morning?"

"It's been strangely quiet upstairs. No stomping, yelling, or complaining from Her Royal Painness."

"Hellspawn?" I asked.

Lorna grinned. "Is that what you call her?"

"I discourage it," Sherry said reprovingly, though her eyes sparkled, "but, yes. Nixy cuts to the chase."

"Well, neither she nor that assistant of hers, Trudy, came down for breakfast. Of course, Hellspawn—oh, I do like that!" Lorna flashed another wide smile at me. "She never eats much, which is probably why she's so foul-tempered. Clark told me she nearly hit Bryan's car yesterday. What a piece of work."

"So she's still upstairs?" I said.

Lorna shrugged. "I don't know. She could've gone out the back way."

"There's a back door?"

"There's an enclosed back staircase. It leads to the alley and parking lot. After café hours, or during them, for that matter, my guests can enter a personal code on the keypad to get in. The back stairs are a holdover from the saloon days, but it's also a fire exit."

"That's a nice safety feature," I said, but I was thinking about Hellspawn being able to sneak in and out of the inn at will.

The check paid a short while later, we thanked Lorna and headed into the spring morning. Businesses were beginning to open their doors, and some hauled merchandise out to display on the wide sidewalks.

We walked the long way around the square where the main drag cut through downtown. The area held more charm now that I had a chance to enjoy it with Sherry. Round concrete planters as high as my knees stood here and there at the edge of the wide sidewalks, and each overflowed with lilies, daisies, and tulips, ivy draping over the sides. Some shops sported flat façades, while others had recessed doorways that emphasized large windows beside the doors. Colorful awnings over the stores invited strollers to stop and window-shop.

I noticed clothing and shoe stores, and, somewhat surprisingly, a computer sales and service store. In the next two blocks, the Happy Garden Florist and Nightlife Restaurant marched alongside multiple attorney, CPA, and insurance offices. Really, for a small town, there were a lot of businesses on the square.

"The antiques store is at the end of this next block," Sherry said, hooking her arm through mine. "Then we'll stop anywhere else you like."

Amazing aromas drifted out of the Great Buns Bakery and Coffee Shop as we strolled past. Next door, Virginia's carried high-end jewelry, and then came Be Sweet, a candy and ice cream store advertising a big sale on boxed chocolates. Gaskin Business Center occupied a larger space, and the store window signs boasted mailboxes for rent, UPS service, packing materials, office supplies, and printing and photocopying services.

As we neared Square Deal Antiques (and Collectibles, the sign read in subtitle), Trudy, Hellspawn's assistant, blew through the door, smiling, almost skipping, and carrying one of Sherry's woven oak baskets clutched to her ample chest. I knew it was Sherry's design because the braided blue gingham fabric handle was my aunt's signature touch.

Trudy spied us and galloped over.

"Mrs. Cutler, I'm so excited!" she said in that deep, breathy voice. "I wanted to buy a basket at the festival, but that didn't work out. I had no idea you sold them out of the antiques store!"

I thought I heard Sherry mutter, "I don't," but Trudy gushed on.

"I hope I can find another one. This one is a gift for my cousin."

Sherry gave Trudy a kind smile. "You're welcome to come to the house to look at what I have left."

"As long as you come alone," I added.

Trudy flushed as her gaze darted between us. "That's very gracious considering, well, just everything. I will come alone, and I am sorry about Jill. I hope your little tree will live."

"If it doesn't, I can get another one. It's not your fault."

"Thank you, ma'am," Trudy said. "I'd better get back to the inn and hide my basket. Y'all have a good day now."

We watched Trudy's awkward-puppy walk as she crossed catty-corner across the courthouse grounds and on to the inn.

"She has to hide my basket?" Sherry asked. "From Ms. Elsman?"

"I would. The woman stomped on your hemp basket. No telling what she'd do to that one."

"Poor Trudy."

"Not so poor if she has an admirer. Isn't that Bryan Hardy on the courthouse steps? He's been staring at her since she crossed the street."

"The young lady is rather well-endowed."

"I can't tell if his expression means he's admiring or astonished."

Sherry gave me a playful slap on the arm. "Likely both. Come on."

A bell rang as we entered the antiques shop where a motherly-type brunette in an apple-print apron stood behind yet another old-fashioned counter. I grinned to myself, wondering if every shop in town had these counters. This one looked like pine instead of oak, which made sense considering yellow pines grew everywhere around here.

"Hello, Sherry Mae," the woman said, hustling to meet us. "I guess you got our notice."

"I did, Vonnie." Sherry indicated my presence. "Vonnie Vance, this is my niece, Nixy."

"You're Sue Anne's daughter, right?"

"Yes, ma'am." I had to smile. Tracing family connections was a way of life in the South.

"Welcome to Lilyvale, honey," she said as she walked to a grouping of retro furniture near the counter and cash register.

We followed and sat on a curved love seat upholstered in an orange fuzzy fabric while Vonnie settled in a turquoise plastic chair. The wood floors had taken a beating over the years but looked original. The beams accenting the ceiling appeared to be original, too, although the ceiling itself and the walls needed fresh paint. I imagined the space as a general store with shelves upon shelves of dry goods, tools, bags of flour and sugar, an old-fashioned pickle barrel near the door, and penny candy jars on the glass-front counter.

"It's a lovely place, isn't it, Nixy?"

"I love it," I returned with a smile, though the sheer volume of furnishings and knickknacks began to make me feel hemmed in. The art gallery was more about negative space. Here it was about cram-filled space.

Vonnie leaned in. "Sherry Mae, I know we didn't give you quite enough notice according to our contract, but with Mary's husband being deployed again, the sooner we move closer to her, the better. Between the four-year-old and the twins, she's having a heck of a time."

Vonnie sounded as tired as her daughter must be, but I was tuned in more to the mention of a contract. Did Sherry own the property?

Sherry waved a hand. "Don't worry about that. I'm just sorry Lilyvale is losing you and S.T."

"Thank you. We're sorry to leave such a nice place."

"What about all your stock?" Sherry asked. "Will you be opening a store in Texas?"

Vonnie's hair brushed her collar as she shook her head.

"No, no. S.T.— that's my husband, Nixy—is in the workroom now making going-out-of-business signs. I'm contacting designers and dealers we know, so that will help. If anything's left"—she shrugged—"it's yours."

"Fred would be in hog heaven," Sherry said with a smile. "How soon will you be leaving? I'd like to take you both to dinner before you go."

"You are so kind." Vonnie patted Sherry's hand. "We plan to be out by June first, but anytime you want to show the building, we'll accommodate you. I keep the living quarters tidy, and I can spruce up a bit more if I have a heads-up. Or will you list with an agent?"

Bingo! Sherry did own the building. That would be another source of income for her. I glanced around the huge space packed with true antiques and collectibles, and with plain old stuff. The place surely generated income if it was easy to lease and the rent fee wasn't eaten up in taxes.

"I've shown it myself in the past," Sherry was saying, "but I may list it with Angela."

"She'd be a good choice," Vonnie agreed just as the bell at the door announced a customer.

Vonnie called out a greeting, then grasped Sherry's hand. "Thank you again, Sherry, for everything. I promise we'll get together before I leave."

She rose to take care of her customer, and Sherry asked if I'd like to look around. I declined. This stop had given me the perfect opening to ask Sherry about her finances.

"I don't mean to pry, Aunt Sherry," I began, my voice low as we stepped onto the sidewalk, "but did I understand right? You own this building? The same one that used to be Stanton's General Store?"

"Yes, and a couple of properties off the square. I charge a modest rent to keep the buildings occupied."

"So you have some alternate sources of income?"

"Have you been worried about my finances, child?"

"I did wonder how much you and your housemates might need to live together to conserve funds. I mean as opposed to wanting to share the house for the company."

"Well, I won't speak of anyone else's business, but we do just fine. All of us," she stressed, and then linked arms with me. "As for my affairs, Granddaddy didn't sell off *all* the land he owned, and Daddy bought more. Most of that is forest land. I'll show you on our tour."

I remembered the many trucks I saw on the drive to Lily-vale that were hauling long logs. "This forest land. Do you harvest the trees?"

Her lips quirked. "I don't, but the logging company does. They rotate cutting among eight properties, but they don't clear-cut. I insisted on an ecological approach."

"That's good to hear."

"Naturally, Daddy left the properties to both Sue Anne and me. Your mama asked me to buy her out when your daddy was so sick, so we arranged a payment plan."

My dad had died of colon cancer the summer I graduated from high school, and I realized with a deep pang that that's where the money had come from to treat Dad and pay for my college education. I worked during college, too, but I suddenly felt humbled and sad that my mother had given up her inheritance to fund my studies.

Sherry patted my arm. "It's what Sue Anne wanted, child, and anyway it will all be yours someday."

I smiled through misty eyes. "Not for a very long time, I hope. I don't want to lose you, too."

And I didn't. Like a punch in the gut, it hit me that the aunt I'd liked but didn't really know had become very important in these last few days.

We strolled on, arms companionably linked, passing a dry cleaner that advertised laundry service and a tailor. Then came Nifty Nails, Helen's Hair Salon, and a beauty supply store, which Sherry said were all owned by two sisters. Men's Unlimited occupied the corner space by the other end of the main drag, and it looked to carry every kind of men's and boys' clothes from suits to overalls. I wondered if Fred bought his overalls there. We window-shopped at the furniture store and another women's clothing store, nearly coming full circle on the square.

By now, cars packed almost every diagonal and parallel parking space. The sidewalks weren't crowded by Houston standards, but we passed shoppers hurrying in and out of stores and citizens heading to and from the courthouse and county annex building.

"Small as Hendrix County is," Sherry said as she pointed to the building, "there isn't nearly enough room in the courthouse for all the offices. The city offices are in the building behind this one, on the other side of the alley. Did you want to stop somewhere, or are you ready to do our driving tour?"

"Let's roll."

I DIDN'T NEED A GREAT SENSE OF DIRECTION IN LILY-vale because the layout was simple. Especially compared to Houston. I had a mental map going as Sherry directed me past the small but modern-looking hospital, the small county library in a cute 1940s building, and the school complex where the elementary, junior high, and high school buildings shared the same sprawling campus.

As a dozen more landmarks flew by, I absorbed the spring smells, the intense greens of the grass and trees, the vivid colors in the gardens and in the roadside wildflowers. Sherry pointed out her yellow pine forest lands—not all of them connected to each other—and we passed several industrial buildings set back off the road closer to town. One firm manufactured lamp shades, Sherry told me. Another made bar soap for boutique hotels. We also passed what Sherry said were branch offices and special labs of a timber and chemical company.

"Did Dab work for that firm?"

"Yes, but not at this location. Take the next turn and we'll have lunch. It's a hole-in-the-wall, but it's the best barbeque this side of Magnolia."

I wasn't all that hungry until the aroma wafted through the open windows. Then my stomach growled so loudly that Sherry laughed.

We toured awhile longer after lunch, but Sherry began messing with her bangs again.

"Do you need a haircut, Aunt Sherry?" She blinked at me as if I'd spoken Greek. "I noticed you fuss with your bangs on and off. If they've gotten too long, we can stop at your salon."

I thought her gaze looked suddenly guarded, but then she smiled. "I'll make an appointment for next week. I'd rather go home and get back to the family relics. We never did find that paperwork to apply for historical designation."

That certainty that something was off about Sherry surged again, but really, what could I do?

Go along with the program, I decided. And I did.

At least I now knew that Sherry had an income stream. Several of them. Huge relief there. And since Sherry said the rest of the Six did "just fine," I had to accept that. Really, their finances weren't my business. I mentally checked that inquiry off my list.

Two concerns down, one to go—get Hellspawn off Sherry's back.

Back home and fortified with tall glasses of sweet tea, Sherry and I began digging through the history-packed trunks again shortly before Eleanor came home. She informed Sherry she'd made copies of the agenda for Tuesday's meeting and that she was going to work on an improved still design for Dab in her room. Minutes later, a horn tooted. The mailman, Sherry said. I offered to run out to the box, but she wanted to check on her crepe myrtle.

When she came back to the parlor, though, she held a clear plastic box of chocolates.

"Someone mailed you candy?"

Sherry grinned. "No, this was on the porch swing. We always get one or two boxes after the festival, but we still don't know who sends them."

"There's a Be Sweet sticker on the box. Why not just ask at the store?"

"Pooh, that's no fun. This way I feel like we have secret admirers. Want one? I believe these are nougats and caramels and creams."

She held the container of six yummy-looking milk and dark chocolates, but my waistband felt tight enough. "Thanks, but I've eaten too much during this visit."

"In that case I'll eat mine and Fred's. He doesn't care for chocolate."

She popped a piece of candy, wiped her fingers, and reached for the folder labeled FAMILY TREE. With the barrette out of her hair, her bangs hanging over one eye, she picked up the magnifying glass and we began cross-checking birth and death dates.

Nearly half an hour later, we'd finished the dates check when Fred, Aster, Maise, and Dab come in the back door.

"We're in here," Sherry called out.

Aster strolled in, smiling. "Did you two have a good day?"

"Aunt Sherry gave me the grand tour," I answered. "How was yours?"

"Excellent." Her gaze landed on the candy box. "Oooh, is that chocolate from Mr. or Ms. Anonymous?"

"You know it," Sherry said, and lifted the box. "Want your piece now?"

"I'll save mine for dessert. I'm going to garden awhile, and Maise's gone up to finish her book before we start dinner."

"We'll be ready to help." Sherry eyed the candy, shrugged, and selected another piece. "What are Fred and Dab up to?"

Aster waved a hand toward the back. "Fred's going to

help Dab set up the one still in the barn. Or, I should say Dab is letting Fred do it because Fred is driving him nuts."

"Eleanor's been upstairs working on a redesign."

Aster chuckled. "I'll let her know what the guys are up to. She'll need to run interference on the project. See you later."

Sherry chewed her candy, then chugged some tea. "What's next, Nixy? Find the historic designation paperwork?"

"Actually, there are probably new forms online by now." I nodded toward the desktop computer sitting on the library desk near the front windows. "Can you run a search for the procedure and forms while I put some of these papers in order?"

"I'd be happy to."

Sherry drained her tea glass, fired up the computer, and was soon clacking away on the keyboard. The magnifying glass helped me examine documents, but I still had to squint at faded ink on birth certificates, letters, and bills of sale.

We worked in silence until the chair Sherry sat in squeaked, and I realized she wasn't typing. "Did you find the information, Aunt Sherry?"

"What?" she said faintly.

Alarm bells went off in my head. I dropped the letter in my hand and rushed to kneel beside her. "Sherry, what's wrong?"

"Sick. Help me. Fred's bathroom. Door over there."

She pointed toward the far corner of the room, her hand trembling even more than her body. I got her in the bathroom, but we only made it as far as the walk-in shower before she sank to her knees and retched. I held her hair back, and when the first spasms passed and she didn't keel over, I grabbed two white washcloths and wet them. One I laid across the back of her neck; the other I used to wipe her face. Her clammy face. Her breath smelled funny, but like what? I shook my head. It would come to me.

"Aunt Sherry, do you have these spells often?"

"Never."

"Do you have diabetes or any other condition?"

"The candy, child. Don't think it . . . was quite—"

I tended to Sherry while she emptied her stomach again, praying that I'd hear Maise come downstairs. Or that someone—anyone—would come in.

Meanwhile, my own gut churned in a mass of gnarled fear, disbelief, and fury because I'd finally recognized the funny odor.

Garlic.

The chocolates hadn't just been off. They'd been poisoned.

Chapter Ten

THE SECOND I COULD SAFELY LEAVE SHERRY CURLED up on the tile floor, I dashed for my phone and yelled for Maise.

My hands shook so hard, I fumbled the phone before I could hit the phone icon and dial 911. I didn't stop there. I ran out to the back deck and screamed for help. Thank God Aster didn't have acid rock blaring today.

The emergency operator answered after what seemed an eternity but was probably seconds.

"I need an ambulance at . . . Shoot, I can't remember the address. But hurry. I think my aunt has been poisoned."

"Poisoned?" Maise's voice boomed behind me. I turned as she rattled off the house address, and I repeated it. Aster stood with her.

"Where?" Maise barked.

"Downstairs bathroom."

"Move out, Aster." They rushed inside and I felt a rush of gratitude that Maise had nursing experience.

I spotted the other housemates hurrying from the barn.

Fred's walker clanked ninety to nothing as he strove to keep pace.

"Stay on the line," the operator instructed. "The EMTs are en route."

"You're going to hear me talk to other people, but I'm here."

I broke the news to Eleanor, Dab, and Fred, even as we heard sirens blaring in the distance.

Eleanor took charge. "Fred, go to the porch and direct the EMTs to the back deck. It'll be easier to handle the stretcher from there. Dab, see if you need to shift furniture to clear a path in the parlor. I'll find Sherry's insurance cards. I do believe I know where she keeps them." She briefly squeezed my arm. "You go back to her."

I did, but Aster barred the bathroom door. "We found her crawling to the toilet, muttering about Bill. She's indisposed right now."

"The ambulance is coming."

"I hear them, honey. The police will be here, too, so better move that candy box somewhere safe."

Could a person feel herself pale? If so, I did.

I whirled, my gaze darting, seeking the Be Sweet box, and finding it under the papers I'd dropped when I'd leapt up to help Sherry. Should I put the box in a bag? Would the police want to lift fingerprints? Sherry had handled the box, and who knew how many others? What the heck.

I grabbed a flat paper bag that held enlarged photographs, dumped the photos and gathered them in a neat pile, and then eased the box inside, touching it only with a pen. Dab gave me an odd look but went back to wrestling with one end of the sofa. I placed the bag on the computer table, then helped Dab scooch the couch out of the way.

EMTs stormed the room a minute later with a stretcher and big black cases of equipment. With Maise and Aster supporting her, Sherry emerged from the bathroom, deathly pale and shaking. The paramedics got her seated and began taking vitals, asking questions, starting an IV line. I answered questions about the onset of symptoms, Maise answered those about Sherry's medical history and her primary physician's name. Rattled as I was, I felt nothing but grateful that Sherry's house-mates had her medical information. My roommate, Vicki, couldn't have provided any fact but my age.

The EMTs were moving Sherry to the stretcher when a large, warm hand landed on my shoulder. I whirled to find Eric Shoar there, his expression grave.

"Nixy, I know you want to go to the hospital, but I need a minute first."

I nodded, and, after I stopped to snag the bagged candy box, we threaded our way through the rescue team and house-mates to the back deck. There the young black Lilyvale officer I'd met at the station stood at attention as if guarding the house.

"Here," I said, handing him the paper bag. "It's the candy Sherry ate before she got sick."

"You told the dispatcher you suspected poison. Why?"

"Because she was fine before she had the two pieces of chocolate. We've been together all day."

"You ate the same things?"

"Not for breakfast at Lilies Café, but we split a barbeque sandwich plate at lunch. Besides, I smelled garlic on her breath after she was sick in the shower. That's a sign of some kind of poison, but I don't remember which one."

"How do you know that?"

"I dated a guy doing a residency in ER medicine. He talked about cases."

He didn't make the smart remark I could see hovering on his tongue. Good thing, or I'd have punched him. The seniors were taking this more calmly than I'd hoped, while I felt like a blubbering mess.

"Do the paramedics know about the odor?"

"One of them checked Sherry's breath."

"Good. Now, did the ladies clean up the emesis? Do you know?"

"You'll have to ask them. Eric, I can't lose Aunt Sherry."

His brown eyes went soft with sympathy, and he enfolded me in a loose, supremely comforting hug. That nearly undid me.

Probably would have, but an EMT pushed the kitchen screen door open and carefully lifted the wheels at his end of the stretcher over the threshold. Sherry looked so frail, eyes closed, and hooked up to an IV and oxygen. I choked back a sob, my chest aching with the effort. But I had to keep it together.

"Come on," Eric cupped my elbow and steered me back inside, where Maise was issuing orders.

"I'll ride with Nixy. Dab, you feel up to driving everyone else?"

"I'll start the car."

"Maise, a moment," Eric said as Aster and Eleanor trotted off to get their purses. "Nixy says Miz Sherry Mae was ill in the shower. Did you clean it?"

"No time, and we figured you'd want to run tests."

"I'm calling in a county CSI tech so I can come to the hospital. You okay with leaving the house unlocked if I leave the officer out back here?"

"Yes, yes," she said dismissively. Eleanor and Aster were back, and Aster handed Maise her purse. "Nixy, where is your bag?"

"Parlor." I spun away, found my purse in the chair. Keys? Clipped to my purse. Phone? In my capris pocket. Focus? No. Determination? Hell yes.

We arrived at the hospital right behind Dab and crew, and all headed straight for the check-in desk, Maise taking the lead.

"Sherry Mae Cutler came in by ambulance," she told the thirtysomething ER receptionist. "We have her insurance cards."

"You're family?"

I stepped closer. "We're all her family."

The woman gave us a skeptical look, then typed on her keyboard. "Mrs. Cutler is being processed in. If you'll take seats in the waiting area, someone from Admitting will be out to get her insurance information."

"Can one of us be with her now?" Aster asked.

"I'm sorry, no."

None of us liked her answer, but we trooped to the open waiting area meant to hold waiting patients and family alike. Except we were the only people waiting. Eleanor handed Maise something as they and the men sat in thinly upholstered institutional chairs along the wall. Aster pulled a small spray bottle from her purse and discreetly spritzed over her head.

"Water-diluted lavender oil," she said and sprayed each of us.

Fred scowled but kept silent, his gray eyes angry slits. Dab didn't look as dapper as usual, but he sat without fidgeting. Eleanor and Maise looked worried. When she finally sat, Aster rested her cupped hands in her lap and closed her eyes. Meditating, I guessed.

I couldn't sit still. I picked up a hospital pamphlet that told me Lilyvale Hospital boasted four ER treatment rooms, twenty beds, a variety of surgical services, and affiliation with the University of Arkansas for Medical Sciences South. Residents in the rural training track specialized in family medicine, delivering patient care in the ER, surgery, even obstetrics. Fine, well, and good, but I wanted the best for Sherry. If we had to transfer her to Magnolia or elsewhere, so be it.

When a middle-aged woman in a poly-blend pantsuit entered the waiting area carrying a clipboard, Maise rose to give her the insurance cards. The woman would've photocopied and returned them, but Maise insisted on tagging along. Something useful to do, no doubt, because Dab was suddenly bent on taking vending machine orders. Eleanor went with him, and they returned with bottled water, colas, crackers, and a coffee for me. The strong, acidic brew wouldn't do my fear-cramped stomach any favors, but sipping it kept my hands busy while my thoughts raced.

Not one of us said a word about who could have poisoned the chocolates. We didn't have to speculate. We had a suspect

in mind, the only suspect that made any sense. Hellspawn
had gone way too far this time.

TIME WARPS IN A WAITING ROOM. IT HAD WHEN I'D
been stuck in one after my mother's stroke, and it did today.
Every minute lasted hours. The outside ER doors opened
now and then. A deliveryman came and went. A couple with
a small boy who sounded like he was coughing up a lung
rushed in. The child and parents were whisked through the
double doors leading to the ER inner sanctum, but no one
came out to speak to us.

The town grapevine must have been at work, too, because
neighbors and friends of Sherry's came by. Aster, Maise, and
Eleanor spoke with them, then kindly sent them away. Desperate
to distract myself, I leafed through old sports and entertainment
magazines. That didn't help much. I could only think of Sherry.
I couldn't go home until I was sure she'd be well and safe.

When the ER whooshed opened again and Shoar strode
inside, I catapulted from my seat to hustle over to him, then
hesitated when a woman dressed in a uniform similar to the
Lilyvale PD's followed him. Was she a county deputy? He
veered toward our group, but the woman stopped in the
automatic door, and then Hellspawn herself stormed in.
Gripping Trudy's arm, she marched to the desk with the
female cop on her heels.

"I need help right now," Hellspawn demanded. "My assistant is sick."

The witch tossed her cap of black hair in that odd asym-
metrical cut, glared at Eric, and abandoned Trudy at the desk.

"Detective, I'm telling you, someone tried to poison me."

Eric nodded. "So you told me and Deputy Paulson outside, but it's your assistant who's ill."

Her eyes narrowed. "The candy was meant for me, I'm
sure. If Trudy hadn't taken it, I'd be at death's door."

Trudy's ashen face lifted and for a moment her eyes blazed. "That's a lie, Jill. You told me to . . . Uh-oh. Bathroom," she choked out as she doubled over.

The ER receptionist pointed down the hall, and the law enforcement lady supported Trudy as she lurched from the counter.

"You need an evidence bag, Paulson?" Eric called after them.

Paulson flicked a hand. "Got it covered."

Hellspawn? She didn't so much as bat an eye at Trudy's distress. Instead she pointed at our group. "These people must be the culprits. If you don't do something about them this time, I'll have your badge."

I think I actually growled as I shot forward. "Knock it off, you bald-faced-lying b—"

Eric threw himself in my path so I couldn't wring her neck.

"Ms. Elsman," he said sternly, "Mrs. Cutler was also poisoned this afternoon, and both the Lilyvale Police Department and the Hendrix County Sheriff's Office are investigating." He took a deep breath. "Do you still have those chocolates?"

She shrugged. "How would I know? Trudy had them in her room, the little thief."

My mouth gaped open so far, the whole state would've fit inside. Before I could gather my wits and give Hellspawn her own good reason to be in the ER, the detective took her arm.

"I need to collect that candy box, Ms. Elsman, and I need you to come with me immediately. Nixy, I'll be back later to check on Miz Sherry Mae."

Hellspawn gave me a departing sneer that bounced right off of me. Because before they got out the door, a young man wearing a white coat and a stethoscope around his neck walked through the ER doors.

"Cutler?"

"Here."

We swarmed the poor man.

"How is she?" Maise barked.

The guy backed up a step and held up a hand. The hospital ID card on his lanyard read R. HAWTHORNE, RESIDENT. "The ER doctor asked me to come tell you Mrs. Cutler is in serious condition."

"Is she conscious?" I whispered.

"On and off, but she's disoriented."

My breath seized and my vision blurred with tears. I almost missed his next statement.

"We've contacted her primary care physician, and he'll be by. Either the doctor or I will be out to update you in a while, but it could be a few hours yet. Due to her age, she'll probably be admitted for further observation."

A dozen questions swirled, but the doc-in-training escaped.

And just then Paulson returned from down the hall with a sack that looked like an airsickness bag. Discreet.

Bless Aster's heart, she immediately asked after Trudy.

"A nurse took her back to the ER directly from the bathroom." Paulson shook her head. "That's a strapping gal, but she's one sick puppy."

With that she left. By unspoken consent, I trooped back to the back-breaking chairs with Sherry's friends.

"Well," Eleanor said firmly, "I do believe we'll want to rotate staying with Sherry tonight."

"No," I jumped in. "I'll do it."

"You think we're too old, missy?" Fred sapped.

I blinked at his scowl. "No, but I should be the one who stays."

"Why?" Dab asked.

"Because I didn't notice she was sick sooner. I didn't stop her from eating the candy in the first place."

Maise snorted. "You don't get between Sherry Mae and chocolate."

"She's right," Aster said with a smile. "I didn't discourage her either, you'll remember. Sherry will be fine. You'll see. Now, about Eleanor's plan."

Aster elected to stay with me until after Sherry was moved

to a room. Eleanor and Maise would go home with Dab and Fred, but be back later to take the night shift. They claimed they'd had power naps in the afternoon. I didn't argue, but Dab and Fred were none too happy about being left out of the rotation.

"It'll be better for women to be there if she wakes in the night," Maise said. "You both can come back with Nixy in the morning."

After the rest of the crew left, Aster sprayed us both with the lavender oil mixture. She assured me Sherry was strong and resilient, and that the scent would keep us from being so overwrought. We talked about her garden, about her passion for making herbal remedies, and about my job and my life. Which would be so very empty without Sherry, but I couldn't dwell on the negative.

We'd drifted to the subject of music when Eric returned.

"Where is Hellspawn?" I asked.

"Why?"

"Because you'll need to arrest me if I have to share this waiting room with her."

He grinned. "She was still at the inn when I left with the candy box."

"Oh dear," Aster said. "Will she come back to pick up Trudy?"

"No idea. Have you heard anything about Miz Sherry Mae?"

We told him what little we knew and that we planned to take shifts so someone would be with Sherry all night.

"You're not worried about Elsman harming her, are you?"

I'd considered it, but it sounded groundless when I heard it aloud.

"We just want her to feel secure," Aster said. "The men will come with Nixy tomorrow, and we women will get ready for the neighbor meeting."

"You're still holding the meeting?" I asked.

"We need to unite now more than ever."

"How about," Eric said, "I run and get y'all some dinner?"

I glanced at the clock on the far wall. Six thirty? In spite of daylight saving time, it felt like midnight.

"That's awfully kind, if it won't take you from your duties."

"I need to eat, too, Miz Aster. Now, what will you have?"

WE CONSUMED SOUP AND SANDWICHES IN A BLISS-fully empty ER. After dinner, Shoar asked me more questions about the onset of Sherry's illness. How long after finishing the pieces of candy did she get sick? General symptoms. Aster chimed in here and there, stressing that a benefactor sent candy after each folk art festival, and the chocolates had never been spoiled, much less poisoned.

"What about the evidence, Eric? Did you find finger-prints? When will you know what kind of poison this was?"

"Yes to fingerprints, though I don't know if they'll be use-ful. Everything goes to the state crime lab, and it could be weeks before we get results. But," he hurried on when I opened my mouth, "the garlic smell points to arsenic, and Miz Sherry Mae and Ms. Henry are being treated accordingly. A small amount makes the victim sick, but it's not lethal."

"That's the best news yet," I said, my smile feeling wan but sincere.

Half an hour later, we got more good news when a white-coated man with tired eyes strolled into the waiting room and headed straight for us. Dr. Lightly introduced himself and gave us good news.

"Mrs. Cutler responded well to treatment and is stable, but we want to keep her overnight. She'll be moved to a room shortly, and the nurses will need to get her settled. When they finish, you can stay with her but let her rest."

Aster thanked him, and the doctor turned to Eric.

"The second poisoning patient—ladies, if you'd step away, please? HIPAA laws, you know."

"No problem there," I said. "We know Trudy."

He eyed our going-nowhere stances and blew out a breath of defeat. Good man to know a losing battle when he saw one.

"The patient"—he stressed the omission of her name—"responded excellently to treatment. She'll be released within the hour, but you can speak with her now if you need to."

Eric nodded. "I won't keep her long."

He followed the doctor but hurried out in less than ten minutes.

"Got a call and need to go," he said. We must've looked frightened, because he added, "It's nothing to do with you. Tell Miz Sherry Mae hi. I'll be in touch tomorrow."

Aster and I sat again, this time near the wall-mounted TV that had been on all day. Aster tuned in to a home improvement channel and critiqued the landscaping choices. About nine o'clock, the new receptionist who'd been on duty a few hours gave us the happy news that Sherry was being transferred to her second-floor room, and we could go up in twenty minutes.

Ten minutes later, a nurse escorted Trudy out.

"There's no taxi service?" I heard Trudy croak.

"No, honey. The driver only works late on church nights. Sorry."

Aster poked me in the arm. "Go offer her a ride back to the inn."

"But Aunt Sherry—"

"Will keep until you get back. Think of it as a chance to snoop once more before our neighbor meeting tomorrow."

There it was. The only reason I could buy into.

Poor Trudy. I thought she'd kiss my feet when I offered to shuttle her back to the inn. After she'd thanked me half a dozen times just on the way to the car, I questioned her just to stop the thanking. Besides, it was barely a five-minute drive to the inn. If I wanted the scoop, I needed to start digging right away.

"Where is Hel—I mean, Ms. Elsman? Did you call her to come get you?"

"I called. She didn't answer," Trudy said, her voice sounding painfully raw. "But that's no surprise. She goes off at all hours of the day and night." She turned toward me. "You think she poisoned your aunt, don't you?"

"It's crossed my mind."

"But then why would she poison her own chocolates?"

"Because she had no intention of eating them?"

Trudy sucked in a breath. "Then she gave me the box because she meant to poison me? Why?"

I put on my detective-show hat. Come on, who doesn't love *Castle*?

"To deflect suspicion from herself to some unknown person."

"But that's horrible."

"Diabolical."

"And sadly believable." She slumped in the seat. "She's going to push someone too far one day."

I let that pass as I turned at a corner. "Trudy, why don't you quit? Tell your boss to shove it?"

"I—I need to keep this job," she said, her voice quavering.

I was quiet a moment, then asked, "What do you do for her?"

"Look up property and tax records, comparable sales, things like that."

"Do you know why she wants land in Lilyvale?"

Trudy hesitated, and I couldn't read her expression in the dark interior of the car. "She hasn't said. Not anything definite anyway."

"But you have your own thoughts on the subject?"

"Right now I can't think straight about anything, Nixy. I just want to go to bed."

I got that. Bed sounded good to me, too, and I'd get there right after I assured myself that Sherry was resting comfortably. Right after Eleanor and Maise relieved Aster and me. I probably wouldn't be able to sleep, but I desperately needed to decompress.

Trudy directed me to a parking area in back of the Inn on the Square, reminding me of what Lorna had said about guests using a code and the back staircase after hours. I'd planned to simply drop Trudy off, but when she stumbled getting out of the car, my conscience kicked in. Plus I could hear Aster in my head saying this was another chance to snoop.

It took Trudy two tries, but she got the code entered, and the door unlocked with an audible click. The staircase was too narrow to climb side by side, so I stayed a step below Trudy, my hand on her back. She turned right at the dimly lit intersecting hallway. At the far end of the hall was an old half-glass door, the glass frosted or textured or both, like I'd seen in noir films. I thought I saw the shadow of a head and shoulders move on the other side of the door, the side where the interior staircase went down to the café, but Trudy stumbled again and I looked away to catch her.

I put an arm around her waist as she lurched down the hall. A few more steps and she fit a key into an old-style lock. Not saloon-days old-style, but one from the 1930s or thereabouts.

The room was spacious enough. Queen bed with a fluffy white comforter and a mound of fat pillows. Two nightstands and a dresser from the 1930s or '40s, nicely refinished. No closet, but a 1930s reproduction wall-mounted clothes hanger with multiple hooks. No bathroom that I could see. An almost-full bottle of water sat on the nightstand nearest to the door.

Trudy must have notice me scanning the room. "I have to share a bathroom. It doesn't matter since no one is staying here right now except Jill and me."

"Let me guess. She got a room with an en suite bath."

"At the other end of the hall."

"You sit. I'll go get you a couple of cool washcloths."

"Um-hmm." She sank to the foot of her bed with a huge sigh, and when I was sure she wasn't going to do a face-plant on the floor, I hustled back out to find the bathroom.

It wasn't far. Another door down, a bathroom with a

pedestal sink, toilet, and shower. Open shelves held scented soaps and fluffy linens. I cranked on the cold water, wet two washcloths, and then grabbed a hand towel for good measure. I paused at the door leading down to the café. An EXIT sign above the door shed a little light, and there had to be dim lights on the other side of it, too. I touched the glass, felt the uneven texture, then put my face close to the surface, attempting to see through. No go. The glass was translucent but not transparent. Whatever I thought I saw was long gone anyway.

I trotted back to Trudy's room. She had flopped back on the bed, so I folded a cold cloth in half and put it on her forehead.

"That's nice," Trudy mumbled.

"Trudy, were you given antinausea medicine?" I asked as I snagged the empty white plastic ice bucket and draped the second cloth over its lip.

"I think so. The nurse said I'd be sleepy."

"That's good, but I've put another wet cloth here on the ice bucket beside your water bottle in case you get sick. I put a dry towel on the nightstand, too. Will you be all right by yourself?"

"Yes. You get back to your aunt. And, Nixy, thank you again for bringing me back."

"Sure, Trudy. You just rest."

I closed her door softly and paused in the hall. I wanted to get back to the hospital, but should I snoop a little more? A second of debate later, I decided to snoop because, hey, who was I to pass up a golden opportunity when it fell into my lap?

I crept down the hall to where Hellspawn's room should be, surprised that the old wooden floors didn't creak. Light leaked from under the last door, so I tiptoed closer. Close enough to suddenly hear Hellspawn's low-pitched voice. I couldn't make out words, but from the cadence, she sounded furious.

Then a voice answered. A male voice. It didn't sound happy either.

Chapter Eleven

I LISTENED FOR ANOTHER MINUTE, HOPING I COULD hear what was being said. No luck. Then someone inside the room moved, cast a shadow in the light seeping from under the door. I scurried back up the hall to the staircase, hoping I'd be long gone before Hellspawn or her visitor came out. Visitor? Hah! That had to be an accomplice.

I eased open the staircase door to minimize noise, but when another door thunked nearby—near enough to vibrate the staircase—I bolted outside.

And heard footfalls in the alley. Hellspawn's accomplice using a different door?

I scanned my surroundings like any wise woman should do, and spotted a man walking briskly down the short end of the alley behind the inn. When he reached the end of it and turned left at the corner, I saw the side of his face in a security light. A face sporting a bushy full beard just like Clark Tyler's.

Had he been in Hellspawn's room? Merely coming out of the back door of the café? I deduced it was a delivery door I hadn't noticed earlier, but why was he here so late? I didn't trot off to find him and ask, but the timing of seeing him sure seemed suspicious. And why was he walking when it made sense to park his car in the lot? Unless he and Lorna lived nearby.

All the way back to the hospital I tried to place that male voice in Hellspawn's room. Was it Clark Tyler's? It could've been anyone. I'd only interacted with a handful of men in Lilyvale, and through a closed, heavy door, I wasn't certain I'd recognize Fred's, Dab's, or Eric Shoar's voices.

Sherry's blue Corolla was in the hospital lot, which meant Eleanor and Maise were here for their shift. I parked and hurried to the second floor, where Maise stood chatting with a woman at the nurse's station. She saw me and waved.

"Go in and see her," Maise said.

I push the extra-wide room door open. The only light came from the bathroom. Sherry was tucked in bed with Aster and Eleanor sitting in more of those hospital-chic chairs. Aster yawned.

"She's doing fine," Eleanor said. "The nurse told us she'd probably be released in the morning after Doc Thorson sees her."

Ah yes. Sherry's primary care physician.

I went to the bed, touched Sherry's limp hand, and then brushed my fingers over her hair. In a flash of memory, I recalled doing the same with my mother, and tears I'd been holding for hours trickled down my cheeks. The light in the room changed, and I heard Maise's sure step.

I turned my head away, wiped my cheeks, and cleared my throat.

"Are you ready to go?" Aster asked softly.

"Ready."

Dab and Fred had waited up for us, which didn't surprise me. Aster filled them in on Sherry's condition. I assured them both they would be welcome to come with me to the hospital in the morning.

* * *

I SLEPT SURPRISINGLY WELL AND AWOKE TO MY phone alarm feeling more upbeat than I had in a week. Not that I'm always Miss Sunshine, but I'm optimistic by nature. I realized that I'd been knocked sideways from the time Detective Shoar demanded I show up in Lilyvale. No matter how valid my concerns about Sherry and company, no matter how justified my anger with Hellspawn, I'd been teetering on emotional ledges, and that just wasn't me.

A quick shower and hair washing later, I put a plan in motion. I dressed in the last of my clean clothes, blue jeans and a cotton tank top, then phoned the art gallery. The message I left for Barbra was hurried. "My aunt was rushed to the hospital and I can't possibly leave her at this point." All true statements, technically. I'd call again later and actually speak to my boss—if she deigned to speak to me. Meanwhile, I'd given her advance notice that I wouldn't be in tomorrow. My work ethic conscience was clear.

My second task was to turn Sherry's room back over to her. She'd rest better in her own bed, right? Right. So I gathered the bed and bath linens and my own dirty clothes. If I had time to shop for a few items, great, but I doubted that would be today. I threw my toiletries, shoes, folk festival finds, and worn-but-not-dirty things in my small suitcase. Finally, with my phone and tablet in my hobo bag, I grabbed the laundry bundled in a sheet and headed downstairs with renewed energy.

Aster, Fred, and Dab were already in the kitchen. Aster and Dab raised brows at me. Fred scowled.

"You fixin' to leave, missy?"

"Nope. I'm fixin' to wash Sherry's sheets and my own gear. I'm about out of clothes."

He blinked. "You're stayin'?"

"You bet your nuts and bolts I am."

"Yeah? Where you sleepin'?"

"On the parlor couch."

"Humph," he grouched and picked up his coffee cup. "Better not snore."

I grinned. "Aster, where's the laundry room?"

"In the basement, but just drop those things over at the door so I can give you the update."

I parked my suitcase on the floor, purse atop the suitcase, and crossed the short distance to the basement door to plop the heap of laundry. Next stop, coffeepot.

"Eleanor and Maise came back at six this morning," Aster said. "I didn't hear them come in, but they left a note that Sherry's vital signs were perfect all night. She slept peacefully and only woke up once."

I paused in the act of pouring coffee, a wave of relief washing over me. "Thank God. Any idea when her doctor will release her?"

"Doc Thorson usually makes his rounds before ten. You could call the nurses' station to check, but have some breakfast first and tell us if you got any information from Trudy. I was too exhausted to ask about it last night."

I snagged an apple and my coffee, sat next to Fred, and nibbled on the apple as I related what little I'd learned from Trudy. I debated mentioning that Clark Tyler had been in the alley, but spilled those beans, too.

The seniors weren't impressed.

"Coulda been out seein' his honey," Fred declared.

"Why, Fred!" Aster exclaimed. "Clark having an affair is just a rumor."

"He's been seen at some peculiar places at peculiar times."

Aster waved that away. "What I find interesting is that Trudy wasn't surprised that we suspected Jill Elsman of poisoning the candy."

Fred snorted. "And I'll bet she knows what that woman wants the land for. You shoulda pushed her harder."

"I couldn't browbeat her, Fred. She was still shaky."

"Even so," Fred said, "if she don't quit that job now, she's gotta be in cahoots with that woman, not just her gofer."

"I don't know." Dab had been quietly turning his cup in a tight circle, looking thoughtful. "I know what it's like to need a job you're not always happy doing. I needed the insurance from my job, especially when my Melba was sick."

"That's true enough, but I can't see the witch payin' much of a salary, much less health insurance. She's got somethin' on Trudy."

Aster rapped her knuckles on the table. "The critical information is Elsman's gentleman visitor. He probably *is* her accomplice and has been doing all the mischief for Elsman. Is it Clark?" She shrugged. "I don't see it. Are you certain you can't place the male voice, Nixy?"

"Sorry. Both of the voices in the room were too mumbled to catch much other than the argumentative tone."

"Hmm. I don't suppose Lorna and Clark have security cameras. Do you know, Fred?"

"No idea, but the police ought to ask that. Could be the poisoner was caught deliverin' the candy."

"Aster, Fred! That's brilliant!" I glanced at the kitchen clock. "I wonder if it's too early to call Detective Shoar."

"Probably not," Aster said, "but call the hospital first. If Doc Thorson comes early, Sherry'll be jumping out of her skin to get home."

Forty minutes later, I'd talked with a nurse on duty and with Sherry herself. In fact, we'd all talked with Sherry. Aster went upstairs to gather some clean clothing for us to take, and I phoned the detective. On his cell, as Aster insisted I do. I got his voice mail, and rather than leave a long, likely convoluted message, I simply asked him to call me.

Aster declared she could very well put fresh sheets on Sherry's bed and clean towels in her bathroom, and that my laundry could wait. I got Fred's okay to use his bathroom to blast my hair with the dryer until it was merely damp. With Fred's gruff admonition not to leave my "girly stuff" in his and Dab's space, I put my hair in a twist and claw-clipped it in place.

Dab got Fred's walker in my trunk—without the tool belt attached. I lifted my face to the light breeze of the perfect spring morning, inhaling the moment of calm. Then we were off.

Sherry looked better than I thought she would, and she insisted on dressing before her doctor came in.

"If he sees I'm ready to go, he won't dare make me stay," she said.

She sure knew her doctor. Fifteen minutes after she'd dressed in navy blue slacks and a pastel blouse, put on lipstick, and pinched her cheeks, Doc Thorson came in with Fred and Dab right on his heels.

I loved the man on sight. He had to be near Sherry's age, not much more than my height, and with a truly caring bedside manner.

"You're a wonder to bounce back so fast, Sherry Mae, and you surely were lucky. I don't suppose this has put you off chocolates?"

"How long have you known me, Doc?"

"Long enough to know that was a foolish question," he said on a chuckle. "You take it easy. Call the office for a follow-up appointment or if you have any questions. And Miss Nix—"

"Call me Nixy, Doctor."

"You watch for symptoms, anything that's not normal. She won't want you to call me, but do it anyway."

He winked. I smiled.

Sherry rolled her eyes, but we soon had her home.

She was a little shaky as she got out of my Camry, and her hands trembled a bit as she ate the light brunch Aster had prepared from the many dishes of food friends had dropped off at the house. Eleanor and Maise were up by then, and Maise must've noticed Sherry's small tremors because she insisted that Sherry go up to her own room to rest.

"I know you've been in bed for hours," Maise said, "but you want to be refreshed and sharp for the meeting this afternoon. Take your shower and have a lie-down."

Sherry grumbled about being hovered over, but I noticed she stayed upstairs until about an hour before the meeting.

In that time, I worked with the seniors to make the parlor company-ready. I carefully repacked the family treasures and stacked papers I wanted to look at again so they'd be handy to snag.

I also got my laundry done and got to see Dab's "moon-shine cellar" in the surprisingly bright and clean basement. The collection of some thirty mason jars and honest-to-goodness old-fashioned brown jugs bore white self-stick labels with a carefully printed year on each. One jug held liquor eighty years old, and I shuddered to imagine how that tasted.

I also called the gallery again. I called from the front porch, and about the time I got my boss on the line, Detective Shoar pulled into the gravel drive. I rushed through my conversation with Barbra, keeping the explanation simple: Sherry was ill and I wouldn't be back at work until at least the following Monday.

When I disconnected, the detective climbed the porch steps and sat beside me. "I got your message from this morning. Were you talking to your boss?"

"She's not happy, but she didn't fire me."

"So you're sticking around?"

"I can't leave until you do something about Hellspawn. She had to have poisoned those chocolates. No one else has a reason to harm Sherry. And," I rushed on, "I overheard her talking to an accomplice."

"You what?" He turned the full weight of his gaze on me. "Where was this? When?"

"Trudy was stranded at the hospital last night, so I took her back to the inn. After I left her in her room, I went down the hall to snoop."

He gave me a black look. "Tell me you didn't intend to break into Elsman's room."

I reared back. "Are you nuts? I just wanted to see if she was there. Trudy says she leaves at night a lot, and Trudy doesn't know where she goes."

"So, in spite of the obvious, that Elsman is on the far side of stable, you thought it was a good idea to hang out in the hall at her door. Let her find you lurking there?"

"I didn't stay but a minute or two."

He shook his head. "Fine. What did you hear?"

"Not enough. I couldn't understand the words, but their tones of voice were angry. Hellspawn hissed, and the man spoke just above a whisper. I can't identify the man, but I did see someone who could have been Clark Tyler in the alley when I left."

"What?" He came partly out of his chair, then fell back. "Spill."

"I heard a door shut as I was opening the back staircase door. I thought it was upstairs, so I hurried outside. That's when I saw a guy walking away fast in the alley. When he turned at the street, I saw a bearded face."

"Did the man see you?"

"I don't think so, but whether it's Clark or someone else, Hellspawn hasn't struck me as the hands-on type. An accomplice could've been doing her dirty work, from the vandalism incidents all the way to the poisoning. What I can't figure is how Elsman could've known about the candy Sherry gets after the folk art festival. Doesn't that make you think a local is involved?"

"It's possible, but Elsman could have overheard one of the vendors mention the tradition. She cruised the festival before she confronted Sherry Mae."

"How do you know that?"

"I spoke briefly with Harold Woods when we first arrived at the festival. You recall that?"

"Vaguely. I was more interested in seeing Aunt Sherry."

"Harold told me Elsman had talked to vendors, and not in a friendly way. So yes, she's on my suspect list, but she didn't buy the candy. Be Sweet had a big sale Monday, and the ladies who work there don't remember who bought what. They only know Elsman wasn't there. No one reported Clark Tyler being there either."

"What do you do now?"

"I have a list of customers the ladies remember being in the store, and I'm tracking down credit card buyers. If it was a cash transaction, I have no way to trace the buyer."

"I guess you checked to see if the store has security cameras."

He gave me a *duh* look.

"How about the inn? If Lorna or Clark—"

"I've checked with them. Neither of them saw the candy delivered, and they don't have working surveillance cameras."

"They should fix that. I'll bet whoever left the box used the back stairs." I sighed. "Did Hellspawn find the candy box in her room?"

"Outside the door, and I think she's telling the truth, but I'm not taking anything at face value." He laid a hand on my arm, gently squeezed, and then let go. "Nixy, listen, please. I'm on this. I can't stop you from snooping, but don't interfere in my investigation. The deputy prosecuting attorney, Bryan Hardy, is hell-bent on finding and frying whoever is behind our crime wave. If you do anything that puts the case in jeopardy, I'll have to arrest you."

"Huh. Then I suppose I shouldn't get a room at the inn." He made a choking sound, so I cut him a break. "Chill, Detective. It was a thought, not a plan. I made Sherry move back to her room, and depending on how long I'm here, the sofa might get uncomfortable."

"I'll recommend a massage therapist in town. Stay away from the inn."

I don't take ultimatums well, and really, who does? But I agreed. And when he thanked me so sincerely, I resolved to keep my word. Unless I came up with a good reason not to.

*   *   *

BY A QUARTER TO FIVE THAT AFTERNOON, THE HOUSE smelled of brownies, and plates and bowls of cookies, pimento cheese finger sandwiches, and chips—much of it food from friends—crowded the folding tables I helped set up. Pitchers of sweet tea and water, paper plates, cups, napkins. Refreshments were ready and then some. The parlor was crammed full with the extra chairs from the dining room and kitchen. Even then, some people attending the meeting would have to stand, and I'd be one of them.

Sherry was ensconced in a corner of the sofa on the far side of the room when the neighbors arrived. With word about her poisoning having spread, a few people brought her flowers, which Aster put on the table with the food.

Every single person exclaimed over the poisoning incident, and threats flew, too. The people I'd seen at the church breakfast led the pack.

Duke Richards pounded a fist on his knee, barely missed hitting the plate he balanced there. "Bog, Big George, and I are of a mind to take Barker and a couple of two-by-fours and go run that woman out of town."

Yikes, the shotgun guy Duke, bald Bog Turner, and Big George the bear nodded as if the plan was a done deal, and so did John Lambert. His wife, Jane, gave him a stern look.

"Too bad the police can't get rid of her for us," said Pauletta Williamson, of the squash blossom jewelry.

"Or they won't," petite Marie Dunn snipped. "I ran into Ida Bollings this morning, and she thinks our city and county officials are up to no good."

"Do tell," Jane Lambert said, leaning so far forward, I thought her bosom would squash the finger sandwiches on her paper plate.

"As you likely know, this Elsman woman threatened to take Ida's rental house land for the unpaid back taxes."

Murmurs of disgust rippled through the room.

"Well, she found her tax receipts and checking account records, and marched down to the courthouse to straighten things out. She talked to that head clerk, Patricia Ledbetter. The one whose child is so sick all the time."

"Bless her heart," Jane Lambert said.

"Yes, and things must be bad with that tyke, because Ida said when she showed Patricia that her property taxes had indeed been paid, and early to boot, Patricia became completely flustered."

"How so?" Sherry asked, her voice a hair too weak for my liking.

"According to Ida, she got real defensive, then angry, and then cried."

Pauletta shook her head. "Ida didn't let it drop, did she?"

"No, but Patricia's boss—y'all know the tax collector, Mac Donel?"

Heads nodded.

"He came charging out of his office, sent Patricia off to compose herself, and told Ida he was looking into the irregularities. Irregulari*ties*, plural. So Ida doesn't think she's the only taxpayer with screwy records, and she thought Mac looked more guilty than concerned about the problem. Why, Ida was so upset, she had to go home and take her medicine."

Every person in the room reflected silently on that flood of information for a moment. I kept an eye on Sherry, who seemed to be wilting. Did I butt in to get the meeting moving?

I caught Maise's gaze and nod. Right, butt in.

"Ladies and gentlemen," I said, "I know you all want to get home, so if we could refocus on the purpose of the meeting?"

"Getting rid of the wicked witch," Big George's voice boomed.

"Without violence," Sherry added.

"Sherry, you're entirely too good," Pauletta said. "Why, that woman tried to kill you!"

"In fairness, we don't know that," I said. "Her assistant was poisoned, too, and Elsman claimed the candy had been sent to her."

"I still think she needs escorting out of town," Duke growled.

"Y'all, please, we are better than that," Sherry said. "If we all pledge not to sell options to her, she'll have to give up sooner or later."

"Needs to be sooner," Bog rumbled darkly. "Before she does kill someone."

I suppressed a shudder that snaked up my spine. "Okay, then, all of you refusing to sell land options is one positive step. Dab and Sherry have filed destruction-of-property complaints against Elsman, and Detective Shoar is investigating those and the poisoning incident. I'm wondering if each of you might be willing to file harassment complaints. Or get an attorney to send cease and desist letters. There's no guarantee those measures would get Elsman to leave town, but it's another proactive step."

"I'm all for it," John said.

"Which choice?" Jane asked her husband.

"Either. Both."

Maise cleared her throat and stepped forward. "We have an attorney who'd be happy to help us with a letter, and I think he'd charge only a modest fee."

"In the meantime," Pauletta said, "I suggest that none of us so much as talks to Elsman. If she comes around again, we slam the door in her face."

No one shouted *Hear, hear*, but that was the consensus. The departing neighbors vowed to contact those who hadn't made the meeting and tell them the plan. Duke, Bog, and George offered to patrol Sherry's property, but Fred and Dab nixed that idea right away.

"If I'm in my workshop at night, I don't want you wallopin' me," Fred told them. They didn't argue with him.

I joined the Six in the kitchen to nibble on leftover finger sandwiches and the slaw Maise hadn't put out for the guests.

We rehashed the meeting as we ate, and the point they glommed on was the tax payments glitch.

"Mac Donel is such a straight arrow," Sherry said, "I can't believe he'd falsify property tax records."

"Or pick Ida's to mess with," Dab said. "She was a court clerk herself. Everyone knows she keeps her papers in meticulous order."

"But I do believe where there's smoke, there's fire," Eleanor mused.

"Yep, somethin's up with somebody at the courthouse. I just hope it gets straightened out in a hurry."

I carried the folding tables back out to the storage room in the barn, Dab along to open doors for me. I got a look at the still that was being reconstructed in the far corner.

"I need to get supplies to finish it to Eleanor's new design, but we'll have it running in no time. And don't worry," he added. "We've set up well away from the gas and the oil products we keep for our machinery. Fred moved those to his workshop."

"Does he really come out alone to work at night?"

"Not since the trouble with Elsman started, I don't think, but he's been known to burn the midnight oil. We seniors sometimes don't sleep as well or as long as you younger folks."

"My mother said the same thing."

He cleared his throat. "Well, I'm glad you're staying a spell longer."

"Me, too," I answered with a smile.

SHERRY TURNED ME DOWN WHEN I OFFERED TO SEE her up to bed, but when Eleanor said she believed she was tuckered out, Sherry allowed it was time for her to go upstairs, too. Maise and Aster followed not long after that, and though Fred and Dab played cards for a while in the kitchen, they retired before ten.

I made up the long sofa and snuggled in. After ten minutes,

I realized I was too wired to sleep. Attempting to read the Stanton patriarch's papers with that faded ink sounded like the perfect way to come down. Or at least tire my eyes enough to sleep.

I began reviewing handwritten notes about Samuel Allan Stanton. Born in 1830 in southwest Missouri, he was already married to Yvonne Ritter and had children before the Civil War began. Sam, one of his brothers, and his wife's brother sided with the South, and Sam moved Yvonne and their five children to Fort Smith. He fought in an infantry unit until wounded and sent home. Several moves later, Sam bought land from a Civil War widow, and they settled down for good. They farmed, had some livestock, and opened a general store in what was barely a crossroad. Eventually the crossroad grew to be Lilyvale.

I peered at Sam Stanton's death date. Was that 1903 or 1905? I rubbed my itchy eyes. Shoot, I couldn't see straight. I'd go check the grave marker tomorrow. Not only were my eyelids drooping, but I didn't entirely trust that Duke wasn't roaming around with his shotgun.

Reading the old papers, the neighbor meeting, and the poisonings fueled my dreams. I woke once to what I thought was a scream or a screeching and a buzz saw. It turned out to be Fred wheezing and snoring. When he didn't quiet down, I crept off the sofa long enough grab my phone and earbuds, and fell back asleep to a nature sounds relaxation MP3.

Next time I awoke, it was to the aroma of bacon cooking. Was Sherry awake yet? How did she feel this morning? I thought about going up to peek in on her, but I needed to change first. And take care of other business.

Neither Fred nor Dab was in the bathroom, so I dashed in and got ready for the day in record time. I wore my cargo shorts again, so I dropped my phone in a leg pocket, then I straightened my belongings and the family papers I'd left out last night. As I finished, Aster came in.

"I thought I heard you up. Breakfast will be ready in ten minutes."

"Is Aunt Sherry awake?"

"Yes, and she seems to feel fine, but Maise says she will tire easily. Keep that in mind when you plan your day with her."

"We'll work on the historical documents. Which reminds me, I need to check a date in the cemetery."

"Then call the others in, will you? They're in the barn."

"At this hour? Why?"

"Looking at Dab's still. Scoot now. Some of us have volunteer jobs to be at by nine today."

As I trooped through the dewy grass, Eleanor, Sherry, Fred, and Dab emerged from the barn door, Fred pausing to secure the padlock. All but Sherry were dressed in senior business casual, Eleanor's outfit elegant as always. Eleanor and Sherry walked with their arms tucked into Dapper Dab's.

"Is breakfast ready?" Sherry asked.

"Aster says just about," I answered as I hugged her and greeted Dab, Eleanor, and Fred. "How are you feeling, Sherry?"

"Hungry," she said.

"So am I, but I'll catch up. I have a quick date with a gravestone."

"I'm not saving food for you, missy," Fred said as he clacked past me.

"You won't have to," I called. Dab escorted the women on toward the house, and I quick-stepped behind the barn.

The huge azalea bushes still bloomed bright pink, and a squirrel chittered at me from one of the oak tree branches spreading over the graveyard. I pulled out my phone to take pictures, something I'd forgotten to do when I came out with Sherry. It wouldn't take long.

I hurried, phone in hand, pausing only long enough to steady the images as I snapped photos even as I reached to open the gate. One step in, and I stumbled in shock.

The small marble tombstones just inside the gate stood drunkenly, or lay on the ground, and the three-foot angel in the children's section of graves was missing a wing.

Fury boiled as I snapped photos of the damage on autopilot.

I didn't see more obvious damage but kept taking pictures as I walked toward the center of the cemetery.

Then I froze, shocked immobile.

A woman lay sprawled on her side across Sam Stanton's grave. Black jeans, black long-sleeved T-shirt, black asymmetrically cut hair matted with blood. Open eyes stared straight at my sneakers.

Hellspawn. Very dead.

Chapter Twelve

I DIDN'T SCREAM. I COULDN'T. I DON'T THINK I
breathed until spots dotted my vision.

What had Hellspawn been doing in Sherry's cemetery?
Well, vandalizing the gravestones, obviously, so I was wrong
about her farming out all her dirty work. Had she slipped on
the wet grass and hit her head on Sam Stanton's three-foot-
high grave marker? Had someone been with her? Killed her?
Geez, surely Duke and company hadn't found her sneaking
around and done this. No, I couldn't see that. But why kill
her, and why kill her here? She must've fallen. Which didn't
change the fact that she was dead and staring at my shoes.

In my peripheral vision, I saw other things that didn't
seem to belong there, but I couldn't look away from those
eyes for a long time. Too long.

I backed up a step, but then paused and took rapid-fire
photos of the scene. Stupid, I knew. I needed to call Detective
Shoar. Right now. I also had to go tell Sherry and her friends.

At least I had some visual evidence. Just in case someone
came along and . . . What? Moved the body?

The body. A fly crawled from the bloody hair just behind her temple across her forehead, and that galvanized me to move. Fast. I sprinted out of the cemetery and around the barn, toward the house, where Eleanor stood at the edge of the deck.

"I was just coming to find—what's the matter?"

I hooked my arm through hers, going for casual in case anyone watched from the kitchen windows.

"You have Detective Shoar's private phone number, don't you?" I asked softly.

She lifted a brow. "Why?"

"We have another situation. Hellspawn is dead."

"Where did you hear that?"

I gulped. "I saw it. In the family graveyard. I'll call nine-one-one, and you call Shoar's direct line. Please."

"But we have to tell the others."

"We will as soon as we make the calls. She's dead on Sherry's property, Eleanor. It'll look suspicious if we put this off any longer."

"Nixy, child, come eat," Sherry called through the open kitchen window.

"Just a minute," I said with a jerky wave. "I need to call, uh, work."

I met Eleanor's eyes, then strode off toward my parked car near the barn. Eleanor followed, her phone in her hand. Guess she'd had it in the pocket of her linen pants.

I spoke as calmly as I could to the emergency operator. After a few questions—including where I was in relation to the injured person—the woman told me to stay put and stay on the line. *Injured person? Lady, she's dead*, I wanted to say, but one doesn't snap at the dispatcher.

Eleanor stood some ten feet away making her. She grimaced as she talked. I figured she was answering questions, too, and when she ended the call, she nodded.

"He's on the way. I'll go break the news to everyone."

"Thanks. I hate to say this, but tell them not to come

outside. I didn't pay attention to footprints, but if there are any besides mine . . ." I swallowed.

"We don't want to compromise evidence." I must've looked surprised because she gave me a ghost of a grin. "I watch my share of cop shows."

CASTLE. BONES. NCIS. IT DIDN'T MATTER HOW MANY crime shows I had watched. The reality of having the authorities descend was chaotic, physically and emotionally. More so than Monday's swarm of emergency and police people when Sherry had been poisoned.

I watched the action from where I leaned against my Camry. A patrol car arrived first, then Detective Shoar in his truck and more patrol cars, then the EMTs and yet more marked and unmarked cars. County deputies came, too, including the woman who'd seen to Trudy on Monday night. I overheard Shoar call her Paulson while he consulted with her and the rest of the officials milling around. The name rang a bell beyond the hospital encounter, but I couldn't place it.

The EMTs didn't stay long. Nothing for them to do besides ask me if I was in shock. I was, but not the kind they treated.

Within thirty minutes, the barrel-chested police chief and the lanky coroner showed up. I didn't know them on sight but asked a passing officer to give me a who's who rundown. With Shoar escorting them, Chief Randall and Coroner Terry Long clomped off behind the barn. An eon later, the chief returned with Detective Shoar.

"You want to call in the state police, do it," I overheard him say, "but I'd like to keep this a local investigation. I want this solved quickly, no matter who is implicated. You understand, Shoar?"

"Yes, sir."

He watched the chief walk away, then crossed to me.

"Are you standing here to catch all the action?"

"I was told not to move."

His eyes narrowed. "By dispatch?"

"And the first officer who got here. He said you wouldn't want to have to hunt me down."

"Nixy, you didn't have to take that literally."

"No, but I'd already been in back," I said, jabbing a thumb over my shoulder. "I didn't pay attention to footprints then, and I didn't want to be accused of messing up any others you find."

"You watch crime shows, don't you?"

"Some, but that doesn't prepare a person to be on the fringes of a real crime scene investigation. Or is it a crime scene? She might have slipped and fallen, right?"

"Nixy, breathe."

I sucked in a breath of spring-morning scent. Exhaled. Inhaled again for good measure.

"You never dated a cop who talked about his work?"

At that, I huffed a breath. "I've never dated a cop, period."

"You should put that on your to-do list."

I blinked at him, saw his slow smile. "There's a dead woman in the family graveyard. Why are you teasing me at a time like this?"

"Because you look ready to jump out of your skin. Come on. You can sit on the deck."

He put a hand at the small of my back and gently urged me forward. When I stumbled, he grasped my elbow.

"You *do* need to eat."

My head whipped up. "Who said that?"

"Eleanor. I talked with her on the front porch. I imagine she's back in the kitchen with your aunt and her friends."

"The Silver Six."

"The what?"

"Silver Six. That's what Sherry calls them. I guess they all call themselves that. I'm babbling, aren't I? I never babble."

"First time I saw a body, I did worse."

I couldn't imagine that, but his deep voice, guiding hand,

and trivial conversation steadied me. Once on the deck, I sat in one of the two white Adirondack chairs. Well, "fell into it" would be more accurate. Just call me Grace.

As I righted myself in the seat, Shoar crossed to the back door. I'm not sure a half second passed before Sherry answered it.

"Is Nixy hurt?"

"Just a little shaken. You can bring her some food, but don't question her. Go right back inside until I can organize officers to interview each of you."

"You can count on us. Oh, and you and your people search wherever you need to."

The detective stilled. "You don't want me to get a warrant, Miz Sherry Mae?"

"No, we've discussed it. Do your duty, but do ask your people to be as tidy as they can."

"You're willing to sign a consent to search the buildings?"

"Absolutely. Do you want me to write up something?"

"We have a form. I'll have someone bring it to the front door."

He headed off, and before he was out of sight, Sherry came out bearing a plate with a steaming omelet, bacon, and crisp buttered toast. Eleanor trailed her with a large mug of coffee in one hand, a TV tray in the other, and a floppy straw hat tucked under her arm.

"Nixy, child, I'm so sorry this has happened." Sherry fussed as she handed me the plate, utensils, and a napkin, then took the TV tray from Eleanor and set it up.

"It's not your fault, Aunt Sherry." I placed the meal paraphernalia on the tray and then hugged her. "How are you?"

"I'm shocked, naturally. I can't imagine what Ms. Elsman was doing in the cemetery unless she was bent on mischief." She stopped, looking stricken. "Oh Lord, did she vandalize the gravestones? Did she smash any?"

"She knocked over some small markers," I said, taking

Sherry's hand, "but the only major damage is to the children's angel. We can get another one."

She closed her eyes briefly and sighed, then squared her shoulders. "Yes, we can. We'd best go back in. We're baking cookies to pass the time."

I nodded. "That's good. Keeping busy, I mean."

Eleanor had put the coffee mug on the tray and now passed the hat to me. "Aster says her gardening hat will keep you from getting sunburned, and Fred says he'll put a fan out here if it gets too hot."

My throat tightened. "Tell them both thanks."

"Holler if you need something," Sherry said. "And don't worry. Eric will get this all sorted out, and we'll put the markers back up. They were beginning to sink and shift in places anyway."

I hadn't noticed sinking and shifting, but if that made Sherry feel better, I was on board.

She and Eleanor hustled back inside, and I dug into my belated breakfast. The aromas and tastes were amazing, but after three bites, I was done. I couldn't get the image of Hellspawn's unseeing eyes and that fly on her forehead out of my mind. My stomach cramped, so I knocked on the door to return the plate but kept the coffee.

Paulson appeared from behind the barn and headed toward me. She carried a black boxy bag and wore a friendly smile.

"I know you told the first officer you didn't touch anything except the gate and latch, but I need to get your fingerprints."

"Sure, but they're on file in Texas. The art gallery required all employees to be printed."

"Now you'll be on file in Arkansas," she said cheerfully.

Her name badge read M. PAULSON, and as she worked, curiosity got the best of me. And nerves.

"I think I met someone else named Paulson at the folk art festival. Do you have relatives here?"

She rolled her eyes. "Everybody has kin here. You probably met my uncle, Mayor Paulson."

"That's it. He bought one of Sherry's baskets."

"Uh-huh, for my mother. I was working that day, so Uncle Pat came to the festival. I'm Megan, by the way."

"Nixy. Nice to meet you."

"Under these circumstances?"

"No, but I won't hold that against you. Uh, about the circumstances. Did Hel—Elsman fall and hit her head?"

"We don't know yet, but nice try," she said on a chuckle, and handed me some wipes. "Think Miz Sherry Mae and company are ready for me?"

"Just be ready to duck questions and eat cookies."

She went in the back door, and I stared at the black screen on my cell phone. Wait. I hadn't looked at the photos of the cemetery. Could my stomach handle them? More, shouldn't I take a peek before I showed them to Eric? I didn't want to show him a bunch of blurs, now, did I?

I angled the screen away from the sun as much as I could, shading it with Aster's hat. In spite of some glare, the pictures weren't blurry. They were all too clear. I enlarged each one, avoiding a too-up-close of Hellspawn's face, and saw those objects my peripheral vision had registered but not recognized.

A black rod with a hooked end appeared wedged against old Sam's marker, and the dirt at the marker's base was disturbed. Looked like a crowbar. By Hellspawn's arm, a smidgen of something off-white showed from under her sleeve. Paper? A sock? I didn't get a good angle on the object, but the last one, near her feet, was clear. A checked scrap of cloth that looked an awful lot like the blue gingham Sherry used in her basket handles. Uh-oh.

Blue gingham wasn't uncommon, but it was Sherry's signature fabric. Who else had easy access to the material?

My thoughts leapt to Trudy skipping out of the antiques store. She'd held a basket with a blue gingham handle. But no. Surely Trudy's basket was still in her room and intact. I hadn't seen it, but if she'd hidden it from Hellspawn, I wouldn't have, would I?

Did Trudy know about her boss yet? I groaned. Who was I kidding? All of Lilyvale likely knew by now. The whole of Hendrix County.

Before my mental leaps bounded completely out of control, boots smacked the deck steps. I hit the home button on my phone, then lifted the hat to shade my eyes to find Shoar standing over me.

"Checking e-mail?"

I shrugged. I had every intention of sharing the shots with the detective. But a little voice told me not now.

He pulled the second Adirondack chair closer to mine. "Tell me what happened this morning and start with why you went to the cemetery."

I took a calming breath and launched into my story. The blow-by-blow truth without mentioning I'd taken photos. Or mentioning the items I'd seen in the photos but not really seen at the scene.

"So you thought she'd hit her head and fallen?" he asked when I finished.

"Didn't she?"

"Where were the Silver Six when you got up?"

I turned my body to face him more fully. "You can't think that any of them killed Hellspawn."

He arched a brow. "Under the circumstances, I'd rethink calling the deceased by that name."

I ground my teeth in frustration. "*What* circumstances? Was she killed?"

"It's a suspicious death. The coroner is conducting his part of the investigation, and the body will go to the state medical examiner for autopsy. He will determine cause of death. Now, back to the Silver Six. Where were they this morning? You know they'll tell me the truth later, so you can do it now."

I inhaled deeply again. "Maise and Aster were in the kitchen. The others were in the barn."

"Why?"

"Aster said they were looking at Dab's still. Not a moonshine still," I added in a rush. "Dab distills Aster's herbs, and it's not even put back together yet. Eleanor and Fred are redesigning it."

He heaved a put-out sigh. "The still hasn't been in the barn all along, has it? It was in the basement. The complainants said they thought the explosions were coming from underground."

"Booms, not explosions, and there were two stills. Faulty valves sort of blew when the old furnace kicked on or off. Something like that. Dab can explain it better. He and Eleanor dismantled them both on Sunday."

"The kitchen fires weren't from cooking either, right?"

"Smoke bombs Maise set off on the windowsill."

He shook his head. "She should know better."

"I'm sure she does, but these people are close. They protect each other."

"Enough to kill?"

"You're saying He—Elsman was murdered?"

"I'm not confirming anything." He ran a hand over his short hair. "Listen, we'll have to search the barn, but I'll let the officers know about the still. Was Miz Sherry Mae, or were her friends, anywhere else on the property aside from the house and the barn?"

"Not that I know of."

"Tell me again what you did when you saw Elsman."

I went through my movements again, but still held back the photos. I knew I should tell him. I'm a law-abiding person, except for driving faster than the speed limit. In Houston, you drive fast or get run over. And, hey, I could e-mail the pictures to him later. *Gosh, in my shock I forgot that I'd taken photos.* Lame, but I really wanted to examine the shots. Something about those three objects teased a memory I couldn't quite grab. Besides, Paulson and other techs were certain to have much better pictures of the entire crime scene, including the items I'd captured on my phone camera.

The good detective reminded me that evidence would go to the state lab and it would be weeks before he had official reports. I wondered about unofficial reports but didn't ask.

"Will you be notifying Trudy?"

"Another officer is doing that, and we'll check with her about next of kin." He stood and subtly stretched his back. "If I have more questions later, will you be around?"

"I'm staying until all this is resolved."

He gave me a cop look. "Good. I have a feeling your aunt is going to need you."

"You saw the gravestones knocked over, right?"

"I did. It appears that Elsman was in the act of vandalizing the cemetery."

I nodded. "That's what I told Aunt Sherry, but I'd like to get the stones reset before she sees the mess. How long before I can do that?"

"Two days or less. Until the investigators collect all the evidence they need and take all the photos, the cemetery and the woods behind the house will be off-limits."

"Complete with yellow tape?"

"And an officer standing guard, so don't give him trouble."

PEOPLE FEED PEOPLE THE WORLD OVER, I GUESS, but I think it's especially true in the South. They don't waste any time either. They hadn't two days ago when Sherry had been poisoned, and they didn't today.

Only hours after the Six had been individually interviewed—even before Hellspawn's body was moved—neighbors began bringing food. Casseroles, cold cut trays, fruit trays, veggie trays, desserts, biscuits, and rolls.

A nonfood aroma permeated the house, too. Aster had set out fresh mounds of lavender flowers, and probably sprayed every room with diluted oil, as well, but the scent failed to calm Sherry. She quickly grew tired and fretful, her trembling hands fussing with her bangs until I insisted she rest. I couldn't get her to go upstairs, so she camped on the parlor sofa and seemed to calm.

Eleanor, Dab, and I took turns going to the front door, exchanging a few words with the bearers of bounty, and then jotting notes as to who brought what on a pad by the door. Though the Six hadn't asked me a thing about discovering Hellspawn's body, every neighbor wanted the scoop. I side-stepped their questions as tactfully as I could, but the strain sct me on edge.

By the time the food flood stopped, the fridge overflowed and the counters were covered. Maise and Aster packed samplings from every dish for old lady Gilroy next door, and I volunteered to make the delivery.

"This ought to feed her for a week," Maise said as she nestled the last of the plastic containers and zipper bags into a box that was longer than it was deep. "Remember, just set the box on the porch, ring the bell, and leave. She won't come out if you wait."

"Will she be able to lift the box?"

"No, but she'll pull it inside. That's what she does when we take over big holiday meals."

The police and sheriff and coroner vehicles were gone, and Sherry's crepe myrtle was upright and holding on to life, but the cars had left tire tracks on the lawn. I shuddered in spite of the pleasantly warm late-afternoon sun on my face. I hoped the coroner would conclude that Hellspawn—okay, Jill Elsman—had fallen, struck her head, and died. After all she'd already been through, Sherry needed a best-case scenario.

The food box was just heavy, long, and awkward enough to need both hands. It bumped gently against my stomach with each step down Sherry's gravel drive and along the short walk next door.

I hadn't paid much attention before now, but old lady Gilroy's small house sat on a slightly wider lot than I thought. Her chain-link fence sagged in a few places and the gate with a simple lift-up latch squeaked. I'd shifted the box to my hip to open the gate, then back to pick my way past the two-foot-wide cracked sidewalk. No twisted ankles or spilled food containers for me.

I took the one step up to the postage-stamp front porch, grasped the box to my body with one arm, and reached to knock. Before my knuckles met wood, the door swung open, and a gnarled hand grabbed mine and jerked me into darkness.

Chapter Thirteen

IT WASN'T PITCH-BLACK IN THE SMALL ROOM, BUT dark enough. I fumbled with the box as my eyes adjusted, and blinked at the elfin woman who stared up at me. Sparse white hair covered her head, and she wore a flower-print housedress that had been out of fashion since the 1960s. Wrinkles on wrinkles, hunched shoulders, piercing gray eyes.

"You know who I am, girl?" she barked.

I blinked. "Ol—I mean, you're Mrs. Gilroy."

"Bernice, but old lady Gilroy will do, and don't think I don't know you caught yourself just then. Now, how old do you think I am, girl?"

I squinted at her and took a shot. "Ninety."

"Hah, I'm ninety-three, and losing time. Get that food to the kitchen."

I couldn't help it. I blinked again, completely befuddled, but followed her without seeing much in the living area besides gloom. She turned right at a doorway and we were in a kitchen with yellow appliances. Yellowed with age, or were they that Harvest Gold color that had once been the rage? Hard to tell with ugly brown curtains blocking light from the back and side windows.

The fridge light nearly blinded me when Mrs. Gilroy pulled the door open. Nothing save a half loaf of bread and a stick of butter sat on the shelves, but it was sparkling clean, as was the rest of the kitchen as far as I could see.

Mrs. Gilroy snapped her fingers in my face. "Don't stand there, girl. Hand me the perishables first."

I placed the box on the 1950s kitchen table, only one sad chair beside it, and began digging through the box. I passed containers to her, and she arranged them in a quickly filled fridge. She wanted only the cookies left out, and I put those on her counter by the sink. When I reached for the empty box, she slapped it out of my hand.

"Leave that. I need it to return the containers, don't you know."

"Aunt Sherry said you don't return them." I had no clue why I challenged her, but she merely cackled.

"Sherry's right. I don't. But you never know what I'll do." She paused and cocked her head at me. "You're Sue Anne's girl, aren't you? You have her look, but you favor Sissy more. You know who Sissy was?"

"I'm Nixy and Sissy was a Stanton ancestor."

"*The* Stanton ancestor, far as I'm concerned. What a pistol she was. She and her husband ran the five and dime for years. You know this house was built by the Stantons for one of their married children?"

"No, I didn't."

"Sissy even lived here. Twice. Once as a young married woman, once when she was older and widowed. A starter home, they'd call it now. Didn't build but two bedrooms, no dining room, but then I imagine they took their main meals at the big house."

"That makes sense," I said, but none of this made sense. Old lady Gilroy, the hermit, educating me about my ancestress Sissy and about the origins of the house while I stood in her kitchen? An alternate universe had opened along with the front door and I'd fallen in.

"I'm reclusive, but I know things, girl." Her eyes narrowed on me, took on a shrewd light. "I know you took on that land woman toe-to-toe."

I glanced at the ugly brown fabric at the side window. "You spied on us through your curtains?"

"I spy on everyone, but the action's at Sherry's. Had the windows open, heard that monster vehicle roar up to the yard, and heard most of the dustup. She never darkened my door. Probably knew I wouldn't answer it. But she drove past so much she liked to have worn ruts in the asphalt out there. Had my bedroom windows open last night. Got up when I couldn't sleep."

It took me a beat to process all that, then it was my turn to give a narrow-eyed look. "Are you saying you heard or saw what happened in the cemetery last night?"

"I have a pretty good line of sight from my bedroom. Car lights came first on the street over, then a flashlight in those woods behind the big house. Flashlight went off, then I heard whispering voices."

I'd forgotten about Hellspawn's Hummer. She sure didn't walk to Sherry's. Had the police found it?

Fingers snapped in my face again. "Think on your own time, talk to me on mine."

"What time was this, Mrs. Gilroy?"

"Two thirty. Three. I got some water and went back to bed."

"And you heard voices. As in more than one?"

"That's what the plural indicates, girl. Keep up. One was deeper than the other. Not much, but I pegged it as male."

"Did you see anything else? Anything that happened in the cemetery?"

She looked away from me as if replaying a scene. "I saw dark figures. Two of them. Didn't see what they were doing other than moving around. But I heard more. Several thunking sounds, like a heavy door closing. Then I heard a short cry. After that, nothing. No noise, no movement."

"I don't suppose you'd tell the detective about this."

"You suppose right. I don't like talking to people."

"You've talked to me."

"I made an exception. You can leave now."

She shooed me through the living room, a room that, now that my eyes were accustomed to the gloom, I saw was furnished with two wingback chairs upholstered in a dull plaid pattern, a stained wood coffee table between them, the chairs facing a flat-screen TV bigger than mine at home.

I planted my feet and faced her. "Did you set that TV up by yourself?"

"A'course. I'm old, not incompetent. Get out now."

She gave me a shove to the door, and I was on the postage-stamp porch, squinting in the sunlight, wishing I had my shades.

I stood there a moment, perplexed that the woman I'd expected to be a frail eccentric had turned out to be just plain eccentric. I hadn't given her much thought before. Now I wondered how she'd shopped for that TV, much less everyday items. I'd like to have the chance to ask someday, not that she'd answer me.

I shook my head. At least I had a sort of witness and her story to give Eric. Because, though I hadn't dwelt on it, seeing that gingham fabric near Hellspawn's body worried me.

I wanted to go around the block to check out that line of sight Mrs. Gilroy mentioned, but Eleanor waved to me from Sherry's porch, where I found the seniors, all six of them, waiting.

"I can't believe Bernice Gilroy let you in her house!" Sherry exclaimed.

"She dragged me in," I corrected as I joined her on the porch swing.

The others sat in the wicker and bent willow chairs, staring at me.

"Report, Nixy," Maise said. "What did Mrs. Gilroy say to you?"

I related our conversation to a rapt audience.

"I'm glad to know she's well," Aster said, "but do you think she really saw or heard a thing?"

"She seemed sure, and that woman is as sharp as I am. Or more so."

"Well, Eric may not need her information," Sherry said. "In spite of everything we went through with Ms. Elsman and the tragedy that she died on our property, the police and sheriff's deputies searched the house and grounds thoroughly. I can't imagine they suspect any of us."

I winced, and Fred noticed. "Out with it, missy. What do you know that we don't?"

I scrambled for a truth I could sell. "I, uh, was just thinking about what the police chief said this morning. That he wants the case solved quickly, no matter who is implicated. Not that I think the police would railroad anyone, but as you said, Sherry, Elsman died on your property. I have a feeling the cops will want to talk with you again."

"I do believe they'll talk to all of us again, but let's not borrow trouble."

"Agreed, Eleanor," Dab said. "Shall we make inroads on that food?"

I didn't have much of an appetite, but neither did the Silver Six. The table talk returned to Mrs. Gilroy, how remarkable it was that she'd let me in her house, and speculation about how she'd gotten the TV in her home, never mind set it up. Then all but Sherry debated whether to go to their volunteer jobs in the morning.

"Please go," Sherry urged. "You know how the instructors depend on you to be there. Nixy and I will stay busy with the historical landmark paperwork, and we'll call if we need you."

"I do believe Sherry is right," Eleanor said. "If we go about our normal business, it will undermine any gossip."

"And show the cops we ain't got nothin' to hide," Fred added.

Maise gave first Sherry, then me, a searching look. "Affirmative, if you promise to call if there are developments."

Sherry and I promised, and then I asked to be excused.

"I want to go check out what I can of Mrs. Gilroy's story before it gets too dark," I explained.

Heads nodded, and Aster pressed a handful of tiny lavender flowers into my hand. "Put them in your pocket and they'll help keep you calm."

"If you'd like another set of eyes," Dab said, "I'll walk with you."

I didn't have the heart to turn Dab down. Besides, he was right.

We left by the front door, Dab hiking his pants up as we descended the porch steps. I put on the light jacket Sherry had insisted I wear, and had my hobo bag with me, my tablet inside. Couldn't hurt to take some photos. Maybe video.

"Thanks for letting me tag along. I was hoping to have a look around back and report to Maise."

"Looking for anything in particular?"

"No, just looking. We're not supposed to ask you about discovering the body, so we'd planned to gather our own intelligence."

"That does sound like a Maise plan."

He grinned, then shook his head. "Let me tell you, it's frustrating to be out of the loop. All the other incidents, the mailbox bomb, the barn being burglarized, we were there to set things right."

Oh, shoot! The barn break-in. The things that had been taken were—nope, I wouldn't rely on my memory.

"Dab, tell me again. What all was missing after the burglary?"

He pulled up his pants, one side, then the other, as he walked. "It took us a while to figure that out, don't you know. The place was a mess. Fred and I had a few tools missing. A crowbar and a hand drill that was my father's."

"What about Sherry's craft supplies? Or Aster's and Eleanor's?" I asked, partly excited, partly dreading the answer. Just knowing the crowbar had been stolen, too, worried me.

"Aster and Eleanor keep most of their supplies in the base-ment. Sherry was missing some white oak slats, some jute and hemp twine, strips of that blue gingham she weaves in with the hemp, and her cotton gloves. The ones she uses when she crochets the jute especially so it won't cut up her hands."

Images whirled. I needed to check again, but the off-white scrap in the photos could be one of Sherry's cotton gloves. It could simply not be coincidence that three items near Hell-spawn's body were among those stolen from the barn just a week or so ago. This wouldn't look good to the police.

"Why are you asking about the burglary? Is this about what you saw in the cemetery with Elsman's body?"

"Dab, it's killing me to keep quiet, but I promised Detec-tive Shoar. Besides, Sherry is still recovering. Hearing details would just upset her more, don't you think?"

"That's a valid point."

In that moment, I realized how valid it was. Seeing the photos I'd taken would only plant ugly images in their minds. Sure had in mine. The seniors were likely tough enough to take it, but that wasn't a great reason to dish it out. Nope, unless an unforeseen, urgent need arose, I'd keep the photos to myself.

We came to the south side of the property line, where the pines and blooming dogwood, more pink azaleas, and low scrub plants grew thick. And where trash had blown and been caught in the vegetation.

"Looks like a critter or two got into someone's garbage," Dab said as he surveyed the line of trees. "Mind helping me police this mess before it gets any darker?"

"You sound like Maise," I teased.

"Yep, but I could do worse."

We picked our way along retrieving torn pieces of com-ics, color ads from circulars, what looked like scraps from a book or magazine page, a fast-food napkin, and a take-out menu. Dab didn't have nearly enough room in his pockets for the debris, so I waded the bigger pieces into balls and stuffed all the trash into the bottom of my bag.

Dusk deepened as we reached the street behind Sherry's, but I pulled out my tablet and began taking video. Since we hoped not to attract the neighbors' attention—or that of the officer stationed nearby—we kept our voices low.

"Did Mrs. Gilroy say which direction the headlights approached from?"

"No, but I think they'd be the brightest in her window and most noticeable if they came from town."

"You don't think the trees would've blocked the lights?"

"Not if the car cleared the trees before the lights were turned off." I dropped my voice more. "Where is the path from here to the cemetery?"

Dab scanned the deeper shadows of the tree line. "See the place where the undergrowth is sparser? I think that's it."

"You think? You're not completely certain?"

"I haven't used it in years."

"I wasn't criticizing. It's just this: if the path is that indistinct while we still have some daylight, how would Elsman be able to find it at full dark, even if there was some moonlight?"

"Good question."

Although I remembered now that Trudy had gone off that way on Saturday, and I'd pondered her knowing about the path when I'd been with Aunt Sherry Sunday afternoon. If Elsman and Trudy had vandalized the barn, they'd both have known where the path came out on the street. And how could two newcomers know about the path? They could've poked around, I supposed, but it was another oddity to put on the back burner of my brain.

Dab rubbed his hands together. "Let's find out what Mrs. Gilroy could have actually seen from her window."

We padded along the street until we stood opposite what I was pretty sure was the back bedroom window. Mrs. Gilroy's backyard was flat, void of trees and bushes, and her window was high enough to offer a better view than I had from the street. The azalea bushes marking the cemetery were easy to see even from here. Shadows moving in the darkness? I wasn't sure.

Dab and I came to the same conclusion. Without standing where Mrs. Gilroy had, there was no way to be sure she had the angle to see squat. Hear voices and noises? That fell into the *definitely probable* column.

Which brought us no closer to knowing who was with Elsman last night, but I had a better sense of the area on this side of the property now.

When we returned, Maise and Aster were having tea in the kitchen, and Dab abandoned us to watch basketball with Fred in Fred's room. Eleanor, Maise reported, had coaxed Sherry to go up for a soaking bath and an early bedtime, but rushed to assure me Sherry was merely tired.

"How are you doing?" Maise asked as Aster poured another mug of tea and pushed it toward me.

"I'm fine."

Maise snorted. "Considering that you found a body, were questioned by the police, and spent time with Mrs. Gilroy, I find that hard to believe." Maise paused a beat. "Nixy, I was a nurse. I've seen more death than Carter had little liver pills. Even if the deceased isn't family or a friend, there is a measure of trauma that goes with seeing death."

Aster placed a gentle hand on my wrist. "You must've experienced that when your mother passed."

I had, and I swallowed hard at the memory of seeing her take her last breath. But my mother's death had been peaceful. She'd even smiled.

"The point," Aster added, "is that if you want to talk about it, we're here."

My thoughts flashed back to Elsman's body. Staring eyes. The fly.

I met concerned gazes, grasped my tea mug tight. When I spoke, my voice came out rough. "How do I get the image of her out of my head?"

Maise gave me a small smile. "You try not to dwell on it, and let time fade the image. Talking about it can help, too."

"Not with us, necessarily," Aster hurried to add, "but as I said, we're here for you if you need us. You're family now."

My throat swelled, and tears prickled my eyes. "Thank you."

"You're welcome," Maise said and rose. "Now, if you'll excuse me, it's been a busy few days, and I volunteer tomorrow. I'm hitting the rack."

Aster took her mug and Maise's to the sink. "I'm going up, too. Oh, and I put a bottle of lavender water by the sofa. Spray it on your pillow and it will help you sleep."

Whether it was due to Aster's lavender spray or plain old exhaustion, I did sleep, and better than I'd thought I could. Especially given that I looked closely and carefully at the photos again before bed.

The white scrap was easier to see without sun glare, and it certainly could be part of a glove. But why did Elsman have them with her if she only meant to vandalize tombstones? To wear while she wielded the crowbar? Why not plain old gardening gloves? And the gingham? Why bring that along? To tie her hair back? Wipe sweat from her forehead? No and no.

I shivered at my next train of thought but followed it anyway. If Bernice Gilroy was right about a second voice, possibly a male voice, and that person killed Elsman, the killer had brought one or more items to the cemetery for a reason. To leave the "clues" to specifically implicate Sherry.

But talk about overkill. I knew about staging, about arranging art for maximum effect. Leaving the stolen objects at the scene smacked of pure staging, and I had to trust that the detective would see that, too.

AT EIGHT THIRTY THE NEXT MORNING, THE SENIORS were up and having breakfast, all but Sherry dressed for a day of volunteering. Eleanor wore another elegantly tailored pantsuit, this one royal blue. Dab looked dapper as ever in a blue polo shirt, his black slacks barely staying on his hips, and Fred had cleaned up again in a white button-down shirt under his tool-stuffed overalls. Aster sported a broomstick skirt and loose tie-dyed cotton blouse, and Maise wore blue jeans and a print blouse under another blinding white apron.

Good to know some things were still predictable, if only the seniors and their fashion choices.

Sherry and I, both in slacks and blouses, did the breakfast dishes, and I called Detective Shoar to report what Mrs. Gilroy had told me. He didn't answer so I left a short message. I still had his card with his e-mail address, but held off on sending yesterday's photos.

By ten thirty, Sherry and I were once more ankle deep into the historical designation paperwork, this time with a freshly printed form.

She unclipped her bangs, letting them hang over her left eye as she attacked the form. "I hate to say it, but there is no pressing need to protect the property now that Ms. Elsman is dead."

"No, but it can't hurt. Elsman could've been the first wave of property speculators." I grinned. "Why, Lilyvale could be on the verge of booming."

She chuckled. "With what industry, do you think?"

"Gambling? Lilyvale as the Las Vegas of Arkansas."

"Arkansas doesn't have any casinos."

"But there's horse racing in Hot Springs. Lilyvale needs to add 'springs' to its name to pull in the tourists and the big bucks." Sherry rolled her eyes at me. "Okay, maybe not. I'd still like to know what had Elsman frothing to option so much land."

"Trudy might tell us, and we owe the girl a sympathy visit."

I grinned. "It *is* the Southern thing to do. Why, we can have lunch with her at the café."

"About one, you think?"

"It's as good a time as any. I don't have a number to call her, though."

"I'll leave a message with Lorna."

"Okay, and then let's knock out this application."

We worked diligently until twelve thirty, finished the form, and gathered the records we'd need photocopied in a file folder. The office supply store on the square could do the job while we ate and tracked down Trudy.

When Sherry went upstairs to freshen her makeup, the crunch of tires on the gravel drive drew me to the front door. Detective Shoar got out of his truck looking troubled.

Uneasiness fluttered in my stomach, but I put on a happy face and met him on the porch. "Did you get my phone message?"

"Yes, but I can't follow up on that right now. Miz Sherry Mae at home?"

This time my stomach flipped. "Upstairs. What's wrong? Did you get the coroner's report?"

He grimaced. "May I come in?"

My stomach full-on clenched as I opened the door. We both stepped into the foyer as Sherry came down the lower staircase.

"I thought I saw your truck from the landing. What can we do for you today, Eric?"

"Miz Sherry Mae," he said slowly, "it pains me to do this, but I need to take you to the station for questioning."

Chapter Fourteen

"YOU WHAT?" I EXPLODED.

"Nixy, child, there is no need to shout. Detective Shoar is doing his job and we will support him in doing it." She peered up at him from under her bangs. "Although I don't know what more I can tell you."

"Is this because of that crow . . ." I checked myself. "Because of what you found in the graveyard with Elsman's body?"

Sherry turned a bewildered gaze on me. "There was a crow in the cemetery? Huh. Well, that's not unusual. There are crows all over Arkansas."

Shoar turned to me. "You didn't tell her what you saw?"

"I didn't tell her or anyone else anything. You asked me to keep quiet."

"What *did* you see, Nixy?" Sherry asked, suddenly looking pale. "The crow. Please tell me it wasn't, ah, picking at Ms. Elsman's remains."

"No, Aunt Sherry, nothing like that." I patted her shoulder and worked to erase *that* mental image. Ick. "The critical question is if you are a suspect. Is she, Detective Shoar?"

"Miz Sherry Mae, due to some physical evidence found at the scene, you are a person of interest. I need you to come with me now."

I snorted. "'Person of interest' and 'suspect' are the same thing. And I happen to know that if you're taking her into custody, you have to read her the Miranda warning. And if you do that, she needs a lawyer."

He sighed. "This information is courtesy of those three lawyers you dated?"

"Darn straight. If you want her to voluntarily come to the station for an interview, I'll drive her. She's still recovering from the poisoning, you know."

"Will you two stop talking over me? I'm right here."

His eyes closed briefly, and I could almost hear him counting to ten. When he opened them again, his gaze rested on Sherry. "Miz Sherry Mae, I'm not arresting you, but I would appreciate it if you'd allow me to drive you to the station. I promise to take good care of you."

"I trust you, Eric." She squared her shoulders. "Nixy, I'll be fine. Just let the others know what's happening. Our cell numbers are taped inside the upper left cabinet by the sink. Start with Eleanor, and she'll notify everyone else."

Shoar and Sherry were barely out the door when I flew to the kitchen in search of Eleanor's phone number. I found it and the other housemates' numbers, along with those for plumbers, electricians, and other tradesmen, although those were faded. Probably because Fred fixed everything now. Everything but the old furnace.

When Eleanor answered my call, I gave her the bare facts, then asked about an attorney.

"We know all the lawyers in town to nod to, but have only worked with Bob Holloway in civil law matters. I'll see who he can recommend."

I thanked her, jumped in my car, and took off. Not speeding, but pushing it. Eleanor called back as I pulled into the police station parking lot.

"Bob referred us to Dinah Souse."

"Souse? Uh, Eleanor—"

"Don't let the last name fool you, Nixy. She's sober as they come, and one tough criminal attorney. She'll meet you at the station."

"Got it. I'm here now."

I didn't dally waiting for Ms. Souse. I marched inside, up to the reception window, and asked to see Detective Shoar.

"He's busy with an interview," the young black officer said. I remembered T. Benton from my first meeting with Shoar.

"Well, please tell him my aunt's attorney is on her way."

"No need. I'm here."

I spun to see the woman who went with the contralto voice. Her skin was the color of a Starbucks white chocolate latte, and she couldn't have been older than her midthirties. Definitely one of the youngest women I'd met in Lilyvale, Dinah Souse looked the epitome of professional. A navy skirted suit paired with a shimmery gray blouse encased her willowy figure. Stylish black medium-heel pumps and a soft-sided briefcase completed her outfit. Dark brown hair was done in a French twist, her eyes were an arresting color of green, and her nails, I noticed when she extended her hand to me, were short and unpolished.

"Dinah Souse, defense attorney," she introduced herself. "You're Sherry Mae Cutler's niece?"

"Nixy," I said with a nod. "Thank you for coming so quickly."

She waved away my thanks. "I'll want to talk with you later, but first, do you have a dollar?"

"Uh, sure." I dug for my wallet and found a five. "Will this do?"

"Perfect. I'm officially retained, and now I need to see my client. Officer Benton," she said as she turned toward the reception window.

"Yes, ma'am. I'll get Detective Shoar straight away."

"I want to go in with you," I said even though I knew the probable answer. "Sherry is recovering from—"

"The poisoning incident. I'm aware." She smiled, really smiled then, and squeezed my arm. "Don't worry, I've got her back. We'll be out shortly."

"SHORTLY" IN LAWYER-SPEAK MEANT SOMETHING more like forever. Waiting for Sherry to come out of the station was only marginally less excruciating than the hospital wait had been. At least I know Sherry was in good health. I trusted Shoar not to make my aunt ill, but I also knew Dinah Souse would protect her health as well as her legal rights. I considered popping over to the Lilies Café to tell Trudy lunch was off, and even paced to the entry door. What I saw outside derailed all other thoughts,

A group of ten or twelve men and women milled in the miniscule parking lot—neighbors and friends of the Six that I'd met at church and at the house when they'd brought food. Pauletta Williamson of the squash blossom necklace, Jane Lambert in a yellow blouse that matched her husband John's shirt, petite Marie Dunn, and even Ida Bollings with her walker were there, along with Bog, Duke, Big George. Several more women who'd been at the neighborhood meeting brought up the rear. The women shook their fingers, the men shook their fists, and a moment later, the entire horde stormed through the front door, voices raised. No one so much as acknowledged me as the tide pushed me against the wall next to the reception window, making a sardine can of the small room.

Poor Officer Benton looked like he would stroke out as Ida Bollings pushed her walker to the front of the crowd.

"See here, Taylor Benton," Ida said. "We understand Sherry Mae Cutler has been arrested. Ridiculous, I tell you. Ludicrous."

"M-Miss Bollings, I can't comment on an ongoing investigation," the officer stuttered.

"Is that right, young man? Does your mother know you sass your elders?

"M-ma'am, I'm not sassing. I'm merely telling you what I can."

"Which is less than nothing," Pauletta said. "Well, sir, we're staging a sit-in until we get answers."

"Pardon my language, ladies, but sit-in, hell no," Big George's voice boomed. "We're holding a confession marathon. Better get someone out here to take our statements."

Benton bolted from his seat and out an interior door, likely into a hall from the footsteps I heard.

Bog began chanting, "Free Sherry Mae," the battle cry echoed by the crowd. In a flash, three uniformed officers rushed from the bowels of the station to confront the crowd.

"Ladies, gentlemen, let's settle down. What's going on?"

John and Jane Lambert in their matching yellow stepped forward. "You're holding Sherry Mae Cutler for killing that awful Elsman woman, and we want her released."

"Mrs. Cutler is not formally in custody," the tallest, oldest officer said. "Now please disburse before we have to charge you with disturbing the peace."

"You are disturbing *our* peace, Dougie Bryant," Ida said to the man.

"Not to mention Sherry Mae's," a voice from the back rang out.

"We all hated that Elsman woman," Bog shouted.

"And we all wanted her gone," another voice rang out as I saw the top of the door to the innards of the station open again.

"So we're all going to confess to killing her," John declared.

"Ah geez."

I snapped my gaze up and found Detective Shoar at the door staring at me with, well, murder in his eyes.

"Are you behind this, Nixy?" he asked over the suddenly quiet crowd.

I drew myself up. "I am not. These formidable citizens are here of their own volition."

"Pardon again, ladies, but damn straight we are, Shoar,"

Big George said, then patted my head. "Hello, Nixy. I didn't see you there."

I flashed a smile as the detective cleared his throat. "Would it help y'all to know that Miz Sherry Mae is merely being questioned?"

People exchanged glances, much like the Six did, then Ida sang out, "Heck no, we won't go."

Voices echoed the new chant until Eric's piercing whistle broke it up.

"Fine. You want to confess? Go outside, organize into groups, and we'll be out to take your statements. Benton," Eric barked at the young officer back behind the reception desk, "call in a couple of patrol units to help out."

The horde turned toward the outer door, exiting with a lot more order than they'd entered with. As I followed them out, overhearing the discussion of who should be in the first batch of confessors, Dab's Caddy pulled into the lot across the street next to the fire station—a lot half-filled with cars belonging to the protestors, I surmised. Sherry's seniors piled out, and I hustled to meet them as they crossed the side street.

"What's going on?" Maise demanded.

"Your friends showed up to confess to Elsman's murder."

"You're kidding," Dab said, eyeing the crowd.

"They're deciding which group will give their statements first."

"Is Sherry still in with Detective Shoar?" Aster asked just as Eleanor said, "Did the lawyer come over?"

"Yes on both counts. Ms. Souse wouldn't let me go in with Sherry, but she said they'd be out shortly."

"Humph, bet that was a while ago," Fred said.

"Thirty or forty minutes," I admitted as patrol cars pulled up. They didn't screech to a stop, but the officers did park at angles in the street to surround those of us standing in the parking lot, like a small SWAT team springing into action. They didn't, thankfully, whip out any weapons.

Several officers from inside the station briefed the patrol officers, and Ida clomped her walker to the officers to inform them which group was to be questioned first. For a woman who didn't want to get out of her car to pick up a prescription, she certainly got around just fine today. Perhaps she'd had a nip or three before she came to town?

Eleanor waved at someone behind me, and I turned to see Pauletta hurry toward us.

"I knew you'd be here as soon as you could shake free from your volunteer jobs," she said. "We've got things under control now. Ida, Marie, and the men are confessing first. The men need to get back to their jobs, and Ida should rest after all this excitement."

"That's lovely, Pauletta," Aster said, "but why are y'all doing this?"

Pauletta blinked. "For Sherry."

"But," Dab said kindly, "the police surely won't take you seriously."

"We don't expect them to. We're making the point that Jill Elsman was thoroughly disliked and that any of us could've done her in."

"That's a brilliant strategy," Maise said.

"Thank you. If the police even thought about pinning this on Sherry just because Elsman was killed on her land, then they'll by golly have to revise their thinking and look for other suspects. Look! Here come reinforcements."

We all turned, watching Pauletta bustle to meet more townspeople. I spotted Vonnie from the antiques store and Lorna from the café and inn.

Lorna, just the woman I wanted to see.

I turned back to the seniors. "I need to talk to Lorna about Trudy, but I'll be right back."

"No need to hurry," Maise said. "We'll do our own recon. See if anyone here knows anything about Elsman's movements the night of her death."

I grinned and headed to intercept my target. "Lorna, thank you for coming over."

"Think nothing of it. I can't believe our police department is arresting Sherry. It makes no sense."

"Fortunately, she isn't under arrest. Just being interviewed. Obviously we missed having lunch with Trudy. How is she taking her boss's death?"

Lorna made a sour face. "Frankly, I wouldn't be surprised if she had a hand in it. Early Wednesday morning, she was packing to leave. Why, I'd just come in to prepare for opening when she burst through the kitchen door."

"No! Why was she leaving?" I asked, not having to feign surprise.

"She said she'd had enough mistreatment. She asked me where she could rent a car. A while later, I hear wails from her room and hurry up there, thinking she's had a relapse from the poisoning. But no. She's throwing a hissy fit because she can't find the basket she bought at the antiques store."

My pulse stuttered. That had to be the basket Sherry made. And it was conveniently missing? "Trudy didn't accuse you of taking it, did she?"

"She pinned the blame on her boss and was mumbling threats under her breath. Of course, that was before she heard the news."

"Is she staying in Lilyvale a while longer? I mean the police must be wanting to question her."

"She *is* staying, and the police *have* questioned her. It put her right on edge, too, when they told her not to leave town. She asked me to have a room ready for some relative who is coming in today or tomorrow."

"Is the relative her ride home?"

"I don't rightly care. Trudy was always polite and quiet, but I'll be glad when this is all over. I'm happy to have rooms rented. God knows we need the money. But Elsman was nothing but trouble. If I'd caught her in another whispered

conversation with Clark, I swear I'd have hit her with the
business end of a skillet."

The anger in her eyes didn't shock me, but the swift
glimpse of fear there did. I filed away the money comment,
though, clearly, cash flow problems were more common than
not. Plus, small towns weren't known for robust economies,
not unless the towns attracted droves of tourists.

"Thanks for sharing with me, Lorna. I hope this relative
settles Trudy's nerves. If you see her, please tell her I'll visit
after I get Sherry back home."

"That would be kind of you." She checked her watch.
"I'd best get back. I left Clark cleaning up that woman's
room from the fingerprint mess the police made. Tell Sherry
Mae hello and hang in there."

While I'd talked with Lorna, the number of people in the
parking lot seemed to have swelled again. Eleanor, Maise,
and Aster mingled with the newcomers. I spotted Dab shaking hands with Big George, Duke, and Bog. Fred escorted
Ida to her Buick, her walker clunking, his clanking. Pauletta,
Marie, the Lamberts, and one of the food ladies were with
officers now, gestures flying as they gave their statements.

I stood alone for a moment, watching the front door of
the building, hoping Sherry and Dinah would emerge. No
such luck. What *was* Eric putting Sherry through in there?
How many ways could she tell him she had nothing to do
with Elsman's death? And why was Dinah allowing her to
continue answering questions at all?

Enough! I was discovering two things about myself on this
trip. One, I didn't like waiting. Two, I *really* didn't like being
in the dark. Time to march into the station and demand answers.

I was mere feet from the station door when it opened and
Sherry exited with Dinah right behind her. I rushed to hug
my aunt even as cheers erupted. The crowd had spotted
Sherry, too.

"Are you all right?" I asked.

"I'm just fine, child," she said with a pat on my back.

"Eric brought in his own desk chair for me. With lumbar support. He wants to talk with you now."

I cut my gaze to Dinah's. "You won't need me," she said. "He wants to follow up on the phone message you left him earlier."

"Are you sure," Aster said as she and the other housemates closed in, "that following up is all he wants?"

"I have his word." Dinah turned to Sherry. "You go home and rest, Mrs. Cutler, and I'll visit with all of you tomorrow."

As Dinah made her way through the crowd, Eleanor spoke.

"I do believe I'll stay here with Nixy. Dab can drive everyone else back."

"Or," Shoar said behind me, "I can drive Nixy home if she's comfortable with that."

"You're the one who'll be uncomfortable, Detective," I snapped. "I have more than a few words to say to you."

"I figured."

Eleanor assured me she'd be happy to drive my car, and I walked Sherry to Dab's Caddy while Eric managed to clear the parking lot of those who still wanted to confess to Elsman's murder. "You can come back tomorrow," I overheard him say. "I'll personally take your statements."

People wandered off, officers climbed into patrol cars, and Eric crooked a finger at me.

"I don't like that."

He raised a brow. "Don't like what?"

I mimicked the finger crooking. "It's condescending, don't you think?"

"That's not how I meant it, but you're not going to much like anything I do or say right now. Come on, let's go get coffee."

"Coffee?" I echoed, but I was talking to his back.

"SO YOU WEREN'T BEHIND THE GANG THAT STORMED the station?" he tossed out as he drove toward the vo-tech college.

"I only talked with Eleanor after you left with Sherry. You should know about the small-town grapevine."

"Yes, which is why I asked you not to reveal what you saw in the graveyard. Thank you for cooperating."

I blinked my surprise. "You're welcome, but you do know all those things in the cemetery had to have been planted. They were stolen when the barn was burglarized. Dab said it took a while to get you the full list of missing items. You have a record of those, right?"

"We do, but we only have their word for it that those items were stolen."

I gaped. "You think they faked the report? What? They thought they'd need alibis for where that stuff was on the off chance they could lure Hel—Elsman into the cemetery and whack her? And then leave the goods behind to set themselves up? That's idiotic."

"I can't talk about an ongoing investigation, but I will tell you this out of respect for Miz Sherry Mae. I'm under pressure to find this killer and make an arrest. Elsman bullied Sherry more than any other landowner. Circumstantial as it is, I have to look at all the evidence. Investigate everyone. No one can get special treatment. That includes your aunt. It includes all of you."

I huffed a breath. "I understand that, but I don't have to like it."

"I expect nothing else," he said as he wheeled up to the fast-food drive-through window.

When we had our orders—black coffee for Eric, a DQ-style latte for me (sue me, I missed Starbucks)—he drove to the campus a few blocks away. Though the weather was mild, he parked under a pine tree on a slight rise that overlooked a baseball field.

"My truck is less conspicuous here," he said as he killed the engine.

"You're concerned about fraternizing with a suspect?"

"I'm conducting an informal interview," he corrected,

unfastened his seat belt, and turned his body toward me. "Nixy, you had your phone with you on Wednesday morning. Did you take pictures of the scene?"

I lifted my chin. "Yes."

"Why didn't you tell me?"

"I figured the crime scene people got better shots than I did. Besides, I didn't get a good look at the photos until that night."

"Let me see them."

I dug in my purse for the cell, encountering the trash from last night I'd crammed in my bag. I had to throw that away. Cell liberated from my bag, I pulled up the picture file and handed Eric the phone. His expression gave nothing away as he scrolled through them.

Then, "A squirrel?"

"A potential witness. You should canvas the neighborhood for him. He'll tell you none of us killed Elsman."

"How do I delete these?"

I snatched my phone back. "You don't."

"Then be sure no one else sees them."

"I'm not flashing my phone around town, you know." I bit my lip at the question I needed to ask, then blurted, "So you didn't show Sherry the crime scene photos?"

He shook his head as he sipped coffee, then swallowed. "We don't do that. We have done re-creations, but we don't show photos. Which is why I wish you'd delete the ones you have."

I ignored that and asked, "Is the cemetery still off-limits?"

"Until tonight or tomorrow. I need to check in with the techs before I have the officer on-site take the tape down. You still fretting about the mess?"

"I'm determined to stand the stones up before Sherry goes out there."

"You want some help?"

I arched a brow. "That's not against the fraternizing rules?"

"Not if I'm investigating a lead. You called about Miz Gilroy. What did she tell you?"

I filled him in on that visit and waited for a response. "Well, what do you think? She saw headlights. Was Elsman's Hummer still parked on the street behind Sherry's?"

He gave me a narrow-eyed look. "The Hummer was in the parking lot behind the inn. What made you think otherwise?"

"Trudy complained that Elsman went off by herself a lot. I just imagined she'd be the one driving to vandalize the cemetery."

"If she did, whoever was allegedly with her took the car back."

"Allegedly? I told you Gilroy heard two voices. I know she's old, but she didn't strike me as hearing impaired."

"Still, I can't categorize her a reliable witness. As for what she did or didn't see, I'd have to stand at the same window to have a reasonably good idea of what she could've witnessed. There's no way she'll let me in."

"True."

"There's no harm in you giving it a try, though."

I gawked, the paper coffee cup inches from my mouth. "I thought you didn't want me snooping."

"I don't, but you can run interference with the potential witness. And, if she lets you in, you'll be my proxy. I can be in the cemetery."

I pictured the scene and the lightbulb brightened. "Ah, because it would help to have someone move around there the way Mrs. Gilroy described to me."

"Exactly."

"Is casual information-gathering within my snooping limits?"

He gave me a wary glance. "How casual?"

"Trudy bought one of Sherry's baskets at the antiques store on Monday. Sherry and I ran into her as she came out carrying it."

"So?"

"When I visited with Lorna outside the station earlier, she told me the basket was missing early on Wednesday morning when Trudy was packing to go home. Very early."

"I didn't know that," he said slowly, "but Sherry's sold dozens of those baskets. They're all over the county."

"Tell me, Detective, was the gingham fabric in the cemetery woven in with hemp? I can't tell from the picture I took."

"Why does it matter?"

"Plain strips of fabric were reported missing in the burglary. And jute and hemp rope, too, as I remember. But, if the fabric was braided in *with* the hemp, it had been attached to a basket because Sherry makes the handles to fit each basket. And if it was a basket handle—"

"It could've come from Trudy's basket. I'm following you, but like I said, Sherry's baskets aren't rare."

I huffed. "Well, will you check it out?"

"I need to talk to Trudy again, so I'll ask her then."

"How about we ask now? Sherry and I were going to make a condolence call on her before you came this morning. You can ask about her basket."

He stared out of the windshield looking toward the baseball field. I swore I saw the grass grow two inches before he turned back to me.

"I'll take you with me so long as you swear to follow my lead."

"I'll do my best."

So what if my fingers were crossed?

Chapter Fifteen

THE LUNCH RUSH—WHATEVER THAT LOOKED LIKE at the Lilies Café—was over when Eric ushered me through the door at two thirty.

That was the good news. The better news was that Trudy sat at a table for four tucked off to the side of the dining room near the interior staircase up to the inn. A woman with black hair sat with her. A woman who looked a lot like Jill Elsman.

My step faltered, and Shoar sucked in an audible breath.

The woman had to be a relative. A sister, I thought, because she looked so much like Elsman. This woman's hairstyle was softer, and her energy seemed calmer. She wore black pants and a white tunic blouse with low heels and reached to pat Trudy's arm. Yep, definitely a kinder person.

While we stared, Trudy looked up, gave us a wan smile, and waved us over. I didn't waste time crossing the wood floor.

"Trudy, how are you?" I said.

"Gosh, Nixy, I should be asking you that! I heard the police arrested your aunt. Which is just stupid," she finished with a glare at Shoar.

"Aunt Sherry Mae was questioned, not arrested, but thank you for your concern. Are we interrupting you?" I asked, glancing at Trudy's tablemate.

"Yes. No." She heaved a deep sigh. "I'm sorry. I'm so out of it today."

"That's understandable," the woman with Trudy said. She stood and extended her hand. "I'm Jeanette Elsman Anders."

Jeanette Anders. I knew that name from having called OJE.

"I'm Jill's sister and Trudy's cousin."

"Elsman was your cousin?" I asked Trudy, even as I shook Jeanette's hand.

"Sadly, yes. This is Nixy, Jeanette, and this is Detective Eric Shoar of the Lilyvale Police Department."

He shook her hand, and Jeanette waved at the empty chairs.

"Would you like to join us?"

I peeked at Shoar.

"Or do you need to speak with me in a more formal setting, Detective?"

"This is fine," he said.

"I'm sorry for your loss," I said as we all sat.

Jeanette's grimace matched Trudy's. "My sister was an obsessively competitive and chronically unpleasant woman. I know she didn't make friends here, and I'm sure she didn't make anyone's life easy."

"Well, ah—"

"Trudy's been filling me in on things. I know what Jill was up to."

"Then perhaps," the detective said mildly, "you could tell me what that was. I know about her wanting to buy options on land, but not the reason behind it."

Jeanette sighed. "We're from Little Rock. My father was Oliver Elsman of OJE Development Company. I've worked for the firm for over ten years, but Jill drifted from job to job for a while, then got her real estate license. She'd only been with OJE about a few months when Daddy died. He had a heart attack out of the blue."

I murmured condolences.

"Long family story short, Daddy left the company to me, and Jill was furious. She didn't hide it, but she did do the work I gave her."

"When she wasn't putting OJE at risk," Trudy interrupted. "You don't need to sugarcoat it, Jeanette. Their mother and mine were sisters."

"Do you work for OJE, too, then, Trudy?" Eric asked.

"Jeanette hired me a few months after Uncle Oliver died. Jill was a year older than me, four years younger than Jeanette, but she was never kind to either of us, or to anyone else. Even as a child she was bossy, sly, and manipulative. The mean girl in the neighborhood and in school."

Eric frowned. "Then why come here as her assistant?"

"That's my fault," Jeanette said. "I asked Trudy to keep an eye on Jill while I was on my honeymoon. I never imagined what she'd get up to."

"What *was* she doing here?" I jumped in.

"My fiancé and I were looking into developing an upscale retirement village, but we wanted to build it in a small town where we'd get better prices on land and pay lower taxes."

"Jill"—Trudy took up the story—"overheard Jeanette and Tom mention Lilyvale as the best candidate to research. Jill figured she'd buy the land options, and when Jeanette got ready to move forward, Jill would own rights to the land and jack up the prices."

"Wouldn't you simply build somewhere else?"

Jeanette gave me a rueful smile. "If the price was too dear, absolutely. But Jill's mind didn't work that way. To her, I'd definitely decided on Lilyvale; my plans were firm. She wanted to best me at any cost."

"She had the cash to pull this off?" Shoar asked.

"Our mother died when we were in high school. We inherited money from her, and some from our dad, so the deals would have been honored."

"Mrs. Anders—"

"Please, it's Jeanette."

He gave her a nod. "Do you and your new husband know anyone in Lilyvale when you discussed it as a location for your project? Did your sister?"

"We've been through the town on short getaway trips, but we only met a few people in passing. I don't know about Jill. She never mentioned anyone. Trudy, do you know?"

The large-boned woman looked like a limp lump. Was she devastated? Exhausted? Relieved to be rid of the evil cousin? Or could she be acting? Maybe *she'd* helped her cuz to a bonk on the head.

"I had the feeling she knew someone here," she was saying, "but only because she'd take off without telling me and be gone for hours at a time."

Shoar turned toward Trudy. "Someone like an old flame?"

Trudy snorted. "I can't see Jill in a torrid affair. She'd eat a mate and spit out the pieces. Sorry, Jeanette."

Jeanette shrugged. "You're probably right. Jill did what benefited Jill. Even in college, she didn't make friends. She cultivated people who'd owe her favors. "

"Trudy, do you remember seeing Ms. Elsman with anyone in particular more than a few times?"

"The landowners." Trudy tapped her chin. "Clark Tyler, the guy who owns this place with his wife. She kept going to the courthouse when we first got here."

"Didn't you tell me," I jumped in, "that doing courthouse research was your job?"

Trudy nodded. "I figured Jill was getting the lay of the land, politically speaking. You know, seeing who she could pump or bully for the lowdown, or who she could bribe."

"But you don't have names?"

"No, Detective. She didn't tell me what she had for dinner, much less confide in me. She kept her papers in a white binder, each one in a plastic sleeve, and the sections categorized with tabs. Oh, but you know that. You asked me about it when you took it for evidence."

"Yes."

"Well, Jill was extremely protective of that binder. I tried snooping in it once or twice when she stepped out of her room to take a phone call, but she came back for it before I could open the cover." She paused. "By the way, you asked me about her phone. Did you ever find it?"

He scowled. "Not yet."

Jeanette cocked her head. "Can't you ping it or something?"

"We're working on that. Trudy, one last thing. I understand you bought a basket that is now missing."

"Uh, yes," Trudy said, darting a glance at Jeanette. "I haven't seen it since Tuesday afternoon, but then I've been resting a lot since the poisoning. Mrs. Tyler has been nice enough to fix light meals for me. Frankly, I was avoiding Jill, too, but I told you that, didn't I?"

"Yes, and you said you last saw her Monday when she took you to the emergency room. Is that right?"

"I heard her in the hall several times on Tuesday, but I didn't see her. She never called me, never knocked on my door."

"Is that why you were up early Wednesday morning packing to leave?"

She sighed. "It's stupid to think Jill would've at least checked to see if I was alive, but, yes, I was miffed that she didn't. And completely fed up. Plus I knew Jeanette would be home from her honeymoon."

"Trudy," Jeanette added, "thought I could rein in Jill before she hurt someone. It's ironic that she was the one hurt."

"All right, thank you both." Shoar pushed back his chair and stood, but I wasn't quite ready to leave.

"Jeanette, will you be staying in town for a while? I know this is awkward, but my aunt will scold me if I don't ask you both to dinner while you're here."

Trudy's eyes opened wide. Jeanette simply smiled. "That's kind, but I'll be going back tomorrow if Detective Shoar allows it. Jill's autopsy is being done in Little Rock, and I want be home with my husband. Which reminds me . . ." She looked at Eric. "Trudy doesn't want to drive the Hummer, and I don't blame her. I was going to take it back and let her drive my car. But will the Hummer be released by tomorrow about noon?"

"I'll need to check."

I'd fought not to flinch at the mention of the autopsy. Now I turned to Trudy. "Are you going back, too?"

She shot a glance at Eric, shook her head. "I don't think I'm allowed to leave yet."

"Then perhaps you can come for dinner. If you're up to it," I finished lamely as I rose.

We said our good-byes and were on the sidewalk outside when I heard thudding footsteps and Trudy's voice behind me. I turned, and my escort stopped as well.

"Nixy, I just wanted to, you know, thank you for the invitation to dinner," she said. "And, uh, the basket I had? That was a gift for Jeanette. Do you think I can get another one?"

I remembered she'd said as much when Sherry and I had seen her on Monday. "Aunt Sherry has a couple left from the sale. Do you want one or two?"

"I'll stick with one."

"All right. They're in the basement, so we can look if you come for dinner, or I can bring one by before you leave. Give me your number."

We exchanged contact information, and then Trudy squeezed my wrist, almost a crushing grip. "Thank you."

Eric was quiet on the way to Sherry's, and that was fine for about two minutes. Then I had to probe.

"So, is Trudy a suspect?"

"No comment."

"I suppose she did have motive, means, and opportunity. Especially if she was in on burglarizing the barn."

"No comment."

"But the night I took Trudy home from the hospital, someone else was in Elsman's room."

"So you said."

"Are you really tracking the missing phone?"

"We don't have ready access to those resources."

"Did you get any clues from Elsman's binder?"

This time I got a sideways look. Hmm, he'd deviated from *no comment*. Had I hit a particular investigative nerve?

"Why are you smiling?"

"No reason. Just that you were a lot chattier before we met Jeanette. I suppose you'll be checking her story, too?"

"Like I told you, I'll look into everyone connected to Ms. Elsman."

"Everyone you know about."

He threw me a sour look and I let the conversation die. Questions bounced in my brain—so many of them, I needed to make a list. Shoar wouldn't be disposed to answer a single one, but Sherry's attorney, Dinah, might dish. If, that is, she knew anything more than I did.

Before I hopped out of Eric's truck, he grasped my elbow. "Remember, if Miz Gilroy will let you in her house to survey her line of sight to the cemetery, call me. I'll come on over if I'm free."

ELEANOR, ASTER, AND MAISE MOBBED ME THE MO-ment I entered the foyer.

"Where have you been?" Aster said.

"I was fixin' to storm the station," Maise declared.

"Sherry has been worried," Eleanor added.

"I'm sorry I didn't call. I was making nice with the detective, *and* I have news. How is Aunt Sherry?"

"I'm in here with the menfolk," Sherry called.

I grinned at the old-fashioned term and trooped to the parlor. With my hobo bag on the desk at the front windows, I joined the others seated around Sherry.

"Did Shoar grill you?" Dab asked.

"Not really. In fact, he encouraged me to go ask Mrs.

Gilroy about looking out her window. You know, to better gauge what she could've seen."

"Well, you can't go over empty-handed," Maise said. "We'll whip up something for her while we're fixing supper. Now tell us the big news."

Six pair of eyes pinned me with expectation and, in Fred's case, impatience. "I saw Trudy, and I met Jill Elsman's sister."

After the exclaiming and the rapid-fire questions died down, I gave them the highlights of seeing Trudy and Jeanette, including the dinner invitation.

"Poor woman," Sherry mused, shaking her head. "To be burdened with such a relative, and now to have her murdered."

Fred humphed. "But why do we have to feed them?"

"Because they'll be more inclined to let information drop in a relaxed setting," I said.

Silence, then understanding *aah*s echoed, even one from Fred.

Eleanor tapped her chin. "Then I do believe we ought to have a list of questions we can slip into conversation."

"We need more than that," I said. "We need to do our own investigating."

"Why do we need to investigate instead of Shoar?" Dab had been quiet, but now pinned me with his gaze. "I thought you trusted him."

"I do trust him, but he has to follow rules and procedures. People will tell us things they probably won't tell him. We'll pass on information if we get any. In fact, we may not have to ask many questions if your friends talk as freely as they did at church."

"That's true," Maise said. "I say we investigate full speed ahead!"

Chapter Sixteen

I MADE NOTES ON A PAD AS WE BRAINSTORMED—THE same pad Eleanor had used to draw the layout of the neighborhood on Sunday afternoon. That seemed like forever ago.

We began with things we wanted to know about Jill Elsman. How to word the questions proved iffier. Sherry and the other women didn't want to sound nosy—or worse, pushy. Not in a time of mourning, they insisted. Dab didn't weigh in on the issue, but Fred scoffed, "Trudy ain't in mournin'."

As we moved on, never-still-for-long fix-it Fred clanked in and out of the entry, front hall, and parlor spraying white lithium on door hinges that didn't squeak as it was. I hadn't really noticed before how restless Fred was, but it was hard to ignore when his every clunk punctuated a point.

I steered the conversation to listing suspects and ran into a wall.

"I can't think of a soul we know who would kill Jill Elsman, no matter how annoying she was," Sherry declared.

"I don't know of anyone either," I said, treading lightly, "but Duke did threaten her with his shotgun."

"Barker?" Fred snorted from the parlor-to-bathroom doorway. "Duke'd blow himself up if he fired that weapon. It ain't worked right in years."

"How about bashing her on the head with it?" I held up my hand when Maise and Aster made protests. "I'm playing devil's advocate here. Duke offered to patrol the property during the meeting on Tuesday. Remember? Y'all said no, but what if he did it anyway, caught Elsman, and conked her?"

"Is that how she was killed?" Dab asked. "Head injury?"

I realized my error and grimaced. "From what little I saw, it was."

"Don't worry about the slip, Nixy," Maise said. "We figured it had to be that or a stabbing. Something quiet. But if Duke had done it, he would've called the police himself."

"Or come to us," Sherry added.

"I didn't say he was a good suspect, but we can ask if he was out late Tuesday night. Ask if he saw anyone sneaking around."

"I suppose we could ask," Sherry said.

"What about that Trudy?" Fred asked, putting his can of lithium and a faded red rag into the tool belt on his walker. "Cousin or no, she could've done it."

"I agree, and she's next on the list. Then there's Clark Tyler."

"I still say he isn't having an affair," Aster said.

"Not with Elsman," Dab said. "Whatever Clark's faults, I don't see him romancing a woman like that."

I cocked my head. "'Whatever Clark's faults'? What does that mean?"

Dab's glance danced from roommate to roommate, then he shrugged. "Story was he had a wild reputation for drinking and gambling in Shreveport before he married Lorna."

"Then Lorna inherited," Maise said, taking up the tale, "they moved here, and Clark supposedly settled down. No more Shreveport gambling."

Could that be the reason for the fear I'd seen in Lorna's eyes today? And her mention of needing money? Did she worry that her husband was gambling again?

Sherry tapped my hand. "Nixy, you can't think Clark killed Elsman."

"I'm looking at potentials. He's not exactly the 'Welcome to Lilyvale' poster boy, plus Lorna told me again today that Elsman cornered Clark more than once."

"That's right. When we ate at the café Monday, she complained about that to us, too."

"Y'all told me you thought Elsman was greasing palms at city hall, and Clark Tyler is on the council. Right?"

"So you think she could've been bribing him?" Eleanor asked.

"Or blackmailing him." That idea met with silence.

"Or manipulating other council members. Detective Shoar told me Elsman had lunch with several of them." Again, silence.

"Listen, I know you don't want to think badly of any of your neighbors or friends or anyone you do business with in town. But we have to think like the police."

"Motive, means, opportunity," Aster said. "Which all of us had, too."

"Correct. Our problem is that Shoar specifically mentioned physical evidence that leads to Sherry first, and to one of us second. Sherry is innocent, and we have to prove it before the detective is forced to arrest her."

"And just how," Fred growled, "are we supposed to pull this off?"

"We start by noting every odd thing that's happened since Elsman came to town, and then we list every person with any power that she could theoretically have bribed or blackmailed or coerced to get what she wanted." I took a breath. "And then we ask questions. They may be hard questions to ask, but the threat to Sherry is urgent."

No one spoke until Maise smacked her fist in her palm. "Damn the torpedoes, Nixy's right. This is a mission to clear Sherry—and all of us."

That fired up the troops. While names and observations

flew, I scribbled madly. By the time our confab broke up an hour later, we had an impressive list of incidences and a shorter one of people to question.

Maise, Aster, and Sherry went to the kitchen to fix supper and a little something for Mrs. Gilroy. Fred headed to the barn with Dab on his heels.

Eleanor gave them a wistful look before Sherry shooed her out, too.

"Nixy will set the table, Eleanor. You run on and ride herd on those two. No telling what they'll come up with if you don't rein them in."

I set the table for the seven of us, remembering to bring in the extra chair for Dab, then asked about a plate for Mrs. Gilroy.

"Right there," Maise said, waving a spatula at the kitchen table. "It's only cold cuts and sandwich bread with potato salad, but it should do. I added two slices of apple pie to clear more space in the fridge."

"Take the food on over to her now," Sherry urged. "I'm eager to see if she'll let you in again."

I was more focused on getting permission to peer out her bedroom window tonight, so I lifted the double-layered and plastic-wrapped paper plates and trooped to Mrs. Gilroy's. As soon as I stepped foot on her porch, I heard Charlie Sheen's voice blaring from inside. I listened a moment. Yep, Mrs. Gilroy had an old episode of *Two and a Half Men* playing. *Mrs. G has a naughty side.* I chuckled to myself, then gasped when the door flew open.

"You already brought me enough food for a week," she snapped. "This must be a bribe."

"It's a foot in your door," I said.

She looked pointedly at the threshold. "Not yet, it isn't. Is that apple cider pie I smell?"

I narrowed my eyes at the elderly elf I was liking more and more. "You can smell pie through plastic wrap?"

She winked. "I can smell the apples, and I saw Connie Jeeter bring food t'other day. She always makes apple cider pie for folks in troubled times."

"Has she ever made it for you?"

"I don't have trouble. Or didn't till I let you in. What do you want?"

I smiled. "Will you listen before you say no?"

She peered up at me. "Must be something I won't want to do if you have to ask me that first."

"I know you value your privacy, and I don't want to impose, but I need your help."

"Because that handsome policeman went off with Sherry Mae today?"

"That's right. I told him what you said about seeing and hearing people in the cemetery, but he needs more proof."

"Thinks I'm blind and deaf, does he? So he wants to look out my bedroom window himself?"

"Uh, no, ma'am, he wants me to look out the window while he moves around in the cemetery."

She pursed her wrinkled lips. "I'd rather have that young, virile policeman in my bedroom, but I'll do this for Sissy."

"You mean Sherry?"

"No, Sissy. The Stanton you remind me of. The one who used to live here. Don't you remember me telling you that?"

"Uh, yes, ma'am."

"Did you ever tell me your name?"

"It's Leslee, but I go by Nixy."

"Nixy, huh? Sissy would've liked that."

"Thank you, Mrs. Gilroy," I sputtered as she whipped the paper plates out of my hands.

"Be here at eight sharp. I'll give you twenty minutes, then I want you out so I can watch my shows."

"Yes, ma'am."

"By the by, are you tossing your cap at that fine policeman?"

"Uh, no. I'll be going home when I'm sure Aunt Sherry Mae is safe."

"None of us is safe all the time, but that manly body warming a woman's bed would sure enough be a comfort."

She shut the door in my face, but not before she winked.

I shook my head as I walked back to Sherry's. Bernice Gilroy giving me dating advice? What a hoot.

I wedged my cell phone from my slacks pocket to call the detective. I would need to do laundry again, and shop, too, if I stayed much longer.

"Mrs. Gilroy is a go," I said when he answered on the third ring. "She'll give us from eight to eight twenty."

"I underestimated your powers of persuasion with her."

That deep, dreamy drawl of his suddenly sounded sexier. Dang Mrs. Gilroy's power of suggestion about his manly body. I cleared my throat.

"Can you come do your end of the experiment or not?"

"Sure. I'll come an hour early. We can reset the grave markers before dark."

GOOD AS HIS WORD, HE PULLED INTO THE DRIVE AT seven on the dot and climbed out of his truck wearing what I'd come to think of as his uniform—jeans, a navy blue T-shirt, and boots. Maise offered him dessert, and Aster offered sweet tea.

"Not now, ladies, thank you. Nixy? You ready?"

"I've got bags of pea gravel and soil in the wheelbarrow," Dab said as he strode beside us toward the barn.

"And I got tools ready, if you need 'em," Fred added, clanking along with the rest of the gang.

"Sherry," I said over my shoulder, "why don't y'all sit on the deck and enjoy the evening while we do this."

She put her hands on her hips. "Detective Shoar, is the cemetery still a crime scene?"

"Matter of fact, I released it."

"Then I'd rather supervise if it's all the same to you both."

Eric shrugged. "Sure, and Fred and Dab can help take down the crime scene tape if they like."

With that, the older men hotfooted it behind the barn, Fred's walker clanking up a storm. Eleanor, Maise, and Aster each grabbed a tool from where they rested against the barn wall—a rigid-tined garden rake, a shovel, a hoe. Eric hefted the wheelbarrow handles, rocked the front wheel to start the momentum, and rolled the bags of topsoil and pea gravel as if he were pushing a load of feathers. And, my, my, I did enjoy the play of muscles bunching under his navy blue T-shirt. Mrs. Gilroy would have vapors at the sight.

"Thanks for including them," I said, walking beside him.

"They need a sense of control."

Which was partly why I wanted them to help me snoop, but I didn't mention that. "Still, you recognized their need, and I appreciate it."

"You're welcome," he said as we rounded the corner of the barn and headed straight on for the cemetery. "I still can't believe you got Miz Gilroy to agree to the plan."

"I think she only did it because I remind her of Sissy Stanton. One of my ancestors," I added when he gave me a puzzled look.

"Yeah, I've heard stories about her. Miz Gilroy knew her?"

I lifted a shoulder. "I haven't worked out the math on how old Mrs. Gilroy would've been when Sissy was alive, but I understand Sissy was a legend here."

Eric tossed me a grin. "I have a feeling you'd be, too, if you stuck around."

I wouldn't touch that comment with a hazmat suit. "Come on, let's get this done so I'm not late to Mrs. Gilroy's."

Sherry wore her bangs fastened in a clip again, and she looked paler than I liked as she surveyed the damage. She gently stroked the angel's one undamaged wing, lips pursed as I approached.

"If I'd known what that woman was up to out here," she

said, fire in her eyes, "I'd have found Fred's .45 and given her what for."

"And I'd have helped you."

She blinked at me in the gathering dusk. "Thank you, child. Now, let's get to work."

Maise called for all hands on deck, and it took less than forty minutes to reset and stabilize the markers. The angel was a lost cause, but Eric carried it and the broken wing to his truck. The man was as strong as he was kind. I scooted in the house to wash up while he helped return the tools and materials to the barn.

I had the detective standing by on his cell when Mrs. Gilroy let me in her home. Tonight, though, the lamp by the sofa and the television screen—sound muted—shed light on the minimally furnished living room.

"Come along," she said, grabbing me by the wrist.

Whereas her kitchen was to the right, she led me into a short hallway that extended behind the living area. A small bathroom was at the end of the hall, the master bedroom to the right.

"There." She gestured across the room, which was nearly as Spartan as the other rooms I'd seen. "I opened the window for you, just like it was that night."

"Thanks, Mrs. Gilroy." I went to the single window, hunched down to approximate her height, and peered through the screen before I put my phone on speaker. "I'm in position."

"Good deal. Start taking pictures."

"Not of my home, you won't," Mrs. Gilroy snapped.

"No, ma'am," I soothed. "I'm just going to snap the view from your window. Nothing inside. I promise. I'm not even using the flash. See?"

I showed her the palm-sized camera Eric had given me to get a better handle of what was visible from the window. No super lens, although the camera had a zoom function. But he didn't want me to use that either.

"Did Miz Gilroy see one flashlight beam or two?"

"One," she said from behind me, then scooted closer to the window.

"Got it. Nixy, what can you see right now?"

"The streetlight is strong enough that I can see some trees near the street. I can see the outline of the azalea bushes, too, but then I know where they are."

"Miz Gilroy is familiar with them, too."

Within half a minute, I saw a stream of yellowish light moving. I took a few photos, and reported seeing the light to Eric.

"You don't see me?"

"Move toward the far corner by the chain-link fence to the children's graves, where the broken angel was. Wait. There. I see you as a figure, but not your features. Hold still while I get shots."

When I finished, he said through the phone speaker, "Let me know what you see next."

I watched his shadowy form move to the corner. "I see you, but I wouldn't be able to identify you as a man or woman. Hold there a minute." I took four photos. "Done. What now?"

"I'm going to whisper. Let me know if you can hear anything at all."

I heard sound, the cadence of speech, but no words. Then I heard another voice, not that much difference in pitch, but the cadence was very slightly different.

Again, I gave my report.

"Is Miz Gilroy there?"

"I am," she said. "Can you hear me?"

"Yes, ma'am. Will you kindly listen this time, ma'am?"

"I heard the voices just now, young man."

His smile came through the phone. "That's great, Miz Gilroy, but will you do it again? I need to know if the whispers were louder or softer than the ones you heard the night of the murder. If you can remember."

I didn't think Eric had thrown the gauntlet consciously, but Bernice Gilroy slowly stood to her tiny full height, eyes blazing. "*If* I can remember? Bring it on."

I smothered a chuckle as he whispered again, using both lower- and higher-pitched voices. Or had he recruited one of the ladies to help? I couldn't have identified either voice.

"The voices I heard that night," Mrs. Gilroy said with great dignity, "were neither considerably louder nor softer than those I just heard. One, however, sounded more gravelly than the other." She paused. "That is the one I thought was a male voice, although from your demonstration I would not be able to differentiate male from female. Now, if you're quite finished, it's time for my shows."

"We appreciate your assistance, Miz Gilroy," he said over the speaker.

"As well you should," she said, then gave me the stink eye. "You can leave now."

"Yes, ma'am." I hit the disconnect button on my phone, and with one last glance out the window, I followed her out. "Thank you, Mrs. Gilroy."

She sniffed. "Like I said, I did it for Sissy. And," she continued as she opened the front door, "if that man takes a superior tone with you like he did with me, I hope you read him the riot act."

I blinked. Smiled. "Don't you worry, ma'am."

Chapter Seventeen

ERIC LEFT AFTER A GLASS OF TEA AND A SLICE OF chocolate cream pie. I wondered how that jibed with fraternizing with suspects, but, hey, that was his problem. I only wish he'd shared thoughts about the Mrs. Gilroy experiment. Like did knowing that she did see and hear something make any difference to his investigation whatsoever?

Eleanor and Dab were high on the experiment because Eric had recruited both of them to whisper. Eric had whispered, too, but he'd changed it up. As they spoke about their roles, I realized that what Mrs. Gilroy had said was true. I couldn't have identified the speakers, and I couldn't hear a marked difference between male and female whispers either.

I spent the rest of the evening finishing my laundry and making plans to both shop for a few essentials the next day and begin my discreet inquiries. First stop: Patricia Ledbetter, the property tax clerk. With a seriously ill child, she would've been an easy target for Hellspawn to manipulate.

Yes, I was back to calling her Hellspawn, at least in my thoughts.

Morning found the seniors dressed in their Friday-go-a'snooping duds, although Eleanor looked no less elegant, and Fred was only marginally more spiffed up. He'd taken a few tools out of his overall pockets.

Dinah Souse arrived for brunch and interviews at eleven on the dot, and I ushered her into the kitchen.

"Where are Eleanor and the men?" she asked as she set her soft-sided briefcase on the kitchen table.

Sherry waved a hand. "They're in the barn tinkering with the still design."

Dinah coughed. "Should I be hearing this?"

"Dab distills my herbs," Aster said. "It's nothing illegal."

She opened her mouth, closed it. Then she turned to me, brown eyes serious. "First, how did the meeting with Detective Shoar go?"

"No problem." I gave her the overview, including our visit with Trudy and Jeanette, and highlights of what Mrs. Gilroy had seen and we'd confirmed.

"Detective Shoar was here last night? He assisted you in this"—she waved her hand in a circle—"experiment?"

"Then stayed for tea and pie," Sherry added.

"That's . . . unusual. Did he share any thoughts afterward?"

"Not a one," I groused. "Is there an official cause of death yet?"

"The coroner doesn't give a cause. That's up to the medical examiner in Little Rock. The newspaper article that ran today reports only that the suspicious death is being investigated."

"When it's official, will you know?"

"Possibly. Let me explain," Dinah said as she opened her briefcase and pulled out a yellow lined legal pad. "The police don't share evidence with the prosecution or the defense until there is an arrest. Sherry Mae is free at the moment because the evidence is likely too circumstantial to make an arrest. However, that could change at any time. My focus right now is to glean information about your encounters with

Ms. Elsman. I heard you butted heads with her several times, Ms. Nix."

"Nixy, and yes, I stood up to her."

"When?" she asked, pen poised over the pad.

I ran through my various encounters with Hellspawn while Sherry, Aster, and Maise put in their two cents now and again. When I finished, she looked thoughtful.

"Detective Shoar came up in your story a great deal. Are the rumors about you two true?"

"What rumors?"

"That he's seeing you socially."

I snorted. "It's Aunt Sherry Mae he's sweet on. She must be his favorite teacher of all time."

Dinah hesitated, then shrugged. "If you say so. Now I understand you took Trudy back to the inn from the hospital on Monday night. Did you see Elsman then?"

"See her, no. I heard her in her room. Or, to be precise, I heard two voices coming from her room. They were speaking softly, but sort of hissing, like they were arguing. I figured one was Elsman, and the other voice sounded male. Although last night I realized that it's hard to judge the sex of a speaker when the person is whispering."

Sherry smiled. "I know that from the classroom. Until I memorized my seating chart, I couldn't distinguish the boys from the girls when they whispered behind my back."

"And yet," I said, "if another woman was in Elsman's room . . ."

"Yes?"

I pursed my lips. "It's just that we thought Trudy most likely helped Elsman pull her stunts. The burglary and such. But Trudy was in her room the night I eavesdropped, so what other woman would help Elsman?"

"We need to put that on the list," Maise said.

"What list?" Dinah asked.

"We made a suspect list with Nixy," Aster told her with pride. "We're going to investigate ourselves."

"That's not a good idea," Dinah began.

"Hogwash," Maise said. "Sherry's neck is on the line, and ours are, too. We left it to the police to find the vandals and they didn't do it. Besides, as Nixy pointed out, people will tell us things they won't tell the police. Nixy's already passed on a passel of information to Detective Shoar. He just has to get his act together."

Dinah took such a deep breath, I could almost hear her counting to ten. Or twenty. "Skipping over that, did any of you ever threaten Ms. Elsman?"

I shook my head. "No threats, but we made it clear that Sherry and most of her neighbors were banding together against selling land options."

"All right. Nixy, I have one more specific question for you. Sherry said Detective Shoar asked you not to talk about what you saw when you discovered the body."

I shot a glance at Sherry and company. "He did."

"You are not legally bound to that, you know."

I wrestled with keeping my word versus helping Dinah keep Sherry out of jail. No contest.

Movement outside caught my eye. "Here come Fred, Dab, and Eleanor. Dinah, let's go to the parlor for a minute."

"Go," Maise said, shooing us. "We'll get brunch on the table."

I SHOWED DINAH THE PHOTOS ON MY PHONE, HAPPY that they had been good for something after all. She didn't say much about them as we scrolled through, and only nodded when I told her the Six had reported the crowbar, glove, and gingham strip stolen a week or so before Elsman's death. When I finished, she asked me if I thought I'd captured anything else of importance in the photos. I told her no, and she suggested I delete all but the shots of the azaleas and the squirrel. I complied. I also remembered to take the wads of paper out of my bag. I'd dig for any smaller pieces of paper later.

Dinah continued to ask questions during the meal, but was so subtle that the exchange flowed like easy conversation. That is, until she asked if Sherry or any of the Six had ever met with Elsman alone. That was pointed enough to make them stop and think.

"We're not attached at the hip, but my friends and I do spend most of our time together. Especially before the folk art festival, when we were finishing our projects. I don't recall even seeing her in passing when I was alone."

"We saw Trudy Monday morning," I added, "but not Elsman."

"That's most helpful to know."

Dinah got a call during our dessert of banana pudding and vanilla wafers. She left after making us swear to call immediately if the detective questioned Sherry—or any of us—again. We swore, we cleaned the kitchen, and we scattered to do our own snooping.

Maise specifically charged Dab and Fred with asking three things. Had anyone seen the Hummer or another car in the neighborhood late the night Elsman was killed? Had anyone seen Elsman or someone else on foot in the neighborhood that night? Did anyone know if Clark was gambling? They'd talk with Big George at his hardware store while they picked up supplies for the still. Then they'd see Duke at the Dairy Queen, and Bog at the barbershop. They'd also catch Councilman B. G. Huff at the furniture store.

"Don't forget Dab and I need to eat early tonight," Fred said as he maneuvered his walker toward the kitchen door.

"Goodness, I'd forgotten about concert night," Sherry said.

"We'll have supper ready at five thirty," Maise assured him.

Fred nodded and clanked out of the house with Dab.

"Concert night?" I asked when the men had gone.

"Concerts on the Square," Eleanor explained. "They only run from seven to nine, but it's a way to bring the community together. We start up after Easter and go through the summer."

"Weather permitting," Aster added.

"What about community togetherness the rest of the year?"

All four women gave me a *duh* look. "We have a few events around Christmas, but fall is high school football season," Sherry answered.

"Oh." And didn't I feel like a dummy, since I'd grown up in Texas, where Friday-night football was sacrosanct.

The women narrowed down the most prime gossip spots. Aster and Maise would take the grocery and shoe stores, and Sherry and Eleanor would visit the beauty salon and dress shops. They'd all go in Sherry's car and ask the same general questions that the men were asking. I hoped Sherry would get a trim at the salon, but when I mentioned it, she gave me a blank stare. I threw up my mental hands. If fiddling with her bangs was a nervous habit, so be it.

My assignment was to hit Gaskin Business Center, where I'd drop off the historical designation paperwork to be photocopied. Then, I'd storm the courthouse. My cover story in seeking out Patricia Ledbetter the clerk and Mac Donel, the tax collector, was genealogical research. I'd wing it from there. In point of fact, I truly was curious about Mrs. Gilroy's property, first because it had once been part of the Stanton spread, and second because she'd told me Hellspawn had never visited her. That had me wondering. Hellspawn had made a nuisance of herself everywhere else. Why not at Mrs. Gilroy's? My inquiring mind wanted an answer.

When we completed our rounds, we women would meet at the Lilies Café. The plan was to talk with Clark if he was there, but with luck we'd also run into Trudy. None of us felt comfortable asking Lorna about her husband's alleged affair or possible gambling, as the men had mentioned, but I'd bite the bullet if I had to. After all, I didn't live here. I didn't want to embarrass Sherry either, but her neck was on the line. I could start with asking about the Hummer. Find out when they closed up for the night and if they noticed the behemoth in the parking lot when they went home. That was an innocuous enough conversation starter.

* * *

I EASED MY CAMRY INTO THE DIAGONAL PARKING
slot halfway between the antiques shop and Gaskin's. The bell
over the door sounded cheerful, and finding Pauletta behind
yet another glass-front dark wood counter was a stroke of luck.
So was the store being empty except for the two of us.

"Surprised to see me?" she asked with a warm smile.

"I didn't realize you worked here."

"I come in part-time now and then. Carter Gaskin owns
the place," she said as she patted her squash blossom necklace, this one with heavily veined light blue stones. "I'm
filling in while he takes his wife—that's Kay—to the foot
doctor in Texarkana. She has terrible pain, bless her heart.
Probably from standing on these concrete floors in high
heels for years. What do you need today, Nixy?"

As my brain caught up to the torrent of words, I thought
about the three-inch heels I often wore at the art gallery and
winced in sympathy with the absent Kay.

"I need some photocopying done," I told Pauletta and set
the red pocket folder with its half inch of paperwork on the
counter. "Two sets should do it."

"Sure thing." She flipped the folder open, read the top
page. "Wonderful! Sherry Mae is finally going to apply for
historical landmark recognition. The traveling judges held
court in her house, you know. For several years before our
courthouse was completed."

"We found a letter about that, but it isn't official."

"Well"—she drawled the single syllable into three as she
leaned across the counter—"I think you'll find more information at the library. Sherry's great-whatever-aunt Sissy gathered
records to get the house landmarked. I saw them when I helped
the library reorganize their historical papers collection, but I
don't think she went through with the application."

"Why not?"

"World War II, dear. And then Sissy died a few years

after the war." She tapped the stack of papers. "You want to investigate those library documents before you photocopy this application?"

"I'll just add anything if I find it." Now I leaned in over the counter. "I'm really more focused on investigating the murder."

Pauletta's hand flew to her chest. "You're actually investigating? Like Jessica Fletcher?"

"Not as efficiently, but yes. Have you heard any rumors about who Elsman was friendly with?"

Pauletta arched a brow. "Friendly? Elsman?"

I grinned. "Point taken."

Pauletta tapped her chin with a manicured finger. "I saw her at the courthouse a good deal when she first came here, and Lorna is still put out with Clark over the woman. That's no secret."

I am not a rumormonger, so I grappled with my conscience two seconds before I said, "You can't mean they were having an affair."

Green eyes rounded. "Nooo. At least . . . No, definitely not. Clark has his faults, but catting around isn't one of them. Besides, I saw them together in passing once at the café, and he sure wasn't starry-eyed."

"Then why is Lorna upset about Clark and Elsman?"

"She thinks Elsman was trying to influence Clark because he's a councilman. That she wanted him to approve whatever scheme she had going and swing other votes when the time came. Clark can be opinionated and surly, but he's shown he has the city's good at heart."

The bell signaled a new customer and Pauletta closed my folder as she called out, "Hello, Mrs. Hardy. I have your order ready. Nixy, I'll have this done in a few hours."

"No rush. I can stop by tomorrow."

I turned from the counter to find Mrs. Corina Hardy staring at me. Deputy prosecuting attorney Bryan Hardy's aunt—I remembered seeing her at church. Her swollen feet crammed into navy shoes with clunky heels, she was two inches taller than I. A wide white belt circled the waist of her navy blue dress, her makeup was troweled on, and she held her nose in the air.

What really got my attention was the bow in her gray hair. The blue gingham bow.

I didn't believe for a second that Mrs. Hardy had killed Hellspawn or stolen a thing from Sherry's barn. But as accessories go, it struck me as odd.

"You," Mrs. Hardy snapped, her tone haughty. "You're Sherry Mae Cutler's niece."

I straightened. "Yes, ma'am, I am."

"Bad business at her place," she pronounced. "Having a graveyard on one's property is tasteless, and look what's happened. A murder. Scandalous. Sherry Mae should move those graves to a proper cemetery immediately."

I seethed at the insult to Sherry but pasted a smile on my face. I guess it was a scary smile because Mrs. Hardy took a small step back.

"The graves," I said calmly but firmly, "are precisely where they should be. In fact, I'm thinking we'll rededicate the cemetery. Invite the city and county dignitaries, and have a lawn party." I turned away, then back. "By the way, that's an interesting bow you're wearing. Blue gingham is my aunt's trademark fabric, you know."

Mrs. Hardy's mouth fell open, and I heard sputtering sounds as I walked out to the tinkling music of the bell over the door. I hoped I hadn't put Pauletta in an uncomfortable position, but from the twitch I'd seen on her lips, she'd weather Mrs. Hardy just fine.

I tried not to dwell on that stupid hair bow. I'd already confirmed via my tablet connection to the Internet that blue gingham fabric was available in different hues, various sizes of checks, and from outlets like Amazon to fabric stores to hobby and craft stores. Mrs. Hardy might've purchased hers ready-made at a drugstore or the beauty salon. The bow didn't have ominous meaning other than to remind me to stay focused.

Downtown traffic was heavier today than it had been on Monday when Sherry and I were in town, but cars stopped for me to cross to the courthouse at the center of the square—likely because I looked like a woman on a mission. I caught myself stomping up the concrete courthouse steps, so I stopped and took a calming breath before I opened the heavy door. Aster would be proud.

Considering all the windows decorating the outside of the building, the courthouse hallway I stepped into was cool and dark. Which made sense when I realized office doors opened from the hall. Sure enough, I opened the door marked TAX COLLECTOR and was nearly blinded by the sunlight streaming in.

Though it was almost two in the afternoon, only one person was in the office, and I was betting it was Patricia Ledbetter. I didn't think she was much older than early thirties, but everything about her spoke of being careworn to a frazzle. Her slumped posture, the clothes sagging on her thin body, her dull pale blue eyes when she stood to greet me, all spoke of heavy burdens.

I felt so sorry for her, I had to steel myself to follow my plan.

"May I help you?" She tried for an inquiring smile and failed.

"I hope you're Patricia Ledbetter," I said cheerfully.

Her expression grew wary. "I am."

"Great. I'm Nixy, and I was told you could help me with research for a genealogy project."

She relaxed. "Who are you researching?"

"The Stantons and the land they owned."

"Mrs. Cutler's family? You must be the niece I've heard about."

"Guilty as charged," I said lightly, though I caught Patricia cringe. "Dare I ask how you know about me?"

She flapped a hand, flustered. "Oh, you know. It's a small town. Word gets around when new people come here."

"Everyone knows everyone else's business?"

She ducked her head, turned back to her desk. "What do you need to know?"

I pulled a pad from my bag. Not the one with the entire suspect list, but a smaller one I'd used to jot notes.

"I want to confirm when the first Stanton bought land here."

She stopped. "That's easy. It was 1867, and Lilyvale was founded in 1868. Although we weren't incorporated as such until later."

"Wow, you know your local history."

She shrugged. "It's sort of my hobby. I wanted to be a history teacher or a historical librarian, but that didn't work out."

"This job has historical aspects, though, and I'm sure you're good it. I was referred to you, after all."

"By whom? Your aunt?"

I took a chance. "No, by Ida Bollings."

She looked pained. "Is there anything else can I help you with today?"

I glanced at my notes. "I need to know the legal description of my aunt's homestead, but I just realized I don't have the address."

"I can look it up," she said, scooting to her computer. Her fingers flew over the keyboard, and she clicked a few times. "Would you like a printout of this?"

"Sure, thanks."

She clicked the mouse again, and I heard the printer whir to life. "Now, let me print the other one for you, too."

"What other one?"

"There's a second address, and it looks like it's the house next door."

Next door? There was no house next door to Sherry except Mrs. Gilroy's.

"Ah, Patricia, I don't mean to offend you, but are you sure you don't have the records mixed up again?"

"You heard about that."

Her voice was flat, angry but without real heat. When she glanced over at me, her eyes brimmed with tears. "This isn't a mistake. Your aunt pays the taxes on her house and the one next door, plus on several commercial properties in town and unimproved land, too," she finished in a rush. "I'll print them all for you."

Patricia clicked the mouse rapid-fire, then shot to stand at the printer, her back to me. When it spit out the last sheet, she snatched them up and crossed to slap them on the counter.

"Patricia, Jill Elsman was behind your tax records mess, wasn't she?"

Panic flooded her expression. "Please, I've fixed that. I'm sorry. Don't get me in trouble. I can't lose this job."

Chapter Eighteen

HER WHOLE BODY QUAKED IN FULL-ON TERROR. I took one of her hands in mine and patted it, hoping to calm her.

"Patricia, I don't want to see you fired or get you in more trouble, but I need information."

"What kind of information?" Her tone dripped suspicion, but she didn't pull away.

I took a breath. "You have a chronically ill child, don't you?"

Her hand twitched. "Davy."

I gulped but forged ahead. "Jill Elsman got you to falsify the tax payments, didn't she? She probably put a lot of pressure on you."

Patricia shuddered. "She was sort of friendly at first, then she was horrible. She offered me a bribe, and she threatened to spread the rumor that I was an unfit mother if I didn't take the money. People here know me. They know better, but she convinced me they'd believe her."

My hand tightened on hers in sympathy. "I'm sorry she put you in a no-win situation. It was cruel, and you did what you had to do. I don't hold that against you, Patricia."

"You don't?"

I released her hand, shook my head. "Not at all, and I don't think you were the only person she was manipulating."

"No?" she said, eyes wide. "Who else was she threatening?"

"Mr. Donel, perhaps?"

"My boss? No way. He was furious about the property tax records being messed up, but he was kind to me about it. Kinder than I deserved, but he knows how distracted I get when Davy has bad spells."

I took another tack. "Do you think Elsman targeted you on her own, or did someone suggest she get to you?"

Patricia spread her hands. "That's puzzled me, too, but she knew about Davy the first time she came in."

"How? Was he here with you? Could she have overheard you talking on the phone about him?"

"No, no. She asked to see a plat book and studied the land division maps for a while before she inquired about some parcels." Patricia looked up and into the distance. "Let's see. When she gave the book back, she said she was staying at the Inn on the Square, and she'd heard about my sick son."

"Did she start nagging you right away?"

Patricia shook her head. "She told me things would get better for us soon, and she left. I guess I thought she heard about Davy and me from Clark or Lorna. She started badgering me the next day, and the next. Then Davy had a bad time again, and that's when I broke."

An outside door shut, and we both jumped.

"Mr. Donel is due back. I—I have to get to work."

"That's okay. Thanks for all your help. Oh, and Patricia?"

She turned back to me.

"Did Elsman come through? Did she pay you?"

Patricia's gaze darted around the office as if someone had materialized to hear us. Satisfied we were still alone, she nodded.

"She gave me cash. I feel guilty spending it, though. I mean, her estate—"

"Her family doesn't need it. Besides, backhanded as it was, it was likely the kindest thing Elsman ever did for anyone."

That got a shy smile out of Patricia, and it looked good on her.

I stepped into the sunshine and stuffed the printouts into my bag. Two missions down, one to go before I met the ladies. Sherry and Eleanor had planned to visit all the dress shops for scoop, but they'd told me Clarra's Closet had a selection of clothes for my age range in petites, so I put that one on my snooping list. The shop was just off the square proper, toward the police station.

I set out in that direction thinking about Patricia's revelations. Not that it was a shocker that Hellspawn had bribed her. Threatening to start a rumor that could take Patricia's child away was pure evil, completely believable, and sadly, no surprise.

On the other hand, learning that Sherry owned Mrs. Gilroy's house, or at least paid the property taxes, was unexpected in the extreme. It certainly explained why Hellspawn hadn't badgered Mrs. Gilroy. I suppose it also explained why Hellspawn had so coveted Sherry's land.

CLARRA'S CLOSET DIDN'T CARRY THE MOST cutting-edge of fashions, but the clothes were well made, classically stylish, and a whole lot less pricey than at similar shops in Houston. In other words, perfect for me. The salesladies didn't dish any dirt, so I gave my credit card a workout buying capris and jeans in blue, one flirty black skirt, and several mix-and-match blouses. A package of bikini undies and a scarf on clearance, and I was satisfied I had outfits enough to see me through the rest of my visit. However long I needed to be here.

Which reminded me I needed to call Barbra again. I'd told her I would be back Monday, but today was Friday. Unless we found the real killer in record time, I'd be in Lilyvale a little while longer.

As I exited the store, I nearly ran into Kate Byrd on the sidewalk. I seized the moment.

"Mrs. Byrd, hello. I'm Nixy, Sherry Mae's niece. I met you at the folk art festival."

"Oh yes. How is your aunt? I heard she was arrested."

"No, just questioned. I heard you had lunch with Ms. Elsman a while back."

Instead of getting defensive, Kate Byrd rolled her eyes. What a pain that woman was. She wanted me to vote in favor of some development, but wouldn't tell me a thing about the project. I blew her off."

"And she didn't harass you or try to manipulate you?"

"Oh, she made noises. She attempted to influence all of us on the council. I know because we compared notes. Informally, not in a meeting. I think the only one of us she regularly cornered was Clark Tyler, and then only because she was staying at the inn. It was much harder for him to avoid her, don't you know."

"Yes, Lorna complained about her, too."

Mrs. Byrd's cell played the sound of a creaking door. "Sorry, but I've got to go. Tell Sherry Mae hi for me."

I stopped at my car to toss my shopping bags in the backseat before hustling to meet the ladies at the café. They were seated at the largest table in the middle of the room, the surface crowded with a tray of assorted pastries, five place settings of small plates, forks, and napkins, and five tall glasses of iced tea.

"What's the occasion?" I ask as I took one of two empty seats.

Sherry flashed a wide grin, and it struck me that I hadn't seen her so happy and relaxed since Sunday's stroll down Stanton family history lane. Could've been the cherry minitart on her plate, but I chalked it up to more.

"Lorna's been baking up a storm for the book club luncheon here tomorrow. We're doing our neighborly duty and testing her new desserts."

"What happened to the early dinner we're supposed to have?"

Maise cut another portion of her lemon bar. "We'll have it, but you know that saying. Life is short."

"Eat dessert first." Aster finished the quote flourishing a forkful of chocolate croissant.

"And I do believe we deserve it," Eleanor said, as she stuck a fork in a flaky apple turnover.

They giggled like carefree schoolgirls. If I hadn't known better, I'd have thought Lorna had put happy herbs in the goodies. Or the ladies had sniffed too much of Aster's lavender.

What the heck. I scooped a chocolate croissant onto my plate and nearly swooned at the first bite.

"So, do you want to hear what we learned?" Sherry asked, her bangs swooping over her eye.

"Sure but . . ." I glanced around the room. "Where is Lorna?"

"She's in the kitchen with Clark. She'll join us in a few minutes."

Now I peered at the stairway to the upstairs inn. "Trudy and Jeanette?"

"Lorna said Jeanette took the Hummer on home to Little Rock, and Trudy drove Jeanette's car to Magnolia."

"Okay, then. What've y'all got?"

"What do we have," Sherry corrected. "On the positive side, the rumor mill was grinding at every stop, but only about the murder in general. No one saw Elsman driving her Hummer the night she was killed, and the neighbors we ran into were in bed during the time she was killed."

"They saw the Hummer rumble through town day and night," Aster added, "but never saw anyone with her except Trudy."

"And those sightings were during the day," Maise supplied. "No one reported a passenger when they saw the car at night."

"I do believe that would be due to the tinted windows," Eleanor said.

"You're right. So you didn't get any real leads?"

"No, but what about your missions?" Sherry asked. "Did you talk with Patricia?"

"She confirmed that Elsman paid her to falsify the property tax records."

"You came right out and asked?" Aster looked as appalled as Sherry.

"We sort of stumbled onto the subject. I saw Pauletta at the business center, and Mrs. Hardy. That woman is a piece of work."

"What did she say to get your back up?" Eleanor asked.

"That Sherry was tacky for having a cemetery in the backyard, and that the graves should be moved."

Maise grinned. "And you said?"

They each leaned in toward me.

"That we should rededicate the cemetery and make a party of it."

They each leaned back, shot glances at each other.

"That's quite a good idea," Eleanor said slowly.

"I was planning to smudge the cemetery anyway."

I blinked. "What?"

"You know, burn cleansing herbs to get rid of the dark energy. I couldn't do it with the detective there."

"The anniversary of the Stanton's coming to Lilyvale is in June," Sherry mused. "Is that a long enough time from the murder to be respectful?"

"Of a woman who didn't respect others?" Maise scoffed. "More than enough, but is it something you really want to do, Sherry Mae? Didn't you have something else planned in June? In Texarkana?"

Sherry blinked at Maise. "That little jaunt? I can work around it. Nixy, do you think you could come back if we plan this?"

"Uh, sure," I answered, but wondered what that byplay between Maise and Sherry was about. I filed that away and got us back to the point. "But let's make sure you stay out of jail first. I talked to Kate Byrd, too. She said Elsman tried to manipulate her and the other council members, but they blew her off. So I got a little information, but nothing really new."

Sherry patted my hand. "It's too bad we didn't get a solid lead, but that's the way the croissant crumbles. Now, I wonder where Lorna got off to. She said she'd join us, but she's taking an awfully long time."

"Do you need her for something special?"

"We need to pay the tab," Sherry said, and reached for her purse.

"I'll go find her. I need to use the restroom anyway."

I went through the opening in the bar to peer in the window set in the swinging door that led to the kitchen. I didn't want to smack the door into Lorna, but no one stood on the other side. I pushed the door open and stepped just inside.

"Lorna?"

Voices came from farther back in the room, behind a door that was cracked just enough for me to catch the strident tones. First I heard the word "money," and then part of a phrase—"what you . . . mutter mumble . . . with that woman." Did I dare tiptoe closer to eavesdrop? In the next moment, something slammed, and I flat chickened out.

"Lorna," I called, louder than I had the first time. Much louder.

The far door flew all the way open. Lorna's haunted gaze found mine, and she frowned at me. "Nixy? What do you need?"

"Sorry to bother you," I said, forcing a nonchalant smile, "but Sherry is ready for the check."

Her expression smoothed. "I'll be right out."

I went back to the tiny hall between the kitchen and interior staircase and on to the restroom. When I exited, Lorna was near the front door chatting with the ladies, and Clark vigorously wiped down the bar. His full beard didn't do enough to hide the strain in his face. I didn't figure he was stressed enough to break the way Patricia had, but I had to put out feelers. Sherry's continued freedom was on the line.

"Hi, Mr. Tyler." His gaze snapped up, but it was clear he didn't recognize me. "I'm Sherry Mae's niece, Nixy. We met Sunday."

"We did?"

"When Jill Elsman almost hit you and Bryan Hardy. You stopped to talk with us."

"I remember now." His body language relaxed, but his expression was more perturbed than friendly. "What can I do for you—Nixy, is it?"

"What time do you and Lorna normally leave for the night?"

He gave me a long stare. "Why do you ask?"

I suppressed a shudder of unease and forged ahead. "I wondered if you saw Jill Elsman's Hummer in the parking lot on Tuesday night."

"Is this about your aunt Sherry Mae?" he asked, his gaze sliding to the group still at the doorway.

"Yes. I ask because it seems odd that Elsman wouldn't have driven herself that night. So, did you see her car in the lot when y'all left?"

"Lorna went home before me that night. I don't remember seeing that crazy Elsman's car or not seeing it."

Huh. He didn't even have to think about his answer when he finally gave it. Had he rehearsed it? He also didn't mention what time he left the café. Had he followed Hellspawn and killed her?

One thing was sure. If this man had an ounce of political charm, I hadn't seen it Sunday, and I wasn't seeing it now.

So much for getting more information. I thanked him, thanked Lorna on my way out the door, and gathered with the ladies on the wide sidewalk.

"I have another errand to run. Do y'all need me to bring anything home?"

"Are you planning," Sherry asked, "to visit a certain detective? Tell him what you found out today?"

"I'm going over there, but I don't know how much I'm going to tell him. I feel sorry for Patricia, and I don't want to get her fired."

"Do what you think best, child. We'll see you later."

I WALKED TO THE STATION, AND SHOAR EXITED THE building just as my feet hit the little parking lot.

"Hey," he said.

"Hey, yourself. You off for the day?"

"Not yet. You need something?"

"To talk, but, um, we might want to do that here."

"Why?"

"There's a rumor circulating about us."

He grinned. "I know, but I need real coffee. Want to hit the Dairy Queen?"

"I'll buy this time."

He assisted me into his truck, wheeled out of the side lot, and then gave me the arched-brow glance that made a few butterflies wake up and happy-dance in my stomach. Dang, he really was handsome. And decent. And—

"You wanted to talk?" he prompted.

"Uh, yes. What happened with the Hummer?"

"I heard Jeanette drove it home."

"Does that mean the techs found evidence in it?"

"It means we finished processing it. Why?"

"Elsman was such a control freak. I can't see her leaving her own wheels behind when she vandalized the cemetery. So I figured you might have found signs of her accomplice in the car. Something that points away from Sherry."

"No comment," he said as he pulled into the drive-through. "Latte?"

"Banana milk shake," I said, as I dug out my wallet. Bananas were a comfort food for me from way back, and I needed comfort about now because I knew he wouldn't share any details with me, but I had to ask questions. I couldn't let up until Sherry was cleared.

When we had our orders, he drove again to the tech college campus. By then I'd sucked down enough banana comfort to calm down.

"What about your search of Elsman's room?"

"What about it?"

"The man I heard in her room. You know, the night I brought Trudy back from the hospital. Didn't you find anything that couldn't be matched?"

"The evidence is at the state crime lab, but hotel rooms are a nightmare for matching samples. Too many people leave traces of their stays, even when the level of housekeeping is excellent."

"Shoot."

"Hey, I know you're worried about Miz Sherry Mae, but don't be. I'm doing my job."

"I know. I just want this over with."

"So you can go back to life in Houston?"

I opened my mouth to answer a resounding "yes," then shut it. I sure didn't miss taking orders from Barbra. Or miss the often temperamental, egotistical artists. Or miss the pretentious art snobs. And the Houston traffic? No. In fact, I didn't even miss my apartment. My own bed was more comfy, but Sherry's couch wasn't so bad.

"Nixy?"

"Yeah?"

"Why did you go to the courthouse today?"

Chapter Nineteen

I BLINKED AND REORDERED MY THOUGHTS IN A hurry.

"I've been gathering family history information, and I wanted to research Sherry's property. The history of Stanton ownership."

"Come on, Nixy. You got Patricia to admit Elsman bribed her."

I snorted. "Elsman threatened to have her son taken away. Wait. How do you know what she told me? Please tell me we weren't overheard!"

"Patricia came by to see me on her break and confessed."

"What are you going to do?"

"Nothing. She didn't kill Elsman. She corrected the tax records. She's welcome to keep whatever Elsman paid her, far as I'm concerned. I call it pain-and-suffering restitution."

"That's it? She keeps her job?"

"She was good at it before. She'll be even more conscientious now."

"That's great, Eric." I bit my lip. "You know, though, if Elsman bribed and bullied Patricia, she probably did the same to others. Like Clark Tyler. The Tylers seem to be having money problems, did you know that?"

"Nixy, I'm going to say this once. Whether it was someone Elsman bribed or bullied or not, someone hated or feared her enough to kill her. You think you're asking innocent questions, but if you say the wrong thing to the wrong person, then I'll have another death on my hands."

"But—"

"I don't want it to be your death."

"But—"

"Or Sherry's. You'd never forgive yourself, and what would Sherry's housemates do without her?"

Mouth open for another "but," I froze. No, I wouldn't forgive myself if Sherry was killed. As for her housemates, after seeing the women giggling together today, I had an even deeper sense of how close they were. Dab and Fred? Well, the ladies treated them like brothers, and the men obviously adored the women as family.

"Nixy," Eric said with a touch of impatience. "You shouldn't have to think twice about putting yourself or the Six in danger."

"I'm not. I've got it. It's just that I hope you're asking Clark Tyler some pointed questions."

"Like what?"

"Like if he has a gambling problem."

"I've heard that rumor," he said, nodding. "What else?"

"If Elsman was bribing or blackmailing him, of course."

"Of course, but if she was, it doesn't mean Clark killed her."

I arched a brow at him. "If you were gambling away family or business money, or both, would you want to face a wife with lethal utensils all over her kitchen?"

He grinned. "Lorna's never struck me as having violent tendencies."

"Funny man, aren't you?"

"Have I made myself clear about staying out of this investigation?"

"You have." Although as long as Sherry was at risk, I'd ignore him.

"Hey," he said, and reached to cover my hand with his. "I'll figure this out. Everything will be fine."

He gave me a slow, sexy smile that about knocked me to the floorboard. Probably to disarm me after he'd chewed me out. It didn't work, and I brought out my own ammunition. I gave him a sugar-high-sweet smile.

"We'd better get back before more rumors fly."

SHOAR DROPPED ME AT MY CAR. I BEEPED MY CAMRY open, threw my bag on the passenger seat, and paced to the driver's side when I noticed Bryan Hardy waving from the courthouse lawn and trotting toward me. Great. What now?

"Ms. Nix," he said when he neared. "Are you well?"

"I'm good, Mr. Hardy. Why?"

"Call me Bryan. I saw Detective Shoar drop you off. Was he interrogating you?"

"Interviewing," I corrected.

His baby face took on a hangdog expression. "I have to tell you how sorry I am about Ms. Sherry Mae. She's always been such a good woman. I know people can snap, but I never thought she had it in her to kill someone."

"Snap?" I echoed, ready to snap him. "You have to be kidding. It's ridiculous to think that my aunt would kill anyone for any reason."

He shook his head. "But the evidence—"

"What do you know about the evidence?" I asked slowly. Dinah had said the prosecution didn't have that information any more than she did.

"It's a small town. People talk."

I narrowed my eyes and stepped into his space. He backed up. "Who talked?"

He stood taller. "I'm not at liberty to say."

"Well, hear this, Mr. Hardy. Anything Detective Shoar has in terms of evidence is circumstantial. If it were solid, he'd make an arrest."

"We'll see."

"Yes, you will see, Counselor." I moved forward again, and he fell back again. If I advanced on him one more time, he'd be in the street. "Sherry Mae is innocent, and I'm going to prove it."

That startled him. His sandy brows flew to his hairline, and something shifted in his hazel eyes.

"I'd be careful about asking questions, Ms. Nix. Obstruction of justice is a serious charge."

"Is that a threat?"

"It's a friendly reminder," he countered, then turned from me when a querulous voice called his name.

"Bryan! Stop talking to that rude Stanton girl and take me home."

He turned back to me just long enough to give me a nod. Good thing he didn't say another disparaging word about Sherry. I'd had it with both members of the Hardy family.

I got in the car, locked the door, and pulled my suspect list pad from under the driver's seat. I'd talked with Patricia and Kate Byrd, and believed neither of them killed Elsman or knew who did. Pauletta gave me some insights about Clark Tyler, and he was the only original name left high on my list.

Although after the confrontation with Bryan Hardy, I added his name under Clark's. Bryan had been fishing for information from me, but why?

Mindful that Dab and Fred would be leaving the house early for the concert, I checked the time on my phone and saw I'd missed a call from Trudy. I took the cell off mute and listened to my voice mail.

"Uh, Nixy, hi. I thought of something that might be important, but I don't want to talk to Detective Shoar until I talk to you. Call me."

As I saved the message, a knock on my window made me jump. It was Vonnie from the antiques store, an apologetic smile on her face.

"I'm sorry I startled you," she said when I put the window down.

"No problem," I said over the sound of my pounding heart. "How are you?"

"Fine, fine. I've started our cleaning out and found some things I want to make sure Sherry gets. Do you mind taking them now?"

Much as I wanted to call Trudy back right away, I gave Vonnie a bright smile. "Not at all."

The interior of the antiques shop didn't seem as jammed with clutter as it had on Monday. In fact, the orange love seat and turquoise plastic chairs were the first things I noticed that were gone. Looked like Vonnie had sold some big items, too, and I hoped she got big money for the pieces. When I commented, she nodded happily.

"Several designers heard I was closing and came in. I sold a breakfront, a Hoosier-style cabinet, some metal lockers, and an entire 1920s bedroom set. I rather hated to let that go. One lady took about half of my mid-century modern things. I loved those, too."

"My mother and I used to go antiquing. I remember a shop owner telling Mom that loving your stock was an occupational hazard."

"She was right. You can't keep it all, but it's hard to see it leave. Except," she added with a twinkle in her eyes, "when you know the right person is getting the right thing. Come on. Let me show you what I want Sherry to have."

I followed her through a thick wooden door set next to an extra-wide metal roll-up door. Which made sense to have if you moved large pieces of furniture in and out of the shop. The back area, what Vonnie had called the workroom, was the size of a three-car garage with duct work and vents running overhead. Part of the heating and air-conditioning system, I guessed, and they made the space look a little like an industrial loft. Workbenches lined two walls, and a huge worktable sat in the center of the room. Another wall was covered with tools hanging on pegboards. Fred would love this place.

A metal door toward the left rear of the building opened onto a flight of steps that led to the apartment, where we walked into a space that functioned as much as a mudroom as a foyer. An antique hall tree with a golden oak patina held umbrellas, coats, and hats. From there, the open-concept living area extended the entire depth of the store downstairs. The living room furniture was traditional-comfy, and the kitchen had been updated in this decade. A fabulous crystal chandelier hung over a Queen Anne–style dining set. A reproduction, I guessed, but the mahogany finish was lovely, and the antiques blended seamlessly with the rest of the décor.

Except for the paneled back wall of the dining room. Not 1970s paneling. This panel job was a work of art, like something out of a mansion. The rich, dark wood looked out of place, and at the same time perfectly at home.

"Home sweet home," Vonnie said beside me. "I'm going to miss this place and this town."

"You've made it cozy, but how on earth did you get this furniture up that narrow staircase?"

She grinned. "We have an old-style lift. See that paneled wall in the dining area? Your relative Sissy had that built to hide the lift and to add storage up here. Clever, huh?"

I did a double take. "Sissy lived here in the loft?"

"You didn't know?"

"Mrs. Gilroy told me about Sissy owning the dime store, but I had no idea she had lived up here."

"She and her husband did until he died. Sissy stayed on for a good while after that. There's just the one bedroom and bath," she said with a wave at two doors across the living room, "but they are quite spacious. What was her husband's name?"

"Josiah Aiken," I supplied, remembering his and Sissy's "in memory of" stones in the cemetery.

"Josiah, yes. Well, come look what I have." Vonnie hurried to the two boxes resting on the dining table. "I hardly believed my eyes when I found this."

She reached for a flattened box about four feet long and two feet wide that had obviously been spliced together and held with brown packing tape. She lifted the top flap with a flair, proudly pointing at a metal sign that read, SISSY'S FIVE & DIME.

"Are you kidding?" With a sense of awe, I touched the cool metal, rusted in places, but not as corroded with time or the elements as I would have expected. "Wow, Vonnie. This is amazing."

"There's a manila envelope under this with pictures of Sissy and Josiah with the sign. Now, the things in here"—she indicated an old hatbox large enough and tall enough to house a ten-gallon hat wrapped all around with twine—"aren't family items, but I thought of Sherry when I saw them."

"I'm sure she'll love your gifts, Vonnie. And this sign is priceless. Sherry will have to hide it from me."

"Von, you up there?" a man called from the top of the staircase.

"I'm here, S.T."

"There's a dealer on the phone. You want to talk to her?"

"I'll be right there. Nixy, I hate to rush you off—"

"It's fine. I need to get home with these treasures."

"Let's take the lift down." She secured the sign box with three lengths of twine that I hadn't seen underneath it. Then she carried her box while I took the hatbox. At the center of the dining area wall, she pushed on a barely there slit in the wood paneling, and two doors swung out to reveal a surprisingly ornate metal grate. Vonnie pulled a handle on one side and the grate opened accordion-style. I admit, I was fascinated, especially when we rode down without undue jerking or clunking.

Back in the shop proper, I told Vonnie to leave the sign box and take her phone call. I'd come back for the second box.

"You're a dear, Nixy. Thanks, and tell Sherry Mae hi for us."

With Sherry's gifts in the trunk a few minutes later, I noticed that the square had all but emptied of cars in the short time I'd been with Vonnie. It was cooler, too, and the wind had risen. Felt like Lilyvale would get an April shower soon. I hoped the rain held off until after the concert.

And, if I wanted to hear Dab's and Fred's reports, I needed to get home. I'd call Trudy from there.

"I CAN'T BELIEVE VONNIE FOUND THESE RELICS OF the five and dime," Sherry exclaimed, tears in her eyes.

Sherry reverently traced her fingers over the letters of the metal sign where it lay on the kitchen table, then picked up the sepia photos of Sissy and Josiah. One showed them in front of the store, holding the metal sign. The other captured them standing under the sign mounted on the building wearing proud, wide smiles.

"Did she say where she stumbled onto these?"

"I didn't get a chance to ask."

"I will when I find her tonight and thank her."

The hatbox Vonnie had sent contained four items, and each one Sherry unwrapped was exceptional. A corncob basket, handwoven with real corncobs, willow, and wicker. Another smaller basket of willow, dark with age, held a tin bird inside it that Fred said was a windup toy from the 1930s. The vibrant blues, greens, yellows, and pinks had faded, but the bird was sweet.

The last surprise had been wrapped in tissue paper and set inside a smaller, well-padded box. When Sherry eased the tissue away, she held a piece of Belleek Irish porcelain in the form of a woven basket. I thought it dated from the 1970s, but the age didn't matter. The soft-ivory-colored basket was exquisite.

"This is too much. I can't accept the Belleek."

"Sherry Mae Cutler, you hush," Maise scolded. "You keep this and you treasure it."

"I do believe Maise is right. Vonnie certainly didn't pack the Belleek basket by mistake. She wants you to have it."

"That would be lovely in your bedroom," Aster offered.

Sherry shook her head, her eyes still brimming with emotion. Dab patted her shoulder. Fred said, "Those are nice things and you deserve 'em, but when are we eatin'?"

"Hold fast, Fred. We'll eat when the casseroles are good and warm." Behind Maise, the oven timer dinged. "Now they're good and warm. You men get to the table. Nixy, Sherry, put those nice things in the parlor so we won't knock into them when we police the kitchen."

We followed orders, and though I'd eaten dessert not two hours earlier, the first bite of chicken artichoke casserole had me nearly swooning.

"It's my recipe," Sherry told me with a proud smile.

"I thought Maise said this was the last of the food the neighbors brought over." Food for troubled times, as Mrs. Gilroy had called it. Trouble food.

"It is, but I've shared the recipe over the years. Jackie Comstock made this dish."

"It's a mite drier than yours, Sherry," Dab observed.

"Well, it could be I didn't share every detail of the recipe with everyone who asked for it." She flashed me a grin. "But I'll give all the secrets to you."

I mumbled a "Yes, please" around the bite in my mouth. Not that I cooked, but I'd consider learning to eat this dish again.

After we'd shoveled food for a few minutes, Eleanor cleared her throat. "I do believe the gentlemen need to make their report. Did you learn anything on your rounds today?"

"Bog, Duke, and Big George were in bed when Elsman was killed, not patrollin' the neighborhood. They never saw a soul but Trudy ridin' along in that Hummer, neither."

"We missed B.G.," Dab said. "He was delivering furniture, but we did hear that Clark goes to Hot Springs once or twice a season with some golf buddies. He doesn't seem to win or lose big, and no one's heard a word about him going to casinos in Shreveport or over in Oklahoma."

"But Duke said Clark and his pals play at them racinos," Fred added.

"What's that?" I asked.

"A sort of casino at the Oaklawn Park Race Track," Eleanor said. Then, "What? I heard about the place from the church group that goes in March."

"Except," Dab said, "there is no live betting. There's electronic blackjack and poker."

I frowned. "I thought there wasn't any gambling in Arkansas except the horse and dog races."

Fred snorted. "The powers that be call it 'games of skill,' but I reckon because the players use a computer thing, it passes as a computer game."

I stared at Fred, not really seeing him, but mulling. His comment and Dab's about computer gambling triggered a memory. I had read an article about online gambling, probably on the Internet via one of my news site feeds. I didn't know squat about how online gambling worked, but the gist of the article was that players can get into deep debt, as much as or more than in person at a casino.

If Clark Tyler was in gambling trouble, what did that really mean in relation to Hellspawn?

"What are you thinkin', missy?" Fred barked.

"Let's say Clark gambles, has sizeable losses, and Elsman knows about it but Lorna doesn't. Elsman could've either blackmailed him to smooth the way for the project, or bribed him to do it, or both."

"That doesn't mean he'd kill her." Dab said. "And I'll tell you straight up, I don't see it."

"Then who else was she blackmailing, bribing, and bullying?"

Six blank faces looked back at me.

"Yeah, I don't know either."

"Talk to that Trudy girl. I still think she's suspicious." Fred pushed his chair back and reached for his walker parked along the wall. "Come on, Dab. We need to tune up with the boys."

I DID NEED TO TALK WITH TRUDY, BUT SHE DIDN'T AN-swer when I called. I'd try again later or maybe run up to her room. I didn't have a code to get in the back way, but I could use the interior stairs if the café was open. First, though, I had to get the ladies settled at the concert.

The entire square had been blocked to traffic, but I found a space on the street behind the Lilies Café. The ladies and I schlepped our folding lawn chairs to a spot just down from the café. Other concertgoers sat in their folding chairs in the streets and on the sidewalks. The evening was cool with a light breeze, and many people wore jackets or wrapped themselves in blankets. A few uniformed policemen wan-dered through the crowd. I recognized the lean, middle-aged Officer Bryant and the young Officer Benton.

"The boys" turned out to be the Pickin' N Grinnin' Boys, each aged fifty and up. I recognized some of them from their having played at the folk art festival on Saturday, and others were new to me. The band was set up on the courthouse lawn, the side facing the café, but a sound system carried the music throughout downtown and beyond.

Aster had told me that Dab played the banjo and Fred played the washboard and some fiddle. "Some" turned out to be an understatement. Dab and Fred were excellent, even as they simply warmed up.

Sherry went off in search of Vonnie. I noticed that the café's CLOSED sign wasn't up, and Clark was inside. He wielded a broom and looked up when I knocked on the door. He scowled but let me in.

"Sorry to bother you, but I can't get Trudy on the phone. Do you know if she's here?"

"Haven't seen her," Clark said. I figured he'd tell me to

get lost, but he motioned toward the staircase instead. "Go on up if you can make it quick. I need to lock up."

I raced upstairs and through the door to the guest rooms, but Trudy didn't answer my knock. The bathroom off the hall was empty, too.

"Not up there?" Clark asked when I came down.

"No, but thanks for letting me check." I started for the door, then stopped and turned back to him. "I'm surprised y'all aren't open on concert night. Seems like you'd have a lot of business."

"Lorna baked all day. She's tired."

"That's right. I had her desserts today. Well, I'll bet you're happy Elsman is gone."

He threw me a sharp glance. "Why?"

"She was bugging you about her project, wasn't she? Lorna said she was driving you crazy."

"I wouldn't kill a body just for annoying me," he said with a level look.

I was taking a chance, but I dove in. "How about for blackmailing you?"

He took a step closer, the hand holding the broom showing white knuckles. "You listen here. I don't care who you're related to, you repeat that and I will sue you for slander. Got me?"

"Got you." I took a breath. "But did you kill Elsman?"

"Hell no."

"Do you know who did?"

He darted a look past me, and I thought he was simply avoiding my gaze until he stiffened. I pivoted but didn't see anyone outside.

"You need to leave."

He headed toward me, broom in hand, and I scampered out the door. He threw the lock behind me.

I stood there on the sidewalk, adrenaline pumping, but proud that I'd seized the opportunity to question Clark point-blank. Did I believe that he didn't kill Elsman? Yes, but I had a strong gut feeling that he knew who did. Trouble was, I couldn't prove a thing.

I called Trudy again, and again got voice mail. Was she all right, or had the killer gone after her, too?

If I didn't reach her in another hour or so, I'd consider alerting Shoar. I wouldn't, however, tell him I'd confronted Clark. No point in getting yelled at twice in one day.

Sherry called me to join her and the ladies as the band launched into their first song. Gradually, I even relaxed enough to enjoy the toe-tapping music. Spending the April evening in Small Town, USA, with Sherry and her housemates, friends, and neighbors was a novel experience. Refreshing. Renewing.

Or it was right up until the band took a break and a scream ripped through the night.

Chapter Twenty

THE SCREAM STOPPED THEN STARTED IN SHORT
blasts and mingled with cries for help. I wasn't positive it came
from behind the café, but I ran that way. Down the half block,
around to the alley, and I stopped short. A light-colored sedan
partly blocked the way. Trudy stood at the front of the car on
the driver's side, arms wrapped around her middle, keening.

"Trudy," I yelled as I edged around the sedan. "Trudy, what's
wrong?"

She swung toward me, eyes wide and wild. "I didn't hit
him. I promise I didn't. He was in the shadows between the
buildings, but I saw him in time. I braked. I know I didn't run
over him."

I reached her and caught only a glimpse of a man's body
sprawled on the cracked pavement before she threw her big-
boned body into my arms, sobbing. But I'd seen the bearded
face. Clark Tyler.

Other people had come to see what was happening. I
heard murmuring around me. No one came close, but the
crowd at the far end of the alley parted for Officer Bryant.

"What's going on?" he called as he trotted toward us.

"I don't have the whole story, but this is Clark Tyler and he's hurt."

Bryant bent to check Clark's neck for a pulse.

"He's alive."

Trudy stood up straight and took a step away from me. "Thank God!"

Bryant called for backup and an ambulance, both of which were already en route. I saw Officer Benton headed our way, and heard sirens. Several someones had undoubtedly called 911 within seconds of Trudy's first scream.

Soon controlled chaos reigned around us. I steered Trudy to the edge of the parking lot, where we'd be out of the way, and that's where Detective Shoar talked to us.

"You two okay?"

"Trudy's shaken but not injured." I glanced to where Clark was being assessed by the paramedics. "Who's contacting Lorna?"

"We have it covered. Just stay here until I come back."

The Pickin' N Grinnin' Boys began playing again, and I hoped the audience had stayed to listen. I really hoped it would deflect some attention from what had happened to Clark, whatever that was. Trudy continued to cry in little hiccups, so I couldn't eavesdrop on the EMTs about Clark's condition. When Sherry hailed me from the street behind the lot where my car was parked, Trudy tagged along.

I filled Sherry in on what little I knew, which was only that Clark was unconscious. She gave me a decisive nod and handed me my purse.

"We'll head on over to the hospital to be there for Lorna. She doesn't have family, you know. How long will you be tied up here?"

"No idea, but take my car," I said as I fished the keys from my bag. "I'll walk to the hospital when I'm free. What about Fred and Dab?"

"They'll be playing for another hour, then packing up. We'll text to let them know where we are."

It was a typically generous and compassionate gesture for Sherry and her housemates, and reminded me what Shoar had said about Lilyvale taking care of its own.

When Clark had been loaded into the ambulance, the detective strode our way, his little cop notebook in one hand, a pen in the other.

"Is Clark going to live?" I asked him.

"The EMTs need to work on him more before they transport. They have better light and a more sterile environment in the truck."

Which didn't answer my question, but he probably didn't have one yet.

"Ms. Henry," he said formally but with kindness. "Are you feeling better now? Can you tell me what happened?"

She grasped my hand in a death grip, swallowed. "I pulled into the alley and saw a big bundle in my headlights. I hit the brakes and got out to see what was there. That's when I realized it was Mr. Tyler."

He made a note. "Did you touch him? Check for a pulse?"

She hung her head. "No. I freaked and screamed."

"It's understandable. So you were coming back to the inn?" She nodded. "Where had you been?"

She looked at the detective, then me, then heaved a sigh. "I went to Magnolia. I know I wasn't supposed to leave town, but I've been here for three weeks, and with Jill dead and Jeanette gone back to Little Rock, well, I don't have any friends here, and I was bored. I just wanted to go somewhere different."

"Magnolia isn't much like Lilyvale, is it?"

Trudy released my hand and gaped. "Are you kidding? The town square is nearly identical, except the buildings there are more brick than limestone."

"I know." He scribbled in the notebook again.

She cocked her head. "You were trying to trick me."

"You need to tell me the next time you want to leave town." She gave him a sheepish look. "How long were you in Magnolia? Where did you go?"

While she recounted her movements, I surreptitiously massaged the hand Trudy had crushed. With luck, I'd have feeling back in a week or two.

"Then I heard about a barbeque place," she was saying, and her expression went euphoric. "The pies were to die for!"

I winced at her choice of words, but Shoar smiled.

"The Backyard Bar-B-Q. I know the place."

"I have all my receipts to prove where I was, and my shopping bags are in the car."

"What did you do the rest of the day?"

"I went to the county library and read a couple of romance novels."

"You read a couple of books?" Eric said sharply. "In one afternoon?"

"I know I don't come off as very bright, but I'm a fast reader. And I happen to like romance novels."

I nearly cheered Trudy. Partly because she stood up for her reading preferences, partly because I like romance novels, too. What's not to like about happily ever after? I didn't make a peep, though. I didn't want to interrupt the questioning. Not yet, but I had to fess up about confronting Clark. I just needed an opening.

"What time did you leave Magnolia?" he was asking Trudy.

"The library closed at six, so I went back to the barbeque place for more pie. I stopped for gas, so I guess I left about seven fifteen. I have that receipt, too."

"Are you certain of the time?"

And there was my cue.

"Detective Shoar, I talked to Clark in the café about seven. A little more than an hour before I heard Trudy scream."

He stopped making notes and whipped his attention to me. "You're just telling me this now?"

I shrugged. "You didn't ask."

The ambulance siren pulsed once just as he muttered something under his breath I didn't quite catch. As the truck rolled out the far end of the alley, people parted for it to pass, but closed ranks again. Uniformed police and deputies kept them back while the crime scene techs, who'd arrived as Eric approached us, began setting up lights to do their investigation.

He told Trudy to wait, then took my elbow to steer me far enough away to talk more privately. "What is your part in this, Nixy?"

I flexed my hand to stimulate circulation.

"Other than being a crying post, I have no part."

"Come again?"

"When I got to the alley, Trudy was standing on the driver's side of the car at the front bumper. She threw her arms around my neck and cried, and that's all I had to do with finding Clark."

"But you talked to him at seven. Why?"

"Trudy called me earlier, but I couldn't reach her when I called back. I saw Clark in the café, and he gave me a minute to see if Trudy was upstairs."

"She wasn't there?"

"No, but I asked Clark some questions when I came back down."

I related our confrontation, and he looked ready to bite my head off when I finished. I quickly repeated the salient point. "I think Clark knew who killed Elsman. Or at least suspected someone."

"And now he's on the way to the ER. Is there a lesson here? Aha, there is. You could be next if you don't stop asking questions."

"Sarcasm doesn't become you, Detective."

His jaw dropped, then he turned away and cursed under his breath. Rather colorfully, too.

"So can I leave?"

He visibly gathered his patience. "You going back to the concert?"

"To the hospital. Sherry and the ladies went over there to be with Lorna, and I told them I'd come, too."

He glanced at Trudy, who stood staring into space, wringing her hands.

"Can you take Trudy with you, then bring her back to the inn later?"

"You don't need to question her more?"

"I'll do *my* job, but I don't think she's involved other than discovering Clark in the alley. I'll get her keys and move her car when the team is finished collecting evidence."

I didn't answer him. I was thinking. Lorna would have enough stress without Trudy's hysterics. So if I was taking Trudy along, she'd have to calm down. I hoped Aster had her lavender spray handy.

"Nixy? Will you take Trudy, or should I find a police-woman to sit with her awhile?"

"I'll take her."

"Good."

He spoke a few words to Trudy, then went to her car. He came back with her purse but asked permission to go through it first. Satisfied she didn't have any evidence stashed in it, he handed it over and went to watch the crime scene team.

THE HOSPITAL WAS ONLY TWO PLUS BLOCKS, BUT as we neared the ER, Trudy's teeth chattered. Must have been shock because the air temperature wasn't that cool. I touched her arm lightly.

"What's wrong?"

She startled. "I don't have good memories of the hospital. And I was thinking that I know now what it must've been like for you to find Jill's body. Horrifying."

I managed not to shudder. "At least Clark Tyler is alive."

"I sure hope he'll recover. I don't much care for him, but Lorna is nice."

My snoopy sense went on alert. "Any reason you don't like Clark?"

She shrugged. "He's unfriendly. Gruff. Plus I overheard Jill say something about having taken care of him and that he'd do what she wanted."

"Trudy!" I exploded. "Why didn't you tell the detective this?"

"I didn't remember it until today," she said, her tone defensive. "She was on the phone. She said the name Tyler, but that was it."

The hospital was in sight now, but I slowed my steps, mulling that information. Trudy slowed, too, and then I stopped.

"Is this why you called me today?"

"No. When I went to the library, before I started reading, I looked around. They have a large collection of state and local historical records. I saw some old yearbooks and remembered that Jill had a folded-up yearbook page in her binder."

"You said you never saw the inside of the binder."

"I know, but it was just once. It was last Sunday, and you know how angry Jill was that day. She ran over the sapling."

"I remember."

"Jill had thrown the binder in the backseat. When we got to the inn again, she told me to get it. The back cover was open and that's when I saw the page."

"Okay, what kind of page?" I asked, thinking back to my yearbooks. "Rows of class photos? A picture of a club or an event? Could you tell if it was from a high school or college?"

"Class photos in rows, and the people looked more college-aged than high school. The thing is, Jill had circled one. I didn't see it but for maybe ten seconds, but the name stuck with me. Trudy, like me, and Whitman like the author. And Jill had written 'RIP' beside the photo."

"You don't think your cousin killed a college kid, do you?"

"What? No, but there's some connection to all this or Jill wouldn't have had that page in her work binder. She wasn't the slightest bit sentimental."

"Did you meet anyone in town who could've been an older Trudy Whitman? I hate to say it, but your cousin could've written 'RIP' for some reason other than this girl being deceased."

"Like a sick joke? It's possible. This is why I didn't want to talk to Detective Shoar about it. He has the binder, so if the page is there, he knows about it and I look like a ninny. But if it's gone—"

"Then did your cousin remove it, or did someone else?"

"I thought before I talk to the detective, you could do a search for Trudy Whitman. Just to see if I should bother reporting it at all."

The ER doors whooshed open, and I realized we needed to get in there before Sherry sent troops to track me down.

"Tell you what. I'll think about this and get back to you. For now, let's go see about Lorna."

I immediately spotted her in the waiting room. Not hard to do since Lorna and the ladies of the Six were the only people there. Sherry held Lorna's hand, and the ladies sat on either side of them. Trudy and I said hello, murmured our concerns. Lorna was too distraught to do more than nod. In fact, she looked like a woman with one foot off a high ledge.

I slipped into a seat beside Aster, and Trudy took the one next to me.

"Do you have lavender spray with you?"

She smiled. "Already used it, though I can't say it helped."

It must not have, because Lorna let out a wail.

"Oh no. The book club luncheon is tomorrow. That's why Clark worked late. To prep for the Saturday menu and clean the café. The book club prepaid. If I have to cancel, I'll have to repay them, and I don't have the money just now. I'll have to close the café entirely."

"Now, Lorna, you must stay positive," Sherry soothed. "About Clark and about the café."

"But I can't. Clark has been gambling again. On the Internet." She paused for only a second before it all came tumbling out. "I found out for sure today, even though I knew we'd been bleeding money. We had a terrible fight. I told him he'd better not have borrowed against the business. It's all I have left of my family."

She looked fierce for a moment, then crumpled. "He said he'd made some back and put it in the bank, but I don't know how he won a dime. He hasn't got a lucky bone in his whole body."

"But he does, Lorna," Sherry said stoutly. "He has you."

"If he lives," Lorna whispered. Her anger had drained, her voice plaintive and frightened.

"Now, Lorna, you just heave to with that thinking," Maise scolded. "Don't worry about the café or the luncheon. We can run the show for you tomorrow."

"That's right," Sherry jumped in. "It's Saturday, and we don't have a thing planned, do we, girls?"

Sherry looked to Eleanor and Aster for confirmation, and they all jumped in quickly and with reassuring enthusiasm.

"I do believe we'd be happy to help," Eleanor declared.

"Maise and I can cook anything on your menu."

"That's right," Sherry said. "Fred can be in charge of drinks and run the counter, and Dab and Nixy and I will serve and bus tables."

"I'll be happy to help, too, Mrs. Tyler."

That got Lorna's attention. She stared at Trudy, who eagerly nodded.

"I waited tables in college. I was good at it."

Lorna met our gazes. "The desserts are made."

"We know."

"And the potpies are prepared. They're on a tray in the large freezer, ready to defrost and reheat."

"Potpies?" Maise echoed.

"Dana likes the luncheon menus to tie into their reading selection." Lorna gave Maise a weak smile. "Everything else for the Saturday menu should be prepped. If Clark finished before he was—"

Sherry put her arm around Lorna's shoulders. "Hush, now. Whatever needs doing, we'll take care of it. Here, give me your set of business keys right now before we get distracted. I'll call Dana and let her know the luncheon is still on. You just concentrate on yourself and Clark."

Lorna's spirits rallied, and she pulled her purse from under the waiting room chair to unhook keys from a D ring attached to the strap.

"Thank you. Thank you all. You make me remember I'm not alone."

Two separate doors whooshed open a moment later, and we all turned our attention to the men who'd entered the waiting room. Detective Shoar strode in from outside, and a doctor came through the ER doors. The same doctor who had treated Sherry. The men exchanged a nod, and the doctor headed toward our group with the detective on his heels. Maise stood to give the doctor her chair beside Lorna. He pointedly eyed the rest of us, but no one moved. He ran a hand through his short hair and sat.

"How is he?" she asked in a small voice.

"Mr. Tyler has a concussion, broken ribs, and he may have damage to his liver or spleen," he said slowly, seeming to weigh his words. "He'll be under observation for at least a few days, unless he should need surgery."

"No offense, Doctor, but does he need to go to a larger hospital?" she asked. "Do you have everything you need here to treat him?"

"At the moment, we do. If he needs surgery, we'll transfer him."

"Is he awake now?"

"He regained consciousness for a few minutes, but he's resting."

"Did he say what happened? Did he get hit by a car? Was he mugged?"

"I'm afraid he wasn't coherent." The doctor glanced at Shoar. "You'll have to ask the detective here what happened."

"Detective?" she said.

"We're not sure yet, Lorna, but you mentioned mugging. Would he have had a cash bag with him tonight?"

She bit her lip. "Probably not."

"Mrs. Tyler, your husband will be moved to ICU soon, and you can stay with him if you like. I'll alert the nurses."

"Yes, please. I want to be with him."

The doctor went back into the ER, Shoar behind him, and for long minutes none of us moved. The only sound in the waiting room was the ER night clerk typing on her keyboard. I wondered what the doctor was telling Eric that he didn't tell Lorna. Not that I imagined he was withholding information about Clark's medical status. Rather I thought he was giving an opinion about how Clark got the injuries.

I finally filled the silence. "Well, if we're running the café tomorrow, I should get Trudy back."

"She's right. With all hands on deck tomorrow, we need to hit the rack early."

"Here, child," Sherry said, and taking my Camry keys from her jacket pocket. "You drop Trudy off, and come back for us."

MY CELL SHOWED THE TIME AS NINE THIRTY WHEN I pulled into the inn parking lot, and judging by the empty streets we'd traveled, the concertgoers had gone home.

The crime scene team had not. They were still at work when I pulled into the near-vacant parking lot and killed the engine.

"Where is Jeanette's car?" Trudy fretted, scanning the lot and the street.

"The police probably parked it out of the way."

"Or the crime scene people have to check it to see if I was telling the truth about braking in time."

"Or that," I agreed because there was no point denying it. Then I glanced in my rearview mirror. "Detective Shoar is already back here, so you can ask him."

Eric jogged straight to the crime scene techs. Trudy sighed.

"Nixy, should I tell him about the yearbook page?"

"You need to make that call."

"Can you look into it first? I don't get a great Internet connection here at the inn."

But I got great service at Sherry's, and seeing Eric walking toward us, I made a snap decision. "I'll see what I can find out, but you tell Detective Shoar about the page anytime you want to."

"As you can see, the techs aren't finished," he said as we exited the car. "I'll have to take you around the front to let you inside, Ms. Henry."

"Call me Trudy, please."

He gave her a short nod. "Nixy, you want to come?"

I was surprised by the invitation, but I shrugged. Maybe I could get more information out of him.

"Sure."

"Where is my car?" Trudy asked as she walked us around to the square.

"We need to have a look at it in the daylight, so it's at the station. I'll bring it over as soon as they finish tomorrow. But," he added, "I put your shopping bags inside."

"You did?" Trudy beamed at him. "Thank you! I'm so tired of wearing the same clothes, I could scream."

He fit the key in the lock and opened the front door with a flourish. Street light filtered through the large front windows, and an old-fashioned sconce lit the bottom steps with a low-wattage bulb. Even softer light shone from higher on the stairs.

"Your bags are over on the staircase, Trudy. Would you like us to walk you to your room?"

"Thanks, but I'll go up on my own. The ghost will protect me."

Chapter Twenty-one

"GHOST?"

"Yeah, I call him Cowboy. So what time should I be ready to work tomorrow?"

"Uh, by six, I think. Six thirty at the latest."

"See you then."

With that, Trudy clomped to the staircase, swept up her shopping bags, and climbed the steps. When the landing door thumped shut, I turned to Eric.

"Ghost?"

He grinned. "It's a long-standing rumor."

"I'm sure that's all it is, but I saw a shadow Monday night when I brought Trudy home from the hospital."

"Where was this shadow?"

"Outside the door on the landing up there. The one that leads from the inn down to the café. It's a half-glass, half-wood door."

"I know. You can't see a thing through that glass."

"Nothing but faint light and the shadow."

"Interesting, but I can't question a ghost. Come on, I need to get back."

I preceded him out, watched him lock up and jiggle the knob.

"Where'd you get the café keys?"

"Fished them out of Clarke's pocket. We needed to be sure the attack didn't happen inside."

"It didn't," I said, and he raised a brow at me. "If he'd been hurt that badly inside, but crawled to the alley, he wouldn't have locked up."

"I'll give you that, but if I'd had to shut down Lorna's kitchen, I wanted to be able to warn her about it tonight."

"Good thing you didn't have to."

"The six-o'clock thing?"

"The seniors, Trudy, and I are working the café first thing in the morning so Lorna won't have to cancel a luncheon that's already been paid for."

"The breakfast and lunch crowds keep the café jumping on Saturdays, so I'm sure she'll appreciate your help."

"Yes, but she'd really like to know what happened to her husband and why."

"You don't have your own theory, Nixy Drew?"

"Aren't you hilarious," I drawled, adding an eye roll for good measure. "I do have several theories, but hey, you're the detective."

His lips quirked. "Good of you to remember."

"As bad as I feel for Lorna," I went on as I stopped at the mouth of the alley, "doesn't this take Aunt Sherry off your suspect list? She was with us from the time I left Clark until Trudy screamed. Two victims of violence in about as many days isn't a coincidence, and since Sherry didn't bash Clark, it's reasonable she didn't kill Elsman."

"It's not that simple. You've seen the physical evidence I have. It implicates Miz Sherry Mae, and it will until I get reports from the state lab."

"I still think Clark knew something about Elsman's killer, and that's why he's been attacked, but it could be something else. Like he owed money to the wrong people."

He held my gaze. "What wrong people? Is this about the gambling rumor?"

"It's not a rumor. Lorna confirmed it tonight while we waited with her. He was gambling on the Internet. They fought about it today."

He looked away. "How angry is she?"

"Not enough to beat up her own husband, if that's what you're thinking. She's frustrated and hurt by his deception, but she's even more frightened."

His mouth tightened. "I'll talk with her. Meantime, work in the café tomorrow. Help Lorna. Watch out for yourself and Miz Sherry Mae and her friends. Let me investigate my leads without worrying about having a next victim."

"Hey, I've helped with leads, you know. Like Mrs. Gilroy being a sort of witness, and—"

He held up a hand. "Conceded, but your help is raising my blood pressure." He put his hands on my shoulders, then trailed them down my arms before he let go. "The best thing you can do to is stick close to the Six and stay safe."

He strode to the crime scene techs, and the breath I didn't realize I'd held came out in a long sigh. Of all the towns in all the world, why had I stumbled into his? And why oh why had Mrs. Gilroy's remark about warm male bodies taken root in my head?

I shook myself and hotfooted it to my car. Pick up the ladies, get home, go to bed, and work hard not to dream of Eric Shoar. That was my plan, and I was sticking to it.

THE SUN WASN'T YET UP WHEN WE ARRIVED AT THE Lilies Café the next morning. We'd taken all three cars in case we needed to make a grocery run or the day got to be

too much for anyone. We each donned aprons from Maise's
stash, too, in case Lorna didn't have enough for all of us.
Fred and Dab wore half aprons, but the women had the full
bib versions. Which I'm sure Eleanor appreciated. She was
dressed to the nines as usual. The rest of us were in working
clothes, me in one of my new pairs of jeans and a stretchy top.

I'd noticed Lilyvale kept its streets clean, and there wasn't
so much as a scrap of paper in the alley to indicate Clark
had been attacked there. Not even the kind of detritus the
paramedics had left behind when they'd treated Sherry at
the farmhouse. I was happy about that for Lorna's sake.

The Six had naturally been disappointed the night before
when I'd told them Clark's attack hadn't erased Sherry from
Shoar's suspect list, but they didn't seem to have a thing on
their minds today except running the café. Trudy had
already turned on the lights, so we all set to work.

I pitched in with Dab and Trudy to set the tables with
utensils and napkins, be sure the salt and pepper shakers
were sufficiently filled, and add packets of sugar and artifi-
cial sweeteners to the white holders.

Fred familiarized himself with the bar area, where the
coffee and soda machines sat and the glasses were stored.
Then, because he'd refused to leave his tool belt at home,
he clacked his walker around the front of the restaurant,
oiling a hinge here, tightening a screw there.

"Told you somethin' would need fixin'," he said to no
one in particular.

At seven, Dab unlocked the front doors, and the stream
of customers began flowing in, despite the fact that it was
barely light. In fact, though sunrise had come, dark clouds
threatened rain.

"'Bout time," one man said. "Been a dry April so far. We
need rain."

And we got it not two hours later in the form of drizzles,
but that didn't hurt business. I consistently scooted to the

kitchen and bar for food and drink orders, bussed my tables, reset them, then started all over again. Trudy and Dab were just as busy, as was Fred. Sherry and the ladies cooked, plated meals, and kept one of the dishwashers running constantly.

Honestly, I didn't know how Lorna and Clark ran the café by themselves.

When I voiced that aloud, Sherry laughed. "It's busier than usual because the town's turning out to support the Tylers. I'm sure Lorna has a load of food that's been left at the house, too."

Ah yes, trouble food. I wondered if Maise would be whipping up something for Lorna or if café duty equaled a covered dish. It sure did for me.

The customers we were most concerned with, the book club ladies, were a breeze to serve. Trudy and I had teamed up to wait on the party of ten, and they raved not only about Lorna's potpies and the decadent desserts, but also the petite side salad and special dressing Maise had whipped up.

Finally, at about two in the afternoon, the crowd thinned, and we took turns breaking for a bite to eat. I was too tired to be hungry, so Maise fixed me half a sandwich made with the last of the roast beef she had found in the industrial fridge. She offered soup, too, but I declined.

As I settled at a table by the bar, my feet propped on a chair, and bit into my refreshingly cold sandwich, I realized I'd been in Lilyvale a full week. A week that felt like a month, but in a good way. I needed to call the art gallery again and tell Barbra not to expect me for another few days. Or a week, I amended and idly wondered if the latest showing was going well. Oddly, I found I didn't truly care. That was a little scary because I enjoyed my career.

I also needed to run a search for Trudy Whitman.

I stood outside under the café awning to call Barbra. Instead I reached my big boss, the gallery owner Felina Gates. When she told me to take my time, assuring me my job was safe, I about happy-danced on the spot.

I Googled Trudy Whitman next, but as the first results popped up, so did my quasi-favorite detective.

"Any coffee left?"

"Fred just brewed a new pot. Come on in."

He followed and I waved him toward the coffee station as I took a seat and closed my phone's search screen. "Everyone is in the back, cleaning. Do you mind serving yourself?"

He grinned. "Waiting tables harder than you thought?"

"Let's just say I'm out of shape for this kind of work," I said as he went behind the bar. "How is Clark? Have you heard?"

"I saw him this morning. Lorna, too."

"Will he need surgery? Is he awake?"

"He's awake, but he's still pretty out of it. He doesn't remember anything from last night. As for surgery, so far, so good. He's being closely monitored."

He came to the table and took the chair next to mine. I noticed then that he looked exhausted and yet a little excited. Or maybe he was just wired on caffeine. He took a few sips of steaming coffee and leaned back in his seat.

"Did you get any sleep?"

"Not much. Between Jill Elsman's murder and the attack on Clark, Chief Randall is on a rant. I understand that. I'm as fed up as he is waiting for information. Waiting for leads to actually lead somewhere. Although we did get one break."

Hope surged so strongly, I nearly leapt into his lap to hear the news. "Did you hear back from the state crime lab about the murder?"

"Not yet. This is about the attack on Clark."

"Well, tell me. Did the crime scene techs find something?"

"They're still cataloging, and everything will go to—"

"Little Rock. I know. That's your mantra. Will you please stop the torture already and tell me about the break? You know you can trust me not to blab."

He nodded and sipped again. "Okay, we got a tip from

some guys out hunting feral hogs in the woods on the far side of Stanton Lake."

"Razorbacks? Somebody hunts those at night? Aren't they dangerous?"

"They don't attack unless defending their dens."

"Okay, so the hunters tipped you to what?"

"One of them tripped over a baseball bat. When they looked at it with their high-powered flashlights, they saw blood and hair residue on the end of it. They'd heard about the attack on Clark before they went hunting, and called their find in to us. The techs and I went out, and we may have a few viable footprints, too."

"The hunters didn't see or hear anyone in the woods?"

"No, I wasn't that lucky, but I'm taking what I can get."

He took a long swallow of the cooling coffee. I didn't dwell on details like his strong jawline or the muscles bunching in his arms. Nope, not me.

He cleared his throat, and I snapped my gaze to his. "So I don't suppose you heard any useful gossip from customers."

"Lots of exclaiming about Clark, lots of sympathy for him and Lorna. A little speculation about needing more officers. That's it."

"Yeah, about now I could use the help." Again he drank, this time in swallows instead of sips, so the coffee must've cooled. Then he reached into his jeans pocket and pulled out keys. "These are for Trudy. Her car was clean, so I parked it in the lot for her."

"She'll be relieved to know that. Thanks."

He stood and pulled out his wallet, but I waved him away. "Go. Your coffee is on the house today."

"Is that an executive decision?"

"You bet, and Lorna would agree."

He smiled down at me. "Don't work too hard."

He ambled out, and you know I paid due attention to that rear view.

I also had a twinge of conscience about keeping the year-book page to myself. Then again, it was Trudy's story to tell. I'd see what I could find, and go from there.

I TOOK MY PLATE AND GLASS, AND TRUDY'S KEYS, to the kitchen. Maise stirred a pot of what smelled like a chicken dish, and Aster checked rolls in the oven. Trudy and Eleanor wiped the stainless steel counters while Sherry, Dab, and Fred perched on metal stools with wooden seats.

"No customers," I said when Dab started to rise. "Detective Shoar was here, but he only wanted coffee."

"Roger that. We're out of most everything except desserts and the chicken and dumplings here. Just put your dishes in the sink."

"I'll wash them. Oh, and Trudy, he brought your car back and parked it in the lot. Here are your keys."

"Thanks, Nixy. I wish he'd tell me I can go home."

"I have a feeling it'll be soon," I said and turned on the hot water. And I mean hot. I adjusted it to the far side of warm and scrubbed.

"What did Detective Shoar have to say?" Sherry asked.

"That Clark is doing well but doesn't remember being attacked."

"No, he doesn't," a familiar voice said.

A chorus of "Lorna!" rang out, followed by hugs.

Lorna looked awful. No makeup, reddened eyes, hairdo smashed on one side. I don't know what kept her upright except willpower.

Sherry steered Lorna to the café. "Let's sit out here so we won't miss any customers coming in."

"Were you busy today?"

"Slammed," I told her. "Everyone said to give you and Clark best wishes."

Lorna's lips tightened and she swallowed. "Lilyvale is a

town of generous-hearted people. Even when the detective had to question me about who could have it in for Clark, he was kind. He put a guard on Clark's hospital door."

My gaze met Sherry's. "Why is that?" she asked.

"He's afraid Clark knows something about Jill Elsman's murder. Something he doesn't know he knows. Eric wants to protect him. And me."

Her voice went raw, and more tears threatened. I handed her a napkin, and she blotted her face.

"I want to thank you, thank you all, for taking over the café today."

"We're happy to help," Dab said with a pat on her hand.

"Reminded me of the time we nurses had to take over the shipboard mess hall," Maise declared.

"We've already discussed it, and we'll run things tomorrow, too," Aster added. "I'm sure the after-church crowd will come in."

Lorna smiled, shook her head. "Thank you, but no. I've decided to close tomorrow. I'll probably close for the week."

"But, Lorna—"

"No, Sherry Mae, I need the time away to focus on Clark. Besides, I've been closed only for holidays for years now. I want a break."

"Then take the time. Your customers will be here when you're ready to reopen. Now, have you eaten? Maise has chicken and dumplings, and there are a dozen lemon bars and turnovers."

"I do believe there are chocolate croissants, too," Eleanor added.

"I need to get back, but I'll take some servings with me. If Clark can have more than liquids for dinner, he'll love the chicken and dumplings."

I stayed at the table with Fred, Dab, Eleanor, and Trudy while the other women trooped to the kitchen. When Lorna came out with a large glass bowl with a lid and a flat rectangular plastic container, Dab rose.

"Let me help you with those, Lorna."

"Appreciate it, Dab. My car is just outside." At the door she turned. "Thank you all again. I'll figure out a way to repay you."

Fred snorted. "Let us know next time you make them turnovers so I can be first in line."

Lorna flashed a grateful smile. "It's a deal, Fred."

"What now?" Trudy asked. "Do we stay open Lorna's regular hours?"

"She told us just now in the kitchen," Sherry said, "to close about four. She asked us to take leftovers home or pack them up along with any other perishables and drop them at the food bank."

"Good, then I'm goin' upstairs to check for squeaky doors. You know of anything else up there that needs fixin'?" Fred directed the question to Trudy.

"Uh, yes, sir. One of the sinks leaks."

"Then you come help me."

"Sure, Mr. Fishner," she said, beaming.

That struck me as odd until I realized she'd been a cheerful ball of energy today. And her comment about being bored and having no friends. I didn't think she'd be counting Fred as a friend, precisely, but she was occupied.

Sherry and the ladies went to the kitchen to begin packing perishables, but I knew they'd hold back desserts for Fred. Okay, for all of us.

Dab had come back, and we set to work looking for the flattened boxes that were in the storage room. We found the tape, too, and as we securely taped the flaps, Dab took them to the kitchen to be loaded with food.

I'd just dragged out two last medium-sized boxes when the bell over the door jangled, and Bryan Hardy strode into the café.

"If you're here to eat, there isn't much left." No, I did not use my polite voice, and he didn't seem to notice.

His glance darted around the room. "I'd hoped to catch Lorna here."

"Why?" I put the box flats on the table with the tape and started assembling them. He moved marginally closer as if to help me, but he didn't lift a finger.

"I went to the hospital to see how Clark is, but the guard wouldn't let me in. Which," he said, spreading his hands, "I guess I understand. The officer is following orders as he should, but I am also an officer of the court."

Huh. Did he sound nervous or just perturbed that the guard hadn't bowed to his position as a prosecutor? I mentally shrugged. Probably the latter. Pinched pride.

"Well?" he demanded. "Have you seen Lorna?"

I ground my teeth at his tone. Had I thought of him as shy? How wrong could I be? He had the arrogant attitude his aunt did. I ripped off a length of tape and applied it to the bottom flaps.

"Lorna was here a while ago. She said Clark is doing well except he doesn't remember anything."

Bryan looked startled and took a step closer. "He doesn't remember being ambushed?"

"Who said he was ambushed?"

He seemed startled, then gave me a pitying look. "It stands to reason," he said slowly, as if talking to an idiot. "Clark would fight back if he saw an attack coming. Does the doctor think he'll get his memory back?"

"It's a head injury. Who knows?" I put a second strip of tape on the box.

He frowned, shook his head. "I hope he'll remember how to play golf."

"Golf?"

"That's how we got to be friends. Playing every Sunday in a foursome. This is the first time he'll miss a round. Guess it'll be a threesome for a while." He gave me a hard stare. "I hope you took my advice to stop asking questions about Elsman's murder."

I stared back. "I'll stop when my aunt is cleared and not a second before."

"Then it's your problem if you end up like Clark."

I opened my mouth to peel a strip off his hide, but Dab came out of the kitchen.

"Nixy, do you have another box ready? Hello, Bryan."

"Dab," Bryan returned.

I handed Dab the assembled box, and Hardy backed up a step.

"Well, I'll be off. Tell Lorna to call me if she needs anything."

I nodded and watched him stroll out, the door banging behind him.

"What was that about?"

"He's ticked that he couldn't get in to see his good buddy, Clark," I said as I quickly taped the second box's flaps down.

"I'm surprised. Other than playing golf, I've never seen them socialize."

"He didn't seem happy with the foursome being a threesome. He acted like he wanted to drag Clark out of the hospital to play."

Dab grinned. "I imagine there's money on the line."

"What?"

"It's not a lot, just a friendly wager. Put ten bucks in the pot and the winner gets the money and buys drinks for the losers."

"Sounds like you golfed. Do you still play?"

"Nah. I was in a couples' league with my wife. It wouldn't be the same."

My heart lurched, and I kicked myself for being flip, although Dab didn't appear to mind. He carried the boxes to the kitchen, and I checked the wall clock. Three forty-eight.

I didn't want to wait any longer to follow up on the yearbook page. If researching the Whitman girl could clear Sherry, I was on board. But Trudy was right about wireless being iffy here at the café, and I didn't want to stand outside in the drizzle. I could do the search at Sherry's farmhouse or—

"Dab, what time does the library close?"

"At five on Saturdays."

"If we're about finished here, do y'all mind if I take off?"

He gave me an appraising look. "You following a clue?"

"It may be a goose chase, but I have to give it a shot."

"Go. We've got this covered."

Chapter Twenty-two

THE LIBRARIAN'S NAME BADGE READ DEBBIE NICOLE Samp, and she was in her early thirties, much younger than I'd expected. Her blonde hair cut in a breezy style, she wore a denim skirt with an embroidered tee and low-heeled pumps.

"Hi, Ms. Samp. I don't have a library card, but—"

"You're Sherry Mae Cutler's niece, right? What do you need?"

Had to love the grapevine. "To research a name, and maybe look at yearbooks from Fairlaine University if you have any."

She brightened. "Fairlaine in Texarkana? I went there, but I doubt we carry any annuals. Most of ours are from Lilyvale High School. Oh, but some old yearbooks are online. How far back are you looking?"

I gave her a range of six years to be inclusive. Good thing I'd remembered to ask Trudy for a few more details—such as where and when Elsman had attended college and what she'd majored in—before I'd rushed over here. Yes, she'd wanted to come with me, but I told her to keep helping Fred with his fix-it jobs. I needed to do this without her.

The library had access to online newspapers, even those that required a subscription to read the actual news. Debbie Nicole set me up at one of their three computer stations. I checked the clock behind the circulation desk. Four fifteen. I had under an hour to discover why Elsman might've kept the yearbook page with Trudy Whitman's photo circled.

Given the "RIP" notation, I began my search with obituaries in Texarkana. Sure enough, I found Trudy Faith Whitman of Texarkana, Texas. With dark hair and a bright smile, she'd been just a day past her twenty-first birthday when she died. The obit didn't give a cause of death, but it wouldn't. I knew that from having written my mother's obituary with Aunt Sherry. The piece, however, did mention that Trudy Whitman had been a dean's list junior at Fairlaine University, studying business.

Hellspawn had not only attended the university in the same time frame as Whitman, she was also in the business program. Score one for the home team. However, Trudy's cousin had been a freshman when Whitman died. Had they known each other personally? I supposed Hellspawn could simply have known *of* Whitman. Had they taken classes together? I'd known a few upperclassmen, especially via the art lab. For all I knew the two women could've roomed together, but my speculation was burning library time.

Next I looked for the university's online yearbooks and struck gold. Well, silver. There was no search feature within the yearbooks, so it took a while to locate Whitman's photo in multiple years of annuals, in sorority pages first. I had a hard time believing a sorority would take Hellspawn, and sure enough her picture wasn't in any Greek group. I tried an "Activities" heading and found a page depicting the business club selling T-shirts to benefit a local homeless shelter. Whitman's bright smile beamed front and center of the photo, and then I did a double take at the younger and—stop the presses—smiling Hellspawn standing beside her.

Okay, so they'd gone to college together, for at least part of a year. I couldn't imagine Hellspawn making actual friends, not from what Trudy and Jeanette said about her, but Whitman was listed as a club officer. Sucking up to her? That I could see.

I had confirmed a connection, but now what? Why circle the young woman's photo? Why keep the yearbook page in that Lilyvale binder? Did it have something to do with how Whitman died?

I went back to the newspaper home page and typed in her name again. Several results came up just as the library lights blinked twice and Debbie Nicole made the rounds to announce she'd be closing in five minutes. I quickly scanned the headlines and partial paragraphs.

Apparent prank turns deadly. Tragic shooting in early hours Thursday. Illegal entry through open window. Honor Student wore a costume helmet. Carried a fake sword. Ms. Whitman. Dead on arrival.

I LEFT THE LIBRARY REELING AND DIDN'T SEE TRUDY until she was right in front of me.

"What are you doing here?"

"Waiting for you," she said, nearly hopping from foot to foot. "I helped your aunt and her friends deliver the food, and then drove over here and saw your car in the lot. I was afraid I'd miss you if you called."

"Why didn't you come inside?"

"I would've interrupted you. So, did you learn anything? Did Jill go to school with the Whitman girl?"

"She did, and I think it's time to tell Detective Shoar about that yearbook page."

"And if he already knows?"

"Then my conscience is clear."

"It's that bad?"

"It isn't good, but I don't know what it all means. I need to call Sherry and let her know I'll be a while longer."

*   *   *

SHOAR MET US AT THE DAIRY QUEEN THIRTY MIN-
utes later. I'd been around food all day and wasn't hungry,
but a banana shake made a start in calming my nerves.

Trudy, on the other hand, had a double cheeseburger,
fries, and a diet cola.

Eric got a black coffee before he joined us in a back booth
I'd chosen so we could be the most private. Not that there
were many diners at the moment, but I was being cautious.

"You two look guilty," he said. "How did you get into
trouble working at the café all day?"

I gave Trudy a go-ahead nod.

"Um, Detective, first, I need to tell you about what I
overheard Jill say on the phone about Mr. Tyler a few
weeks ago."

Good for Trudy. She was laying it all on the line, just like
I'd encouraged her to do.

He didn't look happy when she ended the tale, but he
didn't yell. "I'm glad you told me. Is there something else?"

"It's about that binder of Jill's. Have you looked all the
way through it?"

"I have. All I saw was lists of property owners, addresses,
approximate values, and notes. Why?"

"Were any of the plastic sleeves empty?"

"What's going on?"

"Well, again I didn't think of this until Friday night, after
Mr. Tyler was hurt. Jill had a yearbook page in the back of
the book."

"You told me you never saw the contents."

"Just once," she said, and described to him what she had
to me.

He frowned. "Why are you just coming to me with this?"

She waved a hand. "If you already knew about the page,
you'd think I was an idiot. So I asked Nixy to look up the
Whitman girl."

He leveled those brown eyes on me. "Did you tell Trudy to keep quiet?"

I shook my head, but Trudy answered, "No, she did not. She told me I should do what I felt was right."

He pinched the bridge of his nose. "I take it you did the research, Nixy?"

"Late this afternoon, but the library closed before I could finish."

I filled him in on the Whitman girl and her apparent connection to Elsman. His posture grew rigid as I talked, but his expression went almost blank. When I related the little I'd read about Whitman's death, what I'd pieced together, he looked strung tight enough to snap. I soldiered on with my part of the story. Maise would be proud.

"So, of course, we had to tell you," I finished. "I don't know whether this coed's death over a decade ago has anything to do with Elsman's death now, but you have the resources to take it from here."

"Not to mention that you're locked out of the online newspaper until the library opens Monday."

His tone made me cringe, but he didn't look like he'd have a coronary over my latest round of snooping.

"There is that."

He held my gaze with his laser cop stare, then seemed to lighten up.

"All right, ladies, thank you for your information. I'll follow up this evening."

He tossed back the rest of his coffee and stood.

"Um, Detective Shoar," Trudy ventured, "what should I do now?"

"You go to the inn and stay put. Nixy goes home and stays put."

"I meant is it okay for me to leave Lilyvale? Like tomorrow? I promise you, I don't know anything else."

"And I promise you I'll let you go home as soon as I can. Monday, if everything works out."

With that, he strode from the restaurant with purpose.

Trudy's wide eyes met mine. "Do you think he knows who killed Jill?"

I DROVE TO SHERRY'S WONDERING THE SAME THING but didn't have time to ponder long.

The Silver Six sat at the kitchen table waiting for me.

"Nixy, child, what took you so long?"

I took a deep breath, and it didn't hurt that I inhaled a lungful of Aster's lavender scent. I answered with partial truths.

"I saw Trudy and took her to the DQ."

"That gal can put away the food, can't she?" Fred said on a chuckle. "Must have a hollow leg, just like my mama used to say about teenaged boys."

"Did your library trip turn up anything new?" Dab asked.

"Brief us, Nixy. What did you research?"

I didn't want to share all the down-and-dirty facts, so I skimmed the surface. "You know how we've been looking for who Elsman could've known here in town? Well, Trudy said she attended Fairlaine University, so I looked up old yearbooks online."

"Fairlaine?" Sherry said. "Why, Bryan Hardy went there before he went out west for law school. Who else, Eleanor? Do you remember?"

My ears perked hearing that Hardy went to Fairlaine. Did his years there overlap with Elsman's and Whitman's? I'd look him up later.

"I do believe Debbie Nicole Samp, the librarian, attended all four years, although that was more recently. Is she still seeing Bryan, I wonder?

I about choked. Debbie Nicole was dating Bryan? Would she mention my library visit? What I'd researched? Or was there a librarian-patron confidentiality rule?

"I know there are others your age, Nixy," Sherry chimed

back in, "and some four or five years older who were educated at Fairlaine. You met the older set of residents this trip. Maybe you'll meet the younger ones next time."

"What I want to know," Fred said, "is did your researchin' get you any closer to clearin' Sherry's name?"

I spread my hands. "Honestly, I don't know."

"I'm sure Shoar will solve the case soon," Dab soothed.

"Are you hungry?" Sherry asked. "Oh, but I guess you ate with Trudy."

"Actually, I didn't. After being around food all day, I wasn't hungry."

"I do believe we saved a chocolate croissant for you if you want it."

"With a cup of chamomile tea, it hits the spot," Aster declared.

"That sounds great, but I need to shower first. That is, gentlemen, if you don't need the bathroom for a few minutes."

"Go ahead, missy. Dab and I want to watch a little basketball, then we're for bed."

With that, he snagged his parked walker and preceded Dab to his room.

Sherry looked after them with obvious fondness. "We'll all turn in early, I'm sure, but we're making tentative plans for tomorrow."

"Other than church?"

Her eyes twinkled. "Actually, we're skipping church and going to the flea market in Texarkana."

"We get inspiration for our own projects seeing what's for sale there," Aster said.

"And it's not a far drive," Maise added.

"Fred and Dab like to go to the flea market, too?" I asked doubtfully.

"They do, plus it'll get us away from town for the day."

Eleanor's reasoning sealed it for me.

"Then I'm in."

* * *

AS I SHOWERED AND WASHED MY HAIR, I MULLED. IF Bryan Hardy had gone to Fairlaine when Whitman and Hellspawn were there, had he known one or both of them? I itched to get out my tablet and look up the yearbooks again, but I visited with the ladies while I ate the croissant and sipped tea. Both did wonders to restore my energy, and I had fun listening to the ladies chat about their day.

When they turned in, I wanted to run for my tablet but needed to blow-dry my hair first. Otherwise, I feared disturbing Fred. My arms were so weak from lugging trays of dishes and drinks all day, holding the lightweight dryer felt like wielding a load of bricks.

I reached in my bag to snag my tablet and felt something sticky. A candy wrapper, I saw. Shoot. It was some of the trash Dab and I had picked up Wednesday night. I'd taken out the big wads of paper but forgotten about the smaller pieces. Now they were mixed in with the receipts I'd thrown in my purse for more than a week.

I dumped the contents on the coffee table, flattened them, and sorted the keepers from the trash. When I came to a scrap of glossy paper a little bigger than my palm, I paused. The ragged piece looked like a page torn from a high-end magazine or coffee table book, but the pictures on the swatch were black and white. The image in the bottom right corner was a finial. The photo above and to the left showed part of a woman's lower arm draped with a scarf. She had a small birthmark at the bend of her elbow. I turned the paper over but found only half of a circle. Curious, but time was wasting. I gathered the photo page and other bits, tossed them in the kitchen trash can, and curled up on the couch with my tablet.

First I pulled up the Fairlaine annuals and searched pages for Bryan Hardy. I found him in a fraternity during the same time period Whitman attended the university. Hardy was a class ahead of her, a senior to her junior status. I clicked onto the "Activities" section, but didn't find a photo of Whitman and Hardy together. Not until I stumbled onto issues of the university newspaper that had been included in the yearbooks.

There I found a group shot of students standing on a homecoming float. Whitman was pictured waving at the crowd. And eureka! Bryan Hardy stood next to her. I enlarged the photo on my tablet, even used Sherry's magnifying glass to be certain.

Which didn't mean they actually knew each other, but it documented them being at the same place at the same time at least once.

Hmm. Would the student newspaper have run an article about Whitman's death? I jumped ahead to a spring issue published after her death. The short piece proved skimpy on facts other than listing Whitman's activities and praising her as an outstanding student. It did state that authorities believed she had been the victim of a prank, but others involved had not come forward, and the homeowner who shot her was not being charged.

Something niggled at me, so I went back to Whitman's sorority photo. I studied the page, the entire page, and saw it. I sprinted to the kitchen, fished the piece of paper I wanted out of the trash, and brought it back to compare.

The finial appeared at the bottom right corner of the online yearbook page. Whitman's photo was near it, complete with the scarf draped over her arm, and the birthmark at the bend of her elbow. Same-sized mark. Same shape.

The torn paper in my hand had been part of the yearbook page in Hellspawn's binder. A solid piece of evidence.

I sank against the sofa back and strove to order my thoughts. Okay, so what did this mean?

As Patricia could attest, Hellspawn was a known blackmailer.

Did she blackmail the killer into being her accomplice by showing him the yearbook page?

If so, did that mean Hellspawn's killer was the prankster, or one of a group of them, responsible for Whitman's death?

Following that line of reasoning, the killer had taken the yearbook page and ripped it to pieces to break the connections among him, Whitman, and Hellspawn herself.

Logical, although I'd have buried or burned the pieces.

The only person I knew of who currently lived in Lilyvale and had attended Fairlaine with both women was Bryan Hardy. He had a reputation to protect. A law career to protect, for heaven's sake. True, I'd not heard he was ever seen with Hellspawn, but if they were conspirators, they wouldn't want to look too cozy, now would they?

Memories flashed of my conversations with Hardy. All but accusing Sherry of the murder. Warning me off snooping. Fishing for information about the evidence. Heck, fishing for information about Clark's condition. Afraid his buddy would forget how to play golf? Lame.

I looked at the time on my tablet, shocked that it was almost eleven. Call my detective friend tonight or not? I sighed and called, left a message, and plugged in my tablet and phone to charge for the road trip.

And hoped Shoar would have the case solved tomorrow.

SUNDAY MORNING DAWNED CLOUDLESS AND PLEAS-antly cool, and the Six and I were dressed, fed, and ready to get on the road at ten.

Then I remembered Trudy's basket. I phoned to let her know I'd bring it by, but she didn't answer. Which I found odd, but after all she'd been through, I figured she'd slept in.

"Y'all don't need to wait for me," I told the Six.

"You bring Sherry," Dab said, "I'll drive the rest of us, and Eleanor can call your cell to let you know where to meet us."

"Great. We shouldn't be more than twenty minutes behind you."

Dab and his group took off. As Sherry remembered

something else she needed upstairs my phone rang, and I was startled to see my roommate's photo pop up.

"What's up, Vicki?"

"Nixy, you're going to kill me, but Greg and I eloped this weekend. We're in Vegas."

I fell into a kitchen chair. "What happened?"

"My mother, his mother, and the guest list from hell. We couldn't take it anymore."

"Vicki, I'm not upset. Congratulations."

"The elopement isn't the issue. It's our new apartment. We can get into it early—the fifteenth of May—but that leaves you with our place, and I know you can't swing the rent by yourself."

I bit my lip. "We're renting month to month now, right?"

"Yes, and I can call the manager tomorrow to give our notice. The thing is, can you find a new apartment that fast?"

"I'll have to. Or I'll find another roommate."

"Greg and I will put out the word. Nixy, I'm really sorry to put you in this bind. By the way, when are you coming back?"

"As soon as I wrap things up here, I'll call you."

Sherry was eyeing me when I disconnected and dropped the phone into my hobo bag. "Problem in Houston?"

I didn't know how much she'd heard, but I shook my head.

"Just my roommate, Vicki. She and her fiancé eloped to Vegas to escape the wedding pressures. I'll go get Trudy's basket now."

I didn't turn on the basement fixture because light poured in through the windows. From the top of the stairwell door, Sherry tsked at me, then hovered there in case I needed help finding her stash.

I was on the bottom step when we heard the doorbell peal.

"You go on. I'll get the door."

I found the baskets were right where she'd left them last Saturday. I carried one of the last two by itshemp-and-blue-gingham handle, but stopped cold on the top step at the sound of a muffled voice coming from the front entry.

Chapter Twenty-three

I'D HEARD THAT VOICE BEFORE, AND I KNEW WHEN and where.

Monday night when I'd taken Trudy back to the inn. The voice had argued with Hellspawn in her room at the inn. Same cadence. Same energy.

The voice got louder then, and I nearly dropped the basket.

Bryan Hardy.

What the devil was he doing here? He was supposed to be where Shoar could arrest him.

Then another voice. Trudy, and she sounded frightened.

Last, Aunt Sherry said clearly, "Bryan Hardy, what on earth are you doing with that gun?"

A gun?

Acting on instinct, I quickly pulled the door between the kitchen and basement nearly closed. Just a crack remained, enough to hear Bryan herd Sherry and Trudy toward the kitchen. I looked for a weapon.

Fred, bless him, had installed two wooden racks on the

walls on either side of the stairs. Low enough to reach, but high enough that one didn't bump into whatever was stored there. Several hooks on the lower rack were empty and just wide enough to hang Sherry's baskets.

Another hook held the strap of a long, heavy-duty flashlight, almost a ringer for the kind cops carried. Better than bashing Bryan with a basket, and bash him I would. I just needed a chance.

A soft thud on the table. Papers rustled. I peeked through the slit in the door but caught only a glimpse of the creep.

"Where is that nosy niece of yours?"

"Tending to the cemetery," Sherry answered without missing a beat. "She'll be out there awhile."

"Call her."

I heard Sherry move to the wall phone by the back door. Then my cell rang in my purse.

"Damn it!" I heard what sounded like my bag, phone, tablet, and all hitting the floor. "All right. I'll deal with her when I finish with you two. Sit down. Right there at the table. Backs to the window. Face me."

Chair legs scraped on the wood floor, and I pictured where Sherry and Trudy sat. Bryan would face them from the other side of the pedestal table.

Paper rustled again. "Here, Trudy. Sign your suicide note."

"Jeanette will never believe I committed suicide."

"I said sign it. Now."

"It's all right, honey," Sherry Mae said. "Tell me what's in the note."

"He made me write that I killed Jill and attacked Mr. Tyler because he found out. Then that you and Nixy found me out, so you had to die, too."

"What's the last line?" Bryan barked.

"'I'm so sorry,'" Trudy recited.

"It's not a perfect plan, but a murder charge against you won't stick, Mrs. Cutler. I get that now. That's why you and

Trudy are about to tragically die. And if you don't drink the
lemonade spiked with antifreeze, I'll use the gun. You're
dying today, one way or the other."

I shivered at the surety, the finality in his tone, and tightened my grip on the flashlight.

"But why kill us?" Sherry asked. "Jill Elsman's death
could have been an unsolved crime."

Bryan laughed, and it sounded insane. "I couldn't chance
that. I wouldn't care if you'd gone to prison, Mrs. Cutler. My
aunt would love it, too, the old witch. But your nosy niece
wouldn't leave this alone. I know she looked at old Fairlaine
yearbooks online yesterday. If she hasn't put it together yet, she
will."

"Put what together?" Sherry asked, calmly and reasonably.
"Why did you murder Ms. Elsman? What did she do to you?"

"Do you know where I met that piranha? At Fairlaine.
She was a freshman, I was a senior, and I thought she'd be
easy to snow. She wasn't."

"Snow over what?" Trudy asked.

"I pulled a prank with some other guys. It went bad; the
girl died. Jill had followed us. She offered to keep quiet and
even to give me an alibi if I needed one. For a price. She knew
my political aspirations and said she'd call in the favor someday. I thought she was blowing smoke, because I never heard
from her. Not all through law school. Not after I moved back
here. Not until a few weeks ago, when she showed up in town.
Sneaked into my damned office in a disguise."

"You helped Jill vandalize Mrs. Cutler's property, didn't
you? Everyone thought I did it, but it was you all along." Trudy
sounded more indignant than scared now, and that was good.

"She didn't know I kept some of the crap from the barn."
He chuckled and it sent another chill down my spine. "When
Jill wanted me to send poisoned candy to Sherry, I hired the
same guy who blew up the mailbox to go buy two boxes. It
pays to have friends in low places. A little doctoring, and I
had candy for two. I couldn't believe that went wrong. Hell,

Jill never shared a thing with you, but she gave you the cursed candy. That time I underestimated her. I didn't do it again."

"What about Clark Tyler?" Sherry asked. "Why did you beat him?"

"That fool. He told me Lorna confronted him about Jill and his gambling, and then he hinted that he'd seen me in Jill's room late Monday night. He wanted money from me. Me." I heard a sound of disgust. "I'll have to finish him later After I kill your niece."

By now I had gripped the heavy flashlight so tightly for so long, my fingers were getting numb. I switched the light to my left hand and shook the right to restore feeling. I was going to need it, and soon.

Something slapped the table. "Sign the damn suicide note. I won't ask again."

I heard a rasp, something lightweight being slid across the table. Then a click. I pictured Trudy picking up his pen to sign. Sadly, he'd probably be smart enough to take the pen with him.

"Good. Now we come to the main event. Where are the glasses, Mrs. Cutler? The sooner you tell me, the sooner this will be over. And don't tell me I won't get away with this. I know how to disappear. I'm gone when I'm done here."

"Why don't you simply leave now?" Sherry asked.

"That's right," Trudy said. "Killing us is just slowing you down."

"Yeah, but it's payback for pissing me off. The glasses?"

"The cabinet to the left of the sink."

"See, that wasn't hard."

Hardy finally moved into my line of sight, his back to me. He tucked a pistol in the back waist of his pants, and I saw he wore blue medical gloves. And golf pants, a detail that oddly made my chills more intense.

His hands would be full with two glasses in seconds. Should I rush him now? I gathered myself to push the door open, hoping Fred had been as diligent in oiling these hinges as he had every other one in the house.

Suddenly, Bryan turned back to Sherry and Trudy. "Don't whisper. Don't even look at each other."

I shrank back, my heart rate still pounding, and strove to breathe quietly. I'd get another chance to rush him. I *had* to get that chance.

The cupboard door banged shut, glasses thunk-thunked on the table. Then I heard a short bursts of a screech or scrape. A cap being unscrewed?

Liquid made a glunking sound as he poured the antifreeze-lemonade cocktail. Sherry couldn't drink that. She'd been poisoned a week ago, and who knew what that had done to her kidneys or liver or whatever. Another poisoning, even if she got to the ER within five minutes, could be crippling to her health if not fatal.

Then I heard a ratchet sound that chilled me all over again. Pete the PI's assistant had shown me how to work the slide on his semiautomatic, and it was the same sound.

"Drink," Bryan commanded.

Odds were his back was to me. If nothing else, I could divert his attention from Sherry and Trudy to me. Sherry could run. Trudy just might be able to tackle the slimeball.

I eased the door open, and it didn't so much as whisper a sound. I peered around the corner of the door to see Sherry slowly stand. What the heck?

She clutched at her chest. "My heart. Oh dear, my heart."

Sherry met my gaze right before she folded to the floor. I knew she was faking the heart attack, except she hit her head on a wood chair seat with a wicked crack.

Trudy saw me, too, and heaved the table at the distracted Bryan, then hit the floor.

The thermos and glasses of poisoned lemonade flew at Bryan, and he fired. I rushed him, whacked his elbow, and he dropped the gun with a howl of pain and rage. He charged me, but I sidestepped and kicked the back of his knee. When he fell, I angled the flashlight at his head and swung.

Before I connected with Bryan's skull, strong arms

grabbed me from behind. I fought the hold until yelling penetrated my adrenaline rush.

"Stop, Nixy, stop. The cavalry is here."

"Eric?"

City police and county deputies swarmed the kitchen around us. Hardy lay facedown on the floor, handcuffed but thrashing and cussing a blue streak.

I stilled in Shoar's arms, panting for breath. Then I remembered.

"Sherry. She hit her head when she fell."

I pulled away and rushed to check on my aunt. Paramedics knelt on each side of her, and the rest of the Six hovered nearby.

"When did y'all get here?" I asked, dumbfounded.

"Long story, missy, but we're part of the rescue team."

"Okay." Was I still dazed?

Could be, because my hero detective took my elbow and steered me into the back hall, where Trudy leaned against Officer Bryant. I sagged against the wall.

"He confessed to everything," Trudy was saying. "He killed Jill, beat up Mr. Tyler, and poisoned the candy Mrs. Cutler and I ate." She ended on a sob.

"We'll get your statement. Just calm yourself," Bryant said.

I looked up at Shoar. "How did you know what was happening? That we were in trouble? Did you get the message I left last night?"

"Not until this morning. By then I'd followed the lead you and Trudy gave, made some calls to Texarkana, then had Hardy watched. When Trudy came outside this morning, he was seen forcing her into his car."

"I was going to breakfast," Trudy said. "He made me curl on the floorboard and drove around for a while before he parked."

"I followed them in a borrowed car. He parked a street over, and when Dab drove off with Fred and the ladies, he waited another ten minutes, then drove to Sherry's."

"How did Sherry's housemates get back here so fast?"

"They saw me heading toward the house and turned around. We had a convoy going."

"Bryan would've recognized Dab's car."

"Exactly. When I noticed them, I called Eleanor's cell and asked them to back off."

I gave him a wan smile. "Which they didn't do."

"Not as I wanted, but it worked out."

Just then, two officers escorted the now tight-lipped Hardy out the back door. But not before he shot me a glance of pure hatred.

I shivered, then straightened. "I want to go check on Sherry now."

Eric nodded and let me go, but followed.

"Stop fussing, Eleanor," I overheard as I stepped into the kitchen. "It's a small cut and it's on the other side."

Sherry's voice trembled and her face looked as white as the gauze bandage on the right side of her forehead. She wore a determined expression, though, from the set of her mouth to the steel in her eyes.

Eleanor was pale, too, as were the other housemates, but Eleanor jutted her chin at Sherry.

"I will not stop fussing. What if you've caused more damage to your vision?"

My heart seized all over again. "Aunt Sherry, what's wrong with your vision?"

Chapter Twenty-four

SIX PAIRS OF GUILTY GAZES MET MINE.

Sherry's baby blues blinked at me from the floor where she'd fallen when she'd fake swooned.

"Let me get to the parlor," she said, "and I'll explain."

"I still recommend that you go to the hospital, Mrs. Cutler," the paramedic said as he closed his black satchel. "You're gonna have a powerful goose egg on your head for sure."

"Pooh. I've already been in the ER this week. Once is enough. I'll rest, I'll use the ice pack you gave me, I'll be fine."

The paramedic helped Sherry stand, then Detective Shoar stepped in. Not one of the roommates looked at me as he led Sherry from the kitchen. I didn't know where Trudy and all the officers and deputies had gone, and I didn't care. I needed to find out what was wrong with Sherry.

She sat in the center of the sofa I'd been sleeping on. Aster arranged sofa pillows at her back, and Maise settled an afghan over her legs. The other three—Eleanor, Dab, and Fred—stood behind the couch.

Behind Sherry. Backing her up like bodyguards.

I pulled up an ottoman and took Sherry's hands in mine. "Whatever it is, please tell me."

Sherry's eyes grew teary, but she held her chin high. "First, you can stop imagining worst cases. I don't have cancer or heart disease or anything else potentially fatal."

"Then what do you have?"

"Macular degeneration, child. It's only in my left eye, and when I let my bangs fall over to cover it, I focus just fine using my right eye. I'm being treated, but there is the chance I could become legally blind."

I'm not sure whose hands shook more as I digested that.

"When did you get the diagnosis? Are you seeing a good doctor?"

"A specialist in Texarkana diagnosed me about eight months ago."

"Why didn't you tell me?"

"I didn't know you'd come to visit. When you did, I was afraid to tell you."

"Afraid of what?" I managed to say past the clog in my throat.

"Afraid," Fred snarled, his complexion gaining color by the second, "you'd have some fool notion of making her move to Houston with you."

"Afraid," Maise jumped in, "you'd want to put her in a home."

"But I wouldn't do that," I said, squeezing her hands. "I wouldn't make you move anywhere."

"Well, we weren't to know that," Fred snapped.

"She manages fine," Dab said as he laid his hand on her shoulder. "And I'm working on an herbal blend she can use as eye drops."

"That's why you want a working still?" Eleanor asked while Aster blurted, "That's your secret project?"

"Dab, that's so sweet." Sherry reached up to pat his hand, then turned back to me.

"I don't want you to think you have to take care of me,

Nixy. You're young, you have a job you love, and you already know we Six take care of each other."

"Yes, and you do an excellent job of it, but I hope you won't mind if I visit often. Houston is only about six hours away."

"Unless you have a lead foot," Shoar said from behind me, and I startled because I'd forgotten he was there, "But, Nixy, I need you to stay in town a few more days until I can wrap up loose ends."

"Trudy, too, I imagine," Sherry said.

"Trudy, too."

I sighed and stood to face him. "Do you need Aunt Sherry's statement right now?"

"Matter of fact, I need to get Trudy's first. I can come back for Miz Sherry Mae's statement later today."

"Stay for dinner when you do," Maise offered.

"Okay, then," I said, "let's reorganize. Sherry, you need to put that ice pack back on and rest. Maise can make tea, and Aster, I'm sure your lavender would help."

"I'll spray it all over the house, and I'll smudge, too."

"You ain't burnin' that stuff while I'm inside," Fred grumped. "Me and Eleanor'll help Dab with the still."

"Great, but let's get the kitchen in order first."

Shoar cleared his throat. "I'm afraid not. I have the crime scene techs on standby right outside, and they'll need the space."

"I forgot about that. Can Maise make tea?"

"Tell you what. Brief me on where Hardy stood, what he touched, and I'll have the team cover the areas Maise needs to use first. After that, give them an hour to wrap up."

"That works," Maise said. "Come along, Sherry. Let's get you upstairs. Why, I'll bet Aster has an herb that will help keep down the swelling and pain."

"Comfrey," Aster confirmed as she moved to Sherry's other side. "Just the ticket for bumps and bruises and broken noggins."

Left alone with Eric, I arched a brow. "Ready to debrief me?"

He smiled. "Watch it. You're beginning to sound like Maise."

"I could do worse."

"I guess you could. Let's go."

He called in his team, and they stood by in the back hall as I gave Eric the rundown on where Bryan had stood, what he'd touched, and what I surmised he'd touched.

"I thought you didn't see him," Eric said at one point.

"I did when he went to the cupboard. Otherwise, I saw glimpses of him and tracked him by sound."

Eric squeezed my hand. "You sorry you didn't get to brain Hardy to kingdom come?"

"Yes and no. Prison is a better punishment."

"That it is."

WHILE THE CRIME SCENE TECHS WERE BUSY IN THE kitchen, I straightened the parlor and dining room, then cleaned the downstairs bathroom and gathered damp towels. I did everything possible to avoid thinking about the long-term ramifications of Sherry's eye disease.

Sherry was right and wrong about my job. I had loved it, and if I got that promotion, I'd love it again. Love it more. But I'd also come to love Sherry, Eleanor, Fred, Aster, Dab, and Maise. They did look out for each other. They'd divided chores to suit their strengths. I knew now that they were light-years from senile, and that they were physically healthy overall.

They'd created a family of the heart, and I would put my own butt in a home before I put Sherry in one. She didn't need it. She wouldn't qualify.

And yet, as the Six aged, would they still be able to care for each other? Perhaps they'd do just as well as they did now. Mrs. Gilroy shone as an example of advanced-age independence. How she got normal household supplies, never mind that TV, was a mystery, but she did it. The Six could be as fortunate.

Or they could not be.

And what then?

The techs kindly told me they were leaving, and confirmed we could clean and restore the kitchen to our hearts' content. Before the van left the gravel drive, Dab, Fred, and Eleanor swarmed inside, and we set to work righting the kitchen. The four of us wiped fingerprint dust from the counters and cabinet doors, swept and mopped the floor, and got the table and chairs back where they belonged. I shuddered when I spotted the bullet hole in the wall. The shot Hardy had fired missed shattering the window by no more than a foot.

"I'll spackle that and repaint," Fred declared, and darned if he didn't pull the supplies out of his overalls and his walker tool belt.

I don't know what came over me, but I giggled.

"What's funny?" Fred barked.

"You. You're a walking hardware store."

"'Course I am. I'm Fix-It Fred."

"I'll bet you've got a tiny can of paint in that tool belt."

He peered into a belt pocket. "Yep, I do. Wanna see it?"

This time I laughed and kept laughing until tears came.

"Here now, missy," Fred grumbled. "We'll have none of that."

He clanked his walker nearer, dangled a large white handkerchief in my face. When I took it, he pulled out a chair and sat at the table.

"You saved Sherry," he said quietly. "You should be proud."

I met his eyes, hiccupping back another sob. "No, Fred. You saved her. The door to the basement didn't make a sound when I opened it. If it had squeaked even a little, Hardy would have heard it and killed all of us."

"Nah, Shoar had the kitchen under surveillance the whole time."

"He did?"

"So did we. We was all in hunkered in the trees. Shoar

wouldn't share his binoculars, though. Dab had to hotfoot it back to the car for his."

I sat back on my heels and stared. "You were all watching the house?"

"Sun was high enough, we could see right into the kitchen without the glare." He paused. "'Course, we ain't got no SWAT folks here. I guess you coulda been shot before Shoar got to you and the others."

That bubbled a laugh out of me, which earned a full-fledged smile from Fred.

"Gotta get back to work. You wanna learn to spackle?"

"Why not?"

NEIGHBORS AND FRIENDS BEGAN COMING BY WITH trouble food, and I let the seniors deal with visitors. I didn't want to talk about Bryan Hardy again until absolutely necessary. Like at his trial.

While trotting to and from the basement to run loads of laundry, I retrieved the basket Trudy wanted to buy. I phoned her to be sure she still wanted it. She was still at the police station, so the call went through, and she gave me her code to the back entrance of the inn so I could meet her in an hour. Then took the basket straight to my car parked out by the barn.

I couldn't help but wonder how Sherry could possibly crochet and weave her baskets or braid these handles with her vision impaired. Yes, I'd looked up macular degeneration on my tablet. I hadn't grasped all I'd read, but I wanted to go with her to her next appointment.

I stood near the chain-link fence, staring at the azalea bushes but not seeing them. My mind's eye saw Sherry instead. The joy in her eyes, the animation in her gestures as she recited the Stanton family stories. She'd sparkled, and I wanted her to keep her spark. More, I wanted to see it. If that meant coming to Lilyvale every single weekend, so be it. I could always stay at the inn.

Meantime, I needed to fold the last load of towels, peek in on Sherry, and let the ladies know I was meeting Trudy.

As I turned, I heard, "Sissy!" from right behind me.

I'm sure my eyes bugged out as I whirled around because Mrs. Gilroy, who from all reports never came out of her house, stood at the chain-link fence.

"Hi, Mrs. Gilroy. You do know my name is Nixy, not Sissy."

"Got your attention, didn't I? I called the cops when I saw that Hardy character show up this morning."

"You have a phone? I don't remember seeing one in your house."

She gave me a *duh* look. "I have an iPhone."

I blinked. "How did you get it?"

"I ordered it over the Internet, of course. Don't you e-shop?"

"Apparently not as much as you do."

"Anyway, it was the blue gloves that tipped me off that Hardy was up to no good. You be sure to tell that detective. If he wants to ask me questions, I'll let him in."

I had to grin. "First me, now Detective Shoar? Where will the madness end, Mrs. G?"

She shook her finger at me but her eyes twinkled. "Sassy. Just like your great-great-great-aunt Sissy. You deliver my message to the detective."

"Yes, ma'am."

She toddled off across the yard, arms pumping. The woman was in scary-good shape. I wouldn't be surprised if she'd ordered gym equipment from the Internet. Who knew what she had stashed in the front bedroom I hadn't seen.

And, come on. An iPhone? How had she gotten service activated without going to a store?

MY MEETING WITH TRUDY WAS SHORT. PARKED IN the near-vacant lot behind the inn, I punched Trudy's code into the keypad and found her in the second en suite room the inn boasted. A large suitcase piled with clothes lay open on the bed.

"Hey, Nixy, thanks for coming," she said as she handed me a twenty-dollar bill that had lain on the chest of drawers.

"After all that's happened, I was concerned you wouldn't want the basket. I'm glad you do."

"This basket will be my best memory of Lilyvale."

"Yours? I thought it was a gift for Jeanette."

"I'm buying her something else." She paused a beat. "Your aunt was a wonder today, wasn't she? How is she doing?"

"She'll be fine, and I hope you are, too."

"I was frightened out of my wits, but your aunt gave me courage. Now I just want to be home, and with luck I'll get to leave tomorrow."

"Then good luck."

I let myself out and started to go to my car, then realized I'd never picked up the photocopying. I didn't remember if the office center had Sunday hours, but I noticed a few stores were open as I circled the square. With all the food that neighbors brought, Maise and Aster had dinner handled in spades, and I needed some time alone.

Sunglasses diffusing the midafternoon sun, I went up the alley, crossed to the next block, and passed a few closed stores. Most of the buildings in this stretch housed CPA and attorneys' offices. I supposed Dinah's was here. Bryan Hardy's? Not any longer.

As I suspected, Gaskin's was closed, but Vonnie's antiques store was open, and she happened to be standing outside. She lit up when she saw me.

"Nixy, is Sherry Mae well? What an ordeal I heard you had this morning!"

"She's got a small cut and a bump on her head, but she's fine, thank you. How is your closeout sale going?"

"Better than I expected, but I imagine there will be items left over. Goodness, where is my head? I need to let Sherry Mae know our plans have changed. We need to be gone no later than the middle of May now. Our son-in-law is being deployed sooner than we understood, so we'll stay with our daughter until our condo is ready."

"You're not buying a house?"

"We don't want to fool with a yard and the maintenance. We've been spoiled living here." She looked up at the building and sighed. "This is a wonderful building. I'm going to miss it and this town and most of all the people. In spite of all this recent trouble, we have far more good apples than bad here."

"I'm sure you do," I said.

"I just wish Sherry would use the building herself. I suppose the ladies do their folk art projects in the house, but Fred works in those sheds without heat or air-conditioning, and he's not getting any younger."

I agreed, but I'd never say it aloud. Fred seemed to be the touchiest of all the seniors about his age.

Vonnie's husband called to her about a phone call. "Well, you tell Sherry Mae I said hi."

"And I'll let her know you need to vacate early."

Surprisingly, she gave me a hug before she scurried inside. I stood a moment, looking in the window at a picked-over display of children's toys, thinking about what she'd said. Thinking about the nice apartment upstairs and that huge workroom. Tech school students would jump at the chance to rent the apartment, and the workroom would be an amazing space for Fred to both fix things and store the finished items until the owners claimed them. But what could Sherry do with the rest of the space?

Chapter Twenty-five

DETECTIVE SHOAR SHOWED UP TO TAKE SHERRY'S statement and have dinner looking good in snug jeans, a white cotton shirt, and boots.

Before he began, though, he said he had a surprise for us.

He linked arms with Sherry and led us out back. I trooped out with the seniors, as puzzled as they were. When he headed past the barn to the cemetery, I was completely confounded, but Sherry's smile grew wider.

Through the cemetery gate, he walked on to the section where the children were buried, and then I saw it. A white angel, wings intact.

"Goodness, Eric, when did you sneak that in here?" Sherry asked.

"I came through the back path," he answered. "It's smaller than your other angel, but that one will take a while to be repaired."

"I don't need the other one repaired, dear. I'd rather have yours." She grabbed a handful of his shirt, pulled him down, and planted a kiss on his cheek. "Thank you, Eric."

Back at the house, he was all business. He interviewed Sherry for thirty minutes, alone, with the parlor pocket doors closed. That seemed an excessive amount of time to me, but Sherry was probably asking him questions, too. I hoped he was also outlining the charges against Bryan. If he didn't fill us in, Sherry would spill.

Eleanor had seated Shoar beside me at the foot of the table. We bumped elbows occasionally, but the proximity wasn't uncomfortable.

"So, Detective," Dab said, "I suppose Hardy isn't cooperating."

"He lawyered up, which we expected."

"Is Dinah representing him?" Sherry asked.

"I don't know who he called, but he'll be tried in another county."

"Too much prejudice against him here," Maise said with a nod.

"I do believe his aunt Corina must be up in arms."

"That or mortified half to death," Aster added.

"No, Eleanor nailed it. She threatened the department with everything but Armageddon when we served the warrant to search the house and garage."

"Woman like that, nose all up in the air, her nephew in jail, she'll hightail it out of Lilyvale. Her pride won't take stayin' here."

Slow smiles bloomed around the table, mine included. Mean? Probably, but justifiable. Bryan's aunt was a piece of work.

"Did you find more evidence?" I asked in spite of myself.

"Enough. In fact, Dab, we found your father's hand drill with his initials burned into the handle. I can't return it to you for a while, but it's safe."

"I'll be glad to have it back when the time comes."

Sherry cocked her head, bangs falling over her left eye. The better to see Eric, I suspected. "You never did seriously suspect me of killing Ms. Elsman, did you?"

"No, ma'am."

"Out of academic curiosity," I said, "why not?"

"The angle of the blow that caused Elsman's head trauma and death indicated she was struck by someone taller or she was kneeling when struck. But I don't make that official call." He looked at Sherry. "I'm sorry I had to put you through the uncertainty, but—"

"Pish," Sherry said. "You had to do your job as you saw fit. I wouldn't have it any other way. Besides, we got to investigate like Jessica Fletcher."

He groaned. "Don't remind me."

Maise soon brought out a chocolate cake Pauletta had delivered that afternoon. When we'd polished off our servings, Eric announced he had to leave, and Sherry suggested I walk him out.

He'd parked back by the barn, and given the rumors that had circulated about us, I figured the ladies would be at the kitchen window peering at us. I didn't expect to see Mrs. Gilroy's kitchen curtains twitch, then fully part and the window be thrown open. If there had been a wall handy, I'd have banged my head against it.

"So," he said in that deep, dreamy drawl, "are you going back to Houston tomorrow?"

My gaze riveted on his. "Tomorrow? I thought you said you'd need me to stay a few days. Until you wrapped up loose ends."

He shrugged and moved marginally closer. "They're pretty well wrapped, but you could always stick around. Especially now that you know about Miz Sherry Mae's eye problem."

"I don't know what I'd do here. I can't see my art degree translating well to a small-town business."

"I don't know about that. I'm sure you'd find some way to use your skills if you get creative." He stepped closer still and my pulse sped. "That's what art is about, right? Creative thinking?"

My "Uh, I guess" sounded like a glug-gurgle.

He cupped my cheek. "Nixy, I want to kiss you good-bye."

"You do?" I asked, but was thinking, *Why not?* If he was a lousy kisser, I'd know I wasn't missing anything.

"Yeah. You have a problem with that?"

"Can't think of one."

This time, I stepped closer to him, my gaze going fuzzy as he bent closer.

And then music suddenly blared from Mrs. Gilroy's house. We both froze, listening. He got it before I did.

"Isn't that song from *The Little Mermaid*?"

I closed my eyes, mortified as the chorus of "Kiss the Girl" played to the entire neighborhood.

I felt him chuckle. "Don't mind if I do."

Before I could say boo, he kissed me. Gently, but firmly.

The earth didn't move, but, shoot fire, it was a close thing. Now I knew what I'd be missing when I went back to Houston.

When he pulled back, the music had stopped. Mrs. Gilroy cackled.

Eric just smiled and zoomed in for another quick kiss. "I'll see you."

I BROKE THE NEWS TO SHERRY THAT ERIC DIDN'T need me to stay in town.

"So you're leaving tomorrow?"

"I think I will. I'm sorry, Sherry, but I do need to get back, before Barbra replaces me at the gallery."

"You aren't replaceable, child, but I understand." She squeezed my hand. "You stayed much longer than you intended."

Her bangs swooped over her bad eye. The gauze covered the cut and bump on her right temple. "Will you be okay while the others go to their volunteer jobs? I heard Dab say something about projects that are being judged tomorrow."

"Semester projects. I thought I'd go with them. After all,

we don't do these volunteer jobs for our health. We want to pass along skills to young people. Who knows? They may be the ones carrying on the folk art festival in years to come."

"Then I hope they've learned well."

Word spread to the housemates, and it was more difficult than I thought to know I'd be leaving them. I'd revered Sherry as my aunt before this trip, but now I loved her. I'd come to love the housemates, too.

With promises that I wouldn't leave until after breakfast in the morning, we turned in. Even though I'd bought some clothes, they didn't take long to pack. Neither did my toiletries. I held out the gifts I'd bought at the folk art festival, though. Smelling Aster's soaps and lotions. Tracing the delicate dips and swells of Eleanor's lily napkin rings. Then I picked up the crocheted basket Sherry had given me tonight, one different from her usual type.

This one was made of stiffened white cotton twine, no bigger around at the bottom than the palm of my hand. She'd braided blue gingham ribbon in a small check with soft cotton twine for the handle. A ring basket, she called it. To hold jewelry. And perhaps, she'd added, to let my ring bearer carry if I got married.

I didn't know when she'd made this. I didn't know how she'd made it given her impaired vision. I knew I'd treasure it and that it was time to have her teach me her skills before she was gone.

I dreamed that night of the Silver Six, Mrs. Gilroy, even Sissy, and when I shot off the couch at seven, I had a plan.

I didn't say a word about it. I needed to turn it over in my head. Go to the town square with a critical eye. Consider if the idea was worth pursuing. And I needed to be real with myself about my art gallery ambitions, modest as they were. Was I prepared to give them up to go in a new direction?

I loaded the car, ate and did KP with the seniors, then bid them a tearful good-bye. My tears as much as Sherry's and everyone else's. I thought even Fred got a little misty.

Car loaded. Check. Directions home. Check. Sunglasses. On. Special list I'd lifted from Sherry's desk. In my bag. I was ready.

Because the tech school campus was more or less on my way out of town, and because Dab and Eleanor followed me, I had to drive past the downtown area, wait until they turned off, and double back.

I pulled into the diagonal slot in front of the antiques store, shut off the engine, and stared at the building. I pictured the retail space in my mind. Would it work? We'd need shelves and display cases. Did the glass-front counter stay with the building? I jotted a note to myself. I knew the back space would be perfect with only a little cleaning, some minor rearranging perhaps, and some seating.

I'd want to paint the entire store. The apartment, too, just to freshen it.

By ten o'clock when Vonnie opened, I had a long list of notes and questions. I wouldn't have all of them answered today, but I'd make a start. The idea carried risks. Every new venture did. However, if I pulled this off—correction, if the Silver Six and I pulled this off—I'd be able to stay close to them all and still do what I loved.

A while later, I waved good-bye to Vonnie, then paused outside to gaze up at the building. I could've sworn I saw Sissy in the apartment window for an instant, but it had to be my imagination. I'd been immersed in visualizing how well the building would work with my minor tweaks.

At ten thirty, I went to the courthouse to find Patricia Ledbetter. She helped me pore over records, gave me the scoop on property tax issues, and told me she'd love to bring Davy in if I got the plan to work. She also gave me another idea for growing the business.

I went by the Lilies Café, idly wondering if Trudy had left yet. I less-idly wondered how Lorna's husband was doing, and it was odd to know I cared about people here beyond my aunt and the seniors.

Including Detective Shoar.

Next I stopped at Gaskin's to pick up the photocopies, met Carter and Kay Gaskin, and looked at their Arkansas-themed gift items. Which were fine for what they were, but we'd be offering different products entirely and wouldn't be stepping on their retail toes. Or anyone else's that I knew of. Good deal.

Last, since the day was perfectly warm, I spent the rest of the morning and early afternoon camped out in the small gazebo on the courthouse grounds making phone calls to the people on Sherry's list. The response wasn't universally positive, but most were guardedly enthused by my ideas.

The seniors were due home from the vo-tech college about two thirty, and I wanted to be waiting on the front porch when they arrived. I gathered Sherry's list, my notes, and my phone, and stuffed them in my bag. Then I drove back to the farmhouse, rehearsing my presentation.

THE SILVER SIX SWARMED THE PORCH WHEN THEY saw my car parked in the front yard. I assured them all was well, then sat them down right there in the wicker and willow chairs and on the porch swing to hear me out. As I outlined my idea to open a folk art gallery in the soon-to-be-vacant store space, six pairs of eyes rounded.

My plan was for Sherry and her friends to sell folk art year-round, even teach classes to pass along their craftsmanship, and invite guest artists to teach, too. The back room would be dedicated to Fred for his fix-it business, and for classes. I wasn't so sure about having Dab distill herbs in the workroom, but he claimed to prefer taking over Fred's sheds.

I'd manage the gallery, and I told Sherry I'd pay rent to live in the upstairs apartment. She nixed that, saying we'd dip into Sissy's trust for the renovations and my rent. Since this wasn't the time to argue finances, we settled on me paying the apartment's utility bills. I'd bring up the rent issue again later when we got the venture off the ground.

"A folk art gallery," Sherry said again. "I just can't get over it. Are you certain you want to give up your paying job at that ritzy Houston gallery for an uncertain income here? I'll be unhappy if you move to Lilyvale just for me."

"I'm anxious about this," I admitted, "but I'm excited. And if I didn't want to do it, I'd be back in Houston by now. Besides, I *want* to be close to you. To all of you."

Sherry beamed through her tears, and I knew in my bones this was right. I wouldn't have thought it a week ago, but I was ready for a new home, a new job, and, okay, potentially even a man in my life.

As the seniors chattered and planned, I noticed Eric's truck drive by. He wheeled into the drive, parked, and hurried to the porch.

"Is there a problem? Did your car break down?"

"Everything is wonderful," Sherry gushed, a sly yet joyful sparkle in her eyes. "Nixy is moving to Lilyvale. We're opening a folk art gallery. Isn't it wonderful?"

"What a creative idea," he said with a slow smile.

His deep, dreamy drawl sounded bland, but his brown eyes blazed with warmth when his gaze held mine.

I could hardly wait to call Lilyvale home.

Crafting Tip

From Marsha Knox of Earth Baskets
St. Augustine, Florida

IF YOU ARE NOT A FIBER ARTIST (WEAVER, KNITTER, crochet, or needlepoint artist, etc.), you probably never realized how hard these materials can be on a body's hands. To be specific, working with fibers and various kinds of wood such as those used in basket weaving can be extremely drying. Most materials will suck the moisture and oils right out of your skin.

One remedy is to use 100 percent lanolin. In its purest form, it is a very sticky paste. It seals in moisture beautifully, but leaves marks on your work. Solve that challenge by wearing cotton gloves when you craft. They are available at craft and hobby stores, as well as online. (BTW, you can also use lanolin on your hands—and feet!—at bedtime. After applying, don gloves and socks.)

Lanolin comes from the wool of sheep. Although you didn't need a prescription, in days gone by, you'd ask the pharmacist to scoop some up for you. Most chain pharmacies no longer carry lanolin, but an old-fashioned, nonchain pharmacy may carry it. Lanolin can also be found in most stores with breastfeeding supplies or ordered online. The lanolin helps prevent tender mom parts from becoming dry and cracked, and it works! However you buy your lanolin, you will need very little, as it lasts forever!

Remember, the 100 percent natural lanolin will save your hands from dryness, and cotton gloves will save your projects from being marred. Happy crafting!

facebook.com/EarthBaskets

Recipes

MAISE'S FRIED OKRA
(In Her Words)

*1 pound fresh okra, or however much you want to
    cook (I find smaller pods of okra to cook up more
    tender. Go for the 3-to-4-inchers.)*
Crisco All-Vegetable Shortening—in the can
flour
cornmeal
salt
pepper

Rinse the whole okra, drain, then cut off the ends—unless
you like them. I don't. Then slice the okra into smallish
chunks, about 1/2 to 1 inch. Okra should be slimy when cut,
and that's good. The more slime, the better the okra will
coat in the flour and cornmeal mixture.

   Now, depending on how much okra you're cooking, mix
flour and cornmeal in a large bowl. I start with a cup of each,
but add more if you're making more okra. I make a mess of
it at once, but in batches. Add salt and pepper, and mix those
dry ingredients well. A whisk works, but so does a fork.

That large bowl is important because you'll need room to add the okra and stir and fold those chunks over until they're thoroughly coated. Elsewise you'll have a big mess of flour and such spilling out of the bowl.

Some use eggs, milk, or buttermilk in their fried okra batter. I don't.

Dump your cut-up okra into the flour and cornmeal mixture. Stir and fold those pieces so they get good and coated.

Put a big pot on the stove—a deep one to keep the popping grease to a minimum. I use an old cast-iron pot, but use what you have.

Drop a few tablespoons of Crisco in the pot—about 1/4 to 1/2 cup depending on your pot size. I like the solid Crisco in the can, but I suppose you can use the liquid. None of that olive oil or coconut oil for me. The okra just won't taste the same. And you be sure to get that Crisco real hot before you add the battered okra.

Spoon the battered okra into the hot oil and let it fry up golden brown—or darker if you want. Fred likes his on the burned side. When one side of the okra has begun to brown, turn it and gently stir as needed as you continue frying.

With a metal slotted spoon or spatula, take the cooked okra out of the pot and drain it on two or three layers of paper towels. Add the rest of the okra in batches until it's all cooked. Be sure to change the greasy paper towels for fresh ones as you drain your batches.

Now, I drain my okra on those layers of paper towels, but I also pat the top of each batch with paper towels. Fried okra can be good cold, but not if it's holding grease. I pat the top of pizza with paper towels, too. I may not cook frou-frou healthy, but I know to blot.

SHERRY'S CHICKEN AND ARTICHOKE CASSEROLE

SERVES 10–12

*6 or 7 half chicken breasts, cooked, deboned
  (and cut when cool)*
3 14-ounce cans water-packed artichokes
4 teaspoons olive oil
3 cloves garlic, pressed

MIX TOGETHER:

2 cans cream of chicken soup
1 cup mayonnaise
1 teaspoon lemon juice
1/4 teaspoon curry

Set aside 1 1/2 cups grated cheddar cheese.

MIX TOGETHER:

2 cups Pepperidge Farm crumb dressing
4 tablespoons butter, melted

Drain artichokes, and slice into smaller pieces before or after you mix with oil and garlic.

In a casserole dish, layer artichokes and cut-up chicken. Spread mayonnaise mixture over top layer, then sprinkle cheese over mayonnaise mixture.

Before baking, sprinkle dressing mixture on top.

Bake at 325 degrees for 30 minutes.

Note from Sherry Mae: The casserole should be warmed through when the cheese is melted and the crumb topping is browned. I use a 9 x 12, 3-quart casserole or baking dish when I cook for all of us, but you can divide the recipe to bake in smaller dishes for fewer people.

This casserole freezes and reheats very well, though the crumb topping won't be as crisp. A few minutes under a low broiler might brown and crisp the topping some, but be careful not to overcook.

Keep reading for a preview of Nancy Haddock's

next Silver Six Crafting Mystery . . .

GOODBYE, GOURDGEOUS

Coming soon from Berkley Prime Crime!

"NIXY! NIXY, CHILD, WE'RE WAITING FOR YOU."

"On my way," I yelled down the stairs.

"We" meant my aunt Sherry Mae Stanton Cutler and her five housemates, aka the Silver Six. They lived together in Sherry's farmhouse and were closer than blood family. The Six were in their late sixties and early seventies, but they'd worked every bit as hard and long as I had, because they were every bit as invested in the success of our new folk art and crafts gallery.

Oops. Not a gallery. The Six thought "gallery" sounded too highfalutin, aka expensive. We'd settled on naming our enterprise the Handcraft Emporium.

I paused long enough to eye myself in the large oval mirror in the small entryway of my new over-the-emporium apartment. Yep, I'd applied mascara to both sets of lashes. That should've been a given, but I'd been known to miss a set. Especially since I'd gone makeup-free for the past month. No point in primping when my waking hours had been spent sanding, staining, and sealing nearly every surface of this old building. I'd even learned to wield a power sprayer to paint the twelve-foot walls, the ceilings, and the exposed ductwork. We'd installed three new fire-rated entry-exit doors and two roll-up service doors, and improved the kitch-enette and bathroom in back of the store proper. We'd installed security cameras and alarms, too.

Now the place shone, and we were ready for our grand opening.

"Nixy! Doralee will be here any minute!"

"Coming!"

I clambered down the interior staircase that led to the back room of the emporium. The space now served as Fix-It Fred's workshop, but we'd decided to use it as a classroom as needed. Like for this evening's Gorgeous Gourds class.

Fred scowled at me. "You know you sounded like a thun-dering herd trompin' down them stairs, don't you, missy?"

"Thundering herd?" I echoed, grinning.

"You laugh, but steep as those steps are, you're gonna fall and break a bone someday when nobody's here to help you."

"Point taken, Fred. I'll slow down."

"Nixy, child, how do we look in our new polo shirts?"

I realized the Six were lined up, as if for inspection. We were each outfitted in a white shirt with "Handcraft Empo-rium" embroidered in forest green above the left breast. Sherry, Maise, Aster, and I wore blue jeans and tennis shoes, while Dapper Dab wore his shirt with polyester pants and loafers. Elegant Eleanor, as I liked to call her, had dressed up her shirt with blue linen slacks and low-heeled pumps.

"You look fantastic. Are you comfortable?"

"I am," Dab said.

"I do believe the shirts turned out quite well," Eleanor declared.

Aunt Sherry ran her hand over the short sleeves. "They're wonderfully soft, too."

"I'm so glad we went with the hemp fabric," our throwback

hippie and all-things-herbal expert Aster added. "Hemp is sustainable, you know."

"We know," former Navy nurse Maise grumbled, "You can't bleach hemp in the regular way, though."

"I don't think we'll get that dirty," I soothed. "Does the shirt work for you, Fred?"

"I ain't used to working with a collar around my neck, but it's okay."

I smiled. Fix-It Fred was a walking hardware store in bib overalls. Tonight's dark denim pair partly covered the embroidery on the polo shirt, but he did look spiffy. The many tools he stuck into each of his dozen pockets stood soldier straight.

Maise clapped her hands. "Time's ticking. Is everything shipshape for the class?"

I looked over the room setup. Two four-foot folding tables were in place for Doralee Gordon, the gourd class instructor. She'd face the wall that led into the store. Two similar tables held refreshments at the back of the room. Four eight-foot solid wood tables, which Fred used for workbenches, were positioned in a semicircle to give all the students a good view of Doralee. The arrangement accommodated sixteen students, four per table, a roll of paper towels at each place.

We'd scrounged a variety of barstools to use for classes, and duct taped white plastic dollar-store tablecloths over the workbenches to catch paint spills. They were pretty much beyond harm, but the tablecloths at least made them look clean.

"Looks great. We only have eleven paid students, but this gives us room for walk-ins." If we had any.

Sherry patted my arm. "Eleven is a good turnout for our first guest instructor. It will take time to build a following. Besides, it's June. People are taking vacations."

"I hadn't thought of that."

"Chin up, child. It's all good."

I blinked at Sherry's use of slang and blinked again as all the seniors but Fred headed through the door into the emporium proper.

"Where are y'all going?"

Sherry gave me a wave. "I told Doralee to park out back, but we'll be mingling in the store, where I can watch for her in case she forgets."

"And we're still training the girls," Maise tossed over her shoulder as she and Aster scooted out. "We'll send one of them back to help Doralee unload."

Eleanor followed. "I do believe they're splendid additions to the business. They'll bring in the younger crowd."

"Maise assigned me to pass out name tags as the students arrive," Dab said as he strode out, his pants riding his bony hips.

When the door closed behind the exodus, I chuckled, knowing that the true mission was to rearrange their individual art displays.

I cocked a brow at Fred. "You're not going out front?"

"Nope, out back. Got all my tools and projects locked up," he said, gesturing at the wall and a half of pine cabinets, some open-shelved, some with doors and padlocks. "I told Ida Bollings to park in the lot out there, so I'll go keep a lookout for her."

"You see Ida a lot?"

He winked. "What can I say? I got a weakness for dames with hot wheels."

"Wheels as in her big blue Buick or that new walker she's sporting?"

"Both. Besides, she's bringing her famous pear bread."

With that he clank-clunked his walker, loaded tool belt fastened to the front of it, out the new back door. I didn't know how much Fred needed the walker to steady him versus how much he simply wanted to keep all his tools near to hand, but he lifted the thing more than he scooted it. And had the arm muscles of a weightlifter to show for it.

I took a deep breath and basked in the quiet for a moment.

The last month had been exhausting, and the next week would be another whirlwind. Thank goodness Kathy Blakely and Jasmine Young were doing a work-study program with us. Both were enthusiastic about crafts and eager to learn, and all for miniscule pay, store discounts, and free classes if they wanted to take them. Only Jasmine had opted for tonight's class, which would run from six thirty to eight thirty.

Doralee Gordon should be here any time now, and I sure hoped she would bring all the supplies she'd need. She'd seemed well organized when I confirmed the class details by phone, and what I'd seen of her art pieces lived up to her business name, Hello, Gourdgeous. But if she'd forgotten anything key to teaching the class, we'd have a roomful of unhappy students.

Tomorrow we'd celebrate the first day of our grand opening and host a week of drawings, demonstrations, and discounts that we hoped would bring in buyers as well as lookers. Since three of the Silver Six, including Aunt Sherry, were folk artists themselves, they knew hundreds of other folk artists and craftspeople both in our little part of southwest Arkansas and all over the state. A gratifying number of those artists had agreed to have their work sold in the emporium, and they'd be in the store next week to do demonstrations.

And Sunday, well, we were taking a break from the emporium on Sunday to rededicate the Stanton family cemetery. Aster had already smudged the graveyard to clear negativity by burning sage, cedar, lavender, and something else I couldn't recall now. Sherry, though, had wanted a formal blessing and had sweet-talked her Episcopal priest into doing the honors. She'd also insisted on a reception on the lawn following the short ceremony. Her farmhouse sat on half a city block, so she'd invited the whole town to attend.

I hoped for a much smaller turnout. I still shuddered remembering why we were blessing the cemetery, and I didn't want to spend the afternoon rehashing those events.

I glanced at the oversized wall clock hung near the stairway to my loft apartment. Dang, where was Doralee?

I'd barely finished the thought when Jasmine flew through the store door, nearly bouncing with excitement.

"She's here, Miss Nixy. Just pulling around back."

"GOOD TO MEET YOU, NIXY, JASMINE," DORALEE SAID with a firm handshake when we met at her SUV. "This is my gentleman friend, Zach Dalton. I hope you don't mind me bringing him to the class. We're making a weekend of it in Lilyvale."

"Are you staying at the Inn on the Square?" I asked as Zach went to the back of the car to begin unloading. Jasmine joined him.

"Yes. We haven't checked in yet, but I understand we don't have to. Not in the usual way, I mean."

"You're right." I knew the owners of the Lilies Café and Inn on the Square, so I knew the drill. "Just enter your code at the back door. The room key will be tagged with your name and be in the lock."

"Good to know, thanks. I'd better help Zach."

I followed and took the handle of one rolling bin while Jasmine took the second one. Zach carried the large box of gourds. The box was awkward but not heavy, Doralee told me.

"Even a box of large gourds is fairly lightweight."

Sherry had told me Doralee Gordon was fifty-five, but her short, golden-brown hair and her cheerful smile made her look younger. Zach was probably in his early to mid fifties, too. Trim and handsome, he was dressed as country casual as Doralee. As he helped unload and arrange class materials, I found him to be quiet but not standoffish, with calm, kind hazel eyes almost the same color as Doralee's. I liked Zach immediately.

When all the bottles of paint, the brushes, and the handouts were set on the tables, Doralee greeted not only Sherry and

the gang, but also the students as they came in. We'd made
stick-on name tags printed in large block letters so the students wouldn't be anonymous faces, and she took advantage
of that to call people by name.

The class filed into the workroom, friends chatting with
each other. Dab, Eleanor, and Aster had opted to stay in the
store with Kathy, but to my surprise, Maise decided to take
the class. Sherry did, too.

Sherry, Maise, and Jasmine shared the table closest to the
refreshments so they could hostess at the break. Ida Bollings
also shared their table, taking a seat at the far end where she
could park her new walker out of the way. Fred's walker was
next to Ida's, and he sat beside her on the tractor-seat stool
he'd brought from his old workshop at the farmhouse.

At Sherry's request, I introduced Doralee, then stood in the
back, ready to assist if needed. Zach took an empty spot at the
far table.

"Welcome, everyone," Doralee began. "First, my thanks
to Sherry for inviting me to teach you about gourd art, and
to Nixy for her lovely introduction. Second, thank you for
being here this evening. I hope you'll enjoy the class. Now,
if you have questions as I go along, just holler. Let's begin
with a quick history about the use of hard-shell gourds."

And off she went, telling the class about the different
kinds of gourds, how she came to work with them, and the
ways to craft with gourds. She then passed samples of her
various gourd art around the class, from simple birdhouses
to gourds with designs etched using a wood-burning tool to
beautifully painted gourds. She said gourds had been called
nature's pottery, and I could see why.

"Why is a thick gourd better?" Sherry asked.

"They're more durable and easier to work with, too. The
longer the growing season, and the drier the gourds are
before they're cut from the vine, the better."

"Where do you get your gourds?" a lady in front asked.

"There are gourd farms around the country you can order from, Ann. I get mine from an organic farm in California."

"Is it hard to grow your own gourds?"

Doralee tilted her head. "I can't really speak to that, Megan, because I've never tried. I'm sure the local nurseries, agricultural extension, or the technical college could help you find that information. Be aware that cleaning gourds is a messy process. You always want to wear rubber gloves and a dust mask, if not a respirator. I also wear a mask when I cut and chisel gourds with power tools."

"How many kinds of gourds did you say there are?"

"If I name them all, Ginger, I'll sound like Forrest Gump." The students chuckled and Doralee grinned. "Seriously, there are at least eight to ten kinds of shapes, and some lend themselves to a project better than others. I like to examine the shapes of gourds and let that spark my imagination as to what it will be."

Doralee glanced at her watch. "We're due to have refreshments, and I know you probably want to get to the fun part—painting your gourds. Are there any more questions first? No? Then let's nosh and paint."

I snagged a piece of Ida's pear bread but left the three kinds of cookies Maise, Eleanor, and Aster had baked to the students. We'd opted to serve only bottled water, but no one seemed to mind.

When class resumed, Doralee asked me to pass out gourds.

"Now these bottle gourds are all about the same shape," she said. "I brought a small size so you could finish tonight, and I removed the neck so they'd be easier to handle. You'll find a variety of acrylic paint colors on the table and some summery and patriotic stencils and sponges if you want a design on your gourd but don't want to freehand. I'll circulate to give you help if you need it."

I stood at the back, ready to assist again, which I figured would be about the time students needed to rinse their paintbrushes. Doralee had brought white plastic butter tubs that

I'd put by the utility sink, and I was straightening to go fill them when the emporium door banged open.

A scowling, burly man stomped into the workroom and pointed at Doralee.

"Doralee Boudreaux, why are you teaching classes when you learned everything you know from me?"

WELL-CRAFTED MYSTERIES
FROM BERKLEY PRIME CRIME

- **Earlene Fowler** Don't miss these Agatha Award–winning quilting mysteries featuring Benni Harper.

- **Monica Ferris** These *USA Today* bestselling Needlecraft Mysteries include free knitting patterns.

- **Laura Childs** Her Scrapbooking Mysteries offer tips to satisfy the most die-hard crafters.

- **Maggie Sefton** These popular Knitting Mysteries come with knitting patterns and recipes.

- **Lucy Lawrence** These brilliant Decoupage Mysteries involve cutouts, glue, and varnish.

- **Elizabeth Lynn Casey** The Southern Sewing Circle Mysteries are filled with friends, southern charm—and murder.

M5G0610